CAPE FAREWELL

Recent Titles from Peter Tonkin

The Mariners Series

THE FIRE SHIP
THE COFFIN SHIP
POWERDOWN
THUNDER BAY *
TITAN 10 *
WOLF ROCK *
RESOLUTION BURNING *
CAPE FAREWELL *

The Master of Defence Series

THE POINT OF DEATH *
ONE HEAD TOO MANY *
THE HOUND OF THE BORDERS *
THE SILENT WOMAN *

ACTION *
THE ZERO OPTION *

* *available from Severn House*

CAPE FAREWELL

Peter Tonkin

This first world edition published in Great Britain 2006 by
SEVERN HOUSE PUBLISHERS LTD of
9–15 High Street, Sutton, Surrey SM1 1DF.
This first world edition published in the USA 2007 by
SEVERN HOUSE PUBLISHERS INC of
595 Madison Avenue, New York, N.Y. 10022.

British Library Cataloguing in Publication Data

Tonkin, Peter
    Cape Farewell
    1.   Mariner, Richard (Fictitious character) - Fiction
    2.   Sea stories
    I.   Title
    823.9'14 [F]

    ISBN-13: 978-0-7278-6415-4
    ISBN-10: 0-7278-6415-7

All Severn House titles are printed on acid-free paper.

Typeset by Palimpsest Book Production Ltd.,
Grangemouth, Stirlingshire, Scotland.
Printed and bound in Great Britain by
MPG Books Ltd., Bodmin, Cornwall.

For Cham, Guy and Mark as always.

Acknowledgements

Cape Farewell has been in the planning stage for many years. Consequently it would be impossible to acknowledge all the sources and influences that went into its writing. But it would be unfair not to mention some of the most powerful influences and important sources from my extensive bundle of notes so that anyone wishing to look further behind the story may do so.

David Miller and John Jordan's *Modern Submarine Warfare* was published by Salamander Books nearly twenty years ago. Consequently much of the information it gives – cutting-edge though it was at the time – needs support from more recent sources nowadays. The Internet proved invaluable once again – especially as I was dealing with the Canadian Navy and that organization has a range of detailed and easily accessible websites. Here I found cutaway diagrams of the interior of the Upholder/Victoria Class of submarines as well as details of their crewing, capabilities and equipment. The Canadian Navy also supplied the structure of MARLANT, vessels in the Atlantic Fleet (especially the Tribal Class Destroyers), and lists of Ranks and responsibilities. I simplified the internal structure and workings of the submarine *Quebec,* however, and added an escape pod to the fin that I stole from the ill-fated *Kursk* and the Russian *Typhoon* Class submarines I researched for my earlier Mariner adventure *Titan 10.* I also gained information about the Canadian Navy's preferred small arms. And, of course, together with the CBC website, the details of the *Chicoutimi* tragedy whose influence on the plot is, I am sure, quite clear.

Another old favourite of immense influence was Wilbur Smith's wonderful novel *Hungry as the Sea*. *Sissy* must owe something to Nick Berg's massive tug *Warlock* but she too has a more modern Internet-based source – the SMIT website which gives details of the SMITWJS ocean-going tugs. The same is true of the Yokohama Fenders which, again, have their own website. Though, as with *Sissy* and *Quebec*, I have allowed my own imagination, guided by the requirements of the plot, to vary things a little from the way they are in the real world.

More up-to-date is a source that my son Guy found for me when we were researching conditions in the North Atlantic. Redmond O'Hanlon's terrific book *Trawler* gave me all the details about the crewing and handling of *La Carihuela* – and, in combination with a range of news stories about submarines tangled in fishing nets, the backbone of the plot.

Finally, I must thank a colleague at The Wildernesse, Mark Robertson, who cheerfully gave me much more than just the name, character and appearance of the intrepid Captain of *Quebec*. Mark got into the story because he is Canadian, a Nova Scotian Blue Noser, and he was amused by the idea of being a character in one of my books. When I told him he would be the captain of a submarine, however, he laughed and warned me that the reality of such a situation would be far from what I proposed – for he suffers from uncontrollable claustrophobia. The condition is so fierce, he says, that he cannot even go camping any more because the combination of darkness and restrictive sleeping bags tricks it off. 'If they really put me in a submarine,' he told me, 'I'd flip at once and simply start killing everyone who tried to stop me getting out.'

And so Paolo Ursini was also born – or Psycho Bob as he becomes known to the men and women aboard the ill-fated *Quebec* . . .

Peter Tonkin. Tunbridge Wells. Spring, 2006

One

Rogue

The rogue formed suddenly at the western mouth of the Denmark Strait, where the seabed plunges over a 2,000-metre cliff into the abyssal Labrador Basin, and it then ran swiftly and secretly south-westwards parallel to the Greenland coast from Kulusuk to Cape Farewell.

It was big, even as North Atlantic rogues go, but it was running with the set of the sea, hard in the wake of a moderating storm. So that in spite of its uncanny speed and massive size, in spite of the deadly danger it represented, it was able to creep up on the vessels in its path like Jack the Ripper hunting victims in a Whitechapel alley.

The first of these vessels was the ocean-going tug *Sisyphus* sailing under contract to the Heritage-Mariner Shipping Company and due in the North Sea oilfields in thirty-six hours' time. *Sissy* was sailing south-eastward again after a run into the shrinking Greenland ice fields to test bows that had been recently ice-strengthened for work in the North Atlantic.

The second was the *Victoria*-class submarine *Quebec*, last of the diesel-electric *Upholder* series to be sold by the British to the Canadian Navy. *Quebec* was running in the still waters one hundred feet beneath the storm-surge as she started on her long voyage home to the St Lawrence seaway after a shakedown under the ice cap designed to get the Canadian crew familiar with her systems.

The third was *La Carihuela*, a Spanish trawler designed for the Mediterranean and really a little out of place in this vast, stormy wilderness. *La Carihuela* had just been unceremoniously chased out of Icelandic waters by a couple of gunboats

1

for poaching protected fish stocks, but was still keen to top up her cargo bays with a last haul of redfish, or anything else she could net while she was here.

It was not so much the vessels themselves that made the difference in the end, however – it was the men and women aboard them; particularly those who owned, controlled or commanded them.

And the first of these, aboard *Sissy*, was Richard Mariner.

Richard towered at the right shoulder of *Sissy*'s duty helmsman, the ice-blue dazzle of his eyes half hidden as he squinted forward. His bright gaze searched along the line of their course south-westwards into the North Atlantic, the easy rocking of his sea-wise stance holding his head steady and level even against the pitching of the wave-tossed vessel. Had the man possessed the almost telescopic gaze of the seabirds sailing easily one hundred feet above his foredeck, he might have been able to make out the distant shoreline of Greenland so far away on his right that it was hidden by the curve of the earth. Or the distant speck of *La Carihuela*, concealed by the grey skirts of the storm withdrawing dead ahead. But he did not. Nor did he need to – he had instruments aplenty that could see further even than the gulls.

However, Richard had been looking at little but screens and bowls for far too long. Now he wanted to see the world in all its vivid glory, to focus his weary eyes on something more than a metre distant.

The great cloud-walls of the storm that had been battering *Sissy* for the last eighteen hours were sweeping away west-wards at last, seemingly brushing the heaving surface of the sea itself. Above them, peeking over their stratospheric shoulders like Richard looking over the helmsman's, peeped the westering, early afternoon sun. After days of gloom and storm it was a welcome sight. With the clean, rain-washed, almost French blue of the clear sky, it gave the steadily receding ridges of the waves a touch of colour to relieve the unremitting slate grey of the deep ocean. There were gleams of gold now, and heaves of breathtaking

2

aquamarine running away before them into the cloud-shadows of the vanishing overcast.

A sense of peace began to settle out of the gathering golden brightness, an ageless understanding that after storms there will always come calms. Even though, mused Richard grimly, the sea was still running dangerously high. He noted the fact but felt none of the prophetic shivering that such an observation usually gave him in such conditions – courtesy of some distant Highland witch of an ancestor. Besides, as if to emphasize and explain the fact both at once, the wind buffeted against the aft of the bridge-house, causing *Sissy* to swoop forward as though she had been rabbit-punched.

Richard looked back. Unusually for a vessel of this size, *Sissy* had a clearview carefully located in the after wall of the bridge-house. It was a clever part of the design of the vessel which had made Richard interested in acquiring her for use by his company – and indeed in acquiring the rights to build more vessels such as this one. The clearview looked back along the tug's after sections so that those on watch could oversee whatever was being towed behind as easily as they could see the way ahead – without having to venture on to the open wings that extended the closed weatherproof bridge on either hand. But there was little to see behind *Sissy* at the moment, other than the blinding glare of the bright new sunbeams off the glittering tumble of oncoming waves.

The overpowering physical sensations all too easily drowned any fey foreboding that might have warned Richard of approaching doom. Suddenly, looking out at the day through the clearviews from the steel-walled safety of the bridge was no longer enough. He had to be outside, whelmed in the vast, vivid immediacy of it. 'Steady as she goes,' he ordered the helmsman and the watch officer alike as he strode impulsively towards the bridge-wing door. 'Just a knot or so slower than the oncoming seas – that way we can ride them comfortably and safely. And keep your tiller midships, remember. We'll wait for things to moderate further before we swing back southerly and risk those seas coming in from the beam.' He added the final order as his massive fist closed on the bridge-wing door handle, feeling the whole metal portal throbbing under the combined powers of the big wind outside and the four huge engines down below. 'We're not due back at Brent until tomorrow in any case,' he added, pulling the door wide and stepping over the high sill on to the exposed bridge wing, into the icy brunt of the gale. 'And they'll not be ready for us to take the platform sections under tow for a good while longer – not after this lot,' he concluded, speaking to himself now as he heaved the doorway closed and stood there, looking around.

Or rather, he thought ruefully, *staggered* there, looking around. For the power of the wind coupled with the swooping roll of the big tug's hull combined to make even him unsteady on feet that were usually as well rooted as oak trees. Without thinking, his hands guided by automatic dictates far below consciousness, he clipped his lifeline on to the safety rail before doing anything else at all. Then it was only human nature to turn and glance back along the tug's wake, to see where the wind, weather and waves were coming from. But, almost fatally, one hurried glance was more than enough for him. The brightness of the Denmark Strait was simply dazzling – the white of the sun, glinting like magnesium flares off a thousand tumbling wave-tops as though off shards of steely mirrors stabbed into his forebrain. Tears welled, their crystal gush compounded by the bitter blast which itself was thickened by pellets of sharp salt spray, multiplying the terrible light into something akin to blindness. Richard turned away, blinking and swearing, having seen almost nothing that lay behind them at all.

Even with the wind at his back and the cloud-shadows soothing his eyes it was a while before he would be able to see clearly again. In the meantime, he held on to the steel safety rail that ran at waist height in front of him and rode the bucking *Sissy* like a bronco, tears turning from fire to ice as they flooded down his cheeks.

'My God!' shouted Robin, Richard's wife, some uncounted time later. 'You must be thinking of something really sad, my love!'

Richard's eyes sprang wide with surprise – he had heard nothing and yet she must have opened and closed the door close by, then walked across the bridge wing to his side and clipped on to the safety rail there. He glared down at her now, his expression dictated by the lingering dazzle that gave her dancing golden curls an almost angelic lustre in his still-streaming vision. The wind-blushing oval of her face seemed to swim up at him, her grey eyes as steady as unruffled pools.

Robin misinterpreted his expression – a rare miscalculation brought about by a lingering tension that stood between them. He hadn't wanted her to come aboard on this trip, for the work they were undertaking threatened to be lengthy and tedious as well as hard and dangerous. And under normal circumstances the crew would have backed him, for they were almost as superstitious as trawler men. Female officers might be everyday occurrences on the big commercial tankers that made up most of the Heritage Mariner fleet, and which Robin as well as Richard held current papers to command. Women might be carving out well-earned careers in naval vessels of all sorts and sizes all over the world. But they were still something of a rarity in the rugged macho madness of smaller boat work, even if they were no longer absolutely forbidden to enter this strange environment of tugs and trawlers, supply ships and lighters.

However, Robin had been amongst *Sissy*'s crew before, in that mad dash from Durban to Kerguelen Island, fighting to save the drifting French tanker *Lady Mary*. The beautiful Englishwoman had become something between a ship's mascot and a kind of pin-up for Captain Hollander and his cheerfully unreconstructed South African crew. They had been happy to see her back in the flesh.

Richard had shared with Robin many years of marriage and more tense situations than he cared to recall and he had always believed there was not a jealous bone in his body. Now he wasn't so sure. And this was a situation she seemed to enjoy. Perhaps because their marriage had become so settled – staid. Perhaps because within the last few years she had been nearly killed in an explosion and faced weeks of surgery and months of physiotherapy in recovery – an experience that had shaken even her unthinking confidence in herself. Because he, in the meantime, had contrived to get himself isolated in some very intimate situations with several stunning young women who varied in profession from Canadian Mounties and Russian police investigators to French merchant naval officers, but who did not, as far as Robin could see, vary one little bit in either their attractiveness or their vulnerable availability.

'What?' she demanded shortly, wary of another confrontation.

But Richard shook his head. 'Nothing. I just got the sun in my eyes. I looked back into the Denmark Strait – it's like a supernova back there.'

Without a second thought, Robin did the same, then hissed in pain almost at once. When their eyes met again, hers were as wet as his. And she shared his preoccupied frown. 'Have you got your sunglasses on you?' she demanded.

'I think so,' he answered, patting his pockets one-handed, holding tight to the safety rail. 'Why?'

'I thought I saw something when I looked back there.' She was patting her own pockets too, her frown deepening as the instantaneous vision of what she had glimpsed began to firm up in her head like a photograph taking form in a developing tray. But the first thing that her questing fingers found was her little walkie-talkie. No use for looking through at all.

Sissy settled then, sitting back into a trough between two waves that seemed longer and calmer than the rest. Richard popped open a pocket in his wet-weather gear and pulled out the fortunately indestructible, almost priceless designer eyewear given to him by his friend and colleague Doc Weary to celebrate their successful completion of the Fastnet Ocean Yacht Race a year or two since. He slid the tight black band of plastic and glass round his head and settled the coated lenses astride the great blade of his nose. 'What?' he said again and turned.

Turned and froze, like Lot's wife in the Bible, turned to a pillar of salt by what she saw.

Richard's first impression was that it must be an iceberg it was so high, so sheer, so square, so solid. It appeared to be a standard tabular berg the better part of one hundred feet in height, seemingly sheer, square at the top, and stretching away on either hand farther than he could easily see. Not so wildly out of place in these latitudes, of course.

Except that it was upwind of them and there was no tell-tale odour of cucumbers such as icebergs always give off. And yet the sheer cliff of it seemed so much more absolute, substantial – simply solid – than water could ever be. Especially as the westering sun glinted on the deep-water-green precipice of its leading wall, giving it a heavy bronze sheen that – even through the treated lenses of his sunglasses – made it seem more like metal than anything else. But then he registered the speed at which it was rushing down upon them; and he registered the lack of surf along its cliff-foot – and he knew.

'Rogue,' he grated to Robin, his voice carrying easily in the sudden hissing silence of its wind-shadow. 'It's a rogue.'

Two

Wave

Now the unusual design of *Sissy*'s bridge-house really began to come into its own. In many ways, in fact, it represented one of the sturdy vessel's best hopes of survival. The huge rogue wave was almost upon her. It was travelling much faster than the seas through which she had been sailing. And even these seas had been too fast and too steep to allow her to turn beam-on with any safety. To try and turn now would be instantly fatal. There was no chance of facing their monstrous opponent bow-on, therefore.

But, as with their careful passage south-westward since the storm began to clear, if they controlled their speed and power carefully – perfectly – they might just be able to let it pass safely under them, riding up its sheer face stern-first. As though they were reversing in a motor car up a treacherously icy precipice.

But the waves they had been dealing with so far were ten metres at the most from trough to crest. The rogue was more than thirty. Like a tsunami, it would have engulfed a ten-storey building without breaking into foam and passed on easily. If they got it wrong in any way at all, it would engulf them just as readily. Indeed, if they got it *right* in every detail and regard, the monster still might prove too much for them . . .

'Full ahead all!' ordered Richard, his gravely voice low and tense – not least because Robin insisted on remaining outside on the bridge wing, claiming she could see things more clearly from out there, promising to add her observations via the walkie-talkie. And, short of ripping off her safety line, slinging her over his shoulder and carrying her on to the bridge like a caveman, he had neither the time nor the power to change her mind. Not that he would have had the inclination to do so if she had been any other crew-member aboard, for a lookout on the bridge wing might indeed be a vital help. If he glanced to his left now he could see her through the window in the top half of the bridge-wing door, clutching intrepidly at the after rail, her head tilted back, sunglasses now securely in place, seemingly stargazing as she looked at the oncoming crest of the thing.

Sissy's four huge motors responded to Richard's terse command almost at once and the tug surged powerfully forward. As she did so, Captain Tom Hollander appeared, breathlessly, summoned by the watch-keeper on Richard's first terse word of warning. 'A rogue?' demanded the wiry Capetowner, resuming command of his own bridge.

'Biggest I've ever seen,' confirmed Richard.

Hollander joined him at the rear-facing clearview and said something foul in Afrikaans. Even though he couldn't see its crest, thought Richard, impressed. Or, perhaps, *because* he couldn't see the crest. Which emphasized how Robin's riskier strategy of standing outside where her upward vision was limited only by the sky instead of the window frame and deck head could be vital.

In spite of the fact that they were running at full speed, they were beginning to slide further back down the leading slope of the long trough preceding the rogue. A glance over his shoulder showed Richard that the helmsman was looking up towards the gulls a hundred feet above the deck now; the gulls and the tops of the dark storm clouds away beyond them. And the aft-facing clearview was looking down along the afterdeck towards the bottom of the approaching monster as the crest of it seemed to rise to newer, ever more threatening heights. At least Robin could see the topmost reach of the rogue and have some clear idea of their chances of bobbing up there before it all closed down and sucked them under like *Titanic*.

'There are vessels ahead of us, Tom,' said Richard, almost conversationally. 'Better put out a warning to them.'

'I hope to God there are vessels all over the place,' answered Hollander flatly. 'I'm putting out a mayday. Sparks, did you hear that?'

'Mayday, Captain. Aye.'

'We've enough emergency equipment aboard to get everyone through this – but only if we get a chance to abandon ship,' calculated Hollander grimly. 'But we don't even have time to go to emergency stations. Still, I've ordered the decks clear and everything battened tight . . .' He glanced out at Robin, the only one aboard not obeying his orders at the moment. 'Anything else'd be a waste of time in any case, I'd say.'

'I agree. If there's anyone aboard who wants to pray, though . . .'

'Too right. Just so long as they can do their duty on their knees. You ever been through anything like this?'

'Never.'

'Any theoretical seamanship that might cover the case?'

'Any minute now we'll be right at the bottom of the trough,' observed Richard thoughtfully if apparently irrelevantly.

'With our bows pointing at the North Star by the look of things,' agreed Hollander, brown eyes narrow as he fought to follow Richard's logic.

'Yes. And that's the point I think we want to go into full astern all. We have four huge motors. The propellers they drive are massive and variable-pitch, designed to push us forward no matter what we're pulling behind us. With any luck, we can use all that power to help us pull backwards up the leading edge of the wave.'

'If we go to full astern all when the stern is already settled pretty deep in the trough – probably awash, I'd say – won't that simply pull us deeper under water?' demanded Hollander, understandably wary of further risking his command.

'It might. But if we can stay in control, then that's no bad thing, is it? The deeper the stern sits as we start going up the front of the wave, the more traction the propellers will have. As long as the rudder stays straight amidships and we don't let her head swing round. Surely our greatest danger will be simply to lose our grip and slide back down into the trough so that the wave can wash right over us either from the stern or from the beam. *Sissy* would never survive that.'

'Too right! I can't think of many submarines that would. And *Sissy*'s sure as hell no submarine. Right. Any plan is better than no plan.' An unnatural darkness swept into the bridge at Hollander's heartfelt words. The icy shadow of the wave itself. 'Helm. Full astern all,' he called at once, his voice cracking. 'Maximum reverse pitch. Keep your rudder set dead ahead.'

'Full astern all. Max pitch. Dead ahead. Aye.' The young helmsman glanced lugubriously over his shoulder and added, 'May I pray now, Captain? In our church we do it standing up.'

Whether it was a manoeuvre Richard would ever repeat or ever recommend that other mariners in similar desperate circumstances follow, he was never sure. It probably broke all sorts of laws of nature, physics and seamanship that even he was unaware of. But it seemed to be working – at first, at least. *Sissy*'s stern was already awash as the oncoming rogue began to sweep over her. The reversing of her fully-pitched propellers sucked the strong, square after section deeper under the water, until they could see even the bases of the aft cranes through a bottle-green swell and all her deck furniture almost to midships was lost under a welter of foam. Robin abruptly reported that she thought she could see the big deck hatches above the engine room beginning to buckle, her voice over the walkie-talkie sounding like a whisper in a thunderstorm.

But then, as Richard had grimly calculated, the power of the wave really came into play: the force that makes a ping-pong ball sit on top of a fountain at a fairground shooting gallery multiplied by millions. *Sissy*'s stern was under water but it was watertight as long as the hatches held, immensely strong and full of air. Up the wave it rose, therefore, like a lift-car in the fastest of express elevators.

Sissy tilted forward. Her bow see-sawed down until the heights of the heavens were replaced by the deeps of the ocean in front of the helmsman's staring eyes – and his prayers became audible to more ears than his God's. The bow slammed down into the water as hard as if the wave had really been an iceberg, and Richard fell to his knees with the shock – thanking God Himself that the whole fore quarter had been ice-strengthened so recently. Foam exploded up over the rails at the forecastle head and spattered on to the clearview. As thick as soapsuds, it washed upwards, but, blessedly, fell away again. Because – just for those few crucial seconds – the game tug did not slide forward down the steep slope of the wave front.

And Robin's place out on the bridge wing began to pay some dividends. It also gave them hope because she informed them they were already a third of the way up the wave and going strong.

Like Richard had thought she would, *Sissy* mimicked a motorcar reversing gingerly up a steep and icy slope. Motors screaming well into the red, threatening at any instant to burn out, burst a gasket, throw a bearing, turn a driveshaft into a corkscrew, she inched backwards, the whole of her solid steel fabric throbbing as though it would burst in the grip of these terrible forces like the frailest of balloons.

For one more moment, she hung there, slowing, as the huge wave surged relentlessly forward beneath her. For one more moment. Then for another, before she hesitated.

'*Halfway!*' came Robin's hoarse report. '*There's a hell of a lot of spray coming over the crest but it's not going to break. I don't think it's going to break . . .*'

White water surged across the afterdeck, green water close behind it, threatening to reach the bridge itself and stamp down upon them all like the foot of an angry god. Robin was calling something further over the walkie-talkie but it was impossible to hear her words through the overwhelming sound. Her tone seemed hopeful, though.

Richard looked across at the shuddering bridge-wing door and caught a glimpse of her still standing there. He thought she gave a wave, then events overtook them once again.

The darkness in the bridge lightened. The dark wall behind them suddenly turned to crystal – as green as darkest emerald – then bottle green, then aquamarine. A wall of spray smashed up the length of the juddering vessel. But it was only spray, as Robin had promised – not water after all. And with it came the gale. As though the storm wind had been caged by the massive wave then released into new fury now, it smashed into the jumping vessel now at the very worst of moments.

For it hit *Sissy* as she still hung there, balancing like a see-saw, her bows amongst the gulls that had been a hundred feet above them only mere moments before. The gulls remained unruffled, riding the blast as though the storm had no power over them, eyeing the men and their ship incuriously.

Sissy rocked forward just a little under the terrible power of wind and spray. Then the forward motion of the wave itself came to their aid. Had the rogue been standing as still as a hillside on the ocean, then *Sissy* would indeed have fallen forward. But it was rushing south-westwards, almost as swiftly as the storm itself. And as *Sissy* rocked on its foaming, wind-whipped crest, the rogue rolled onwards towards Cape Farewell and the game vessel toppled backwards instead.

Engines still racing in full astern, it settled back, digging deep into the after slope of the water mountain it had just climbed so miraculously. The racing propellers gripped. The weight of the vessel itself reversed the force that had got it here so far, and *Sissy* slid incredibly swiftly down the longer slope of the wave's back. A slope that was longer – but no less high, of course. The gradient might be easier but the fall was still one hundred feet. One hundred feet into the face of a thirty-footer close behind.

'Reverse your motors!' yelled Richard, still on his battered knees.

And Captain Hollander bellowed, 'Full ahead all!'

The helmsman, the only one still standing on the bridge – perhaps the only man left standing aboard – obeyed. The shrieking motors calmed, rumbled, reversed their thrust and began to build back to that steady throb that had got them safely this far.

13

The next wave in the smaller storm swell arrived and, although its crest washed all along the length of *Sissy*'s weather deck, it passed. And the intrepid tug settled back on to her south-westerly course as the dark wall of the rogue's wide shoulder swept away from under its ice-strengthened bow and off into the drizzling murk which was all that remained of the departing storm so far ahead.

Richard picked himself up more than a little stiffly. Relief at their survival was bursting into dizzy elation in his breast. He lingered at the helmsman's shoulder as he caught his breath, watching the dark line of the water-wall recede and vanish. 'You'll need to do a detailed inspection after that,' he called to Captain Hollander as the wiry Capetowner bounced back on to his feet.

'Every plate and every rivet, every blessed nut and bolt,' agreed the South African, his tone more animated than Richard had ever heard it.

'Every man aboard as well,' added Richard cheerfully. 'You'll be lucky not to have some halt and lame after all this rattling about.' As he spoke, he crossed to the bridge-wing door. He had someone to check on himself, he thought cheerfully. The elation in his massive chest became a warmer feeling altogether. He pulled open the door thinking that she had been right all along. Right to insist on staying aboard. Right to remain out here in spite of the terrible danger. They had been so close to disaster that perhaps her intrepid count-down had been the thing that made all the difference. He stepped out on to the bridge wing, his face creasing into a forgiving smile, his arms automatically reaching out. Not for the safety rail this time, but reaching out for her.

But the windswept, foam-spattered bridge wing was empty.

'Robin?' he called, foolishly, as though she could be hiding somewhere among the open, Spartan functionality of the place. His eyes swept over the metal-floored platform once, seeing only deck rails, observation pillar for binoculars and so forth, small winches, attachment points for lines and such-like. Attachment points for the self-inflating life raft. The Denmark Strait beyond with Greenland lying just below the horizon to the north.

14

Richard took off his near-priceless fashion-victim designer sunglasses and looked around again, his eyes flooding with scalding tears once more.

But she simply wasn't there any longer.

Robin was gone.

Three

Catch

Everyone hated Paolo Ursini. They had a range of reasons for doing so. He was Italian. He had been put aboard *La Carihuela* by the bankers in Malaga who owned the mortgage on her hull. He had been put aboard so that the trawler could continue to sail in spite of the fact that Paolo's solid Spanish predecessor had quit amid muttered warnings that she was little more than a death trap. He had come aboard in the face of Manuel Bosola's opposition – a desecration of the proud young captain's rights finally allowed because only subservience would stop the bankers foreclosing on the debt of nearly €3,000,000 carried by Bosola himself as owner and commander of the vessel.

And, worst of all, Ursini was the engineer.

Of the eight men aboard the Spanish trawler, the engineer was the only one on a salary instead of a share. He was the only one whose livelihood did not depend on dragging catch after catch out of the unforgiving ocean and getting them safely back to Malaga docks. He was the only man aboard – it was clear – with a safe berth no matter what. For Captain Bosola was famously ruthless and anyone falling even slightly beneath his exacting standards would be on the beach and unemployed in an instant. But the men could understand – perhaps even forgive – the captain: €3,000,000 was a lot of debt to carry around with you; and the only way to survive under such a burden was to bring home the biggest and best catches with almost mechanical regularity. Any man who did not help in this endeavour did not deserve his place aboard. Any man who did, of course, could grow rich on his share of the proceeds. Any crewman, that is – but not the engineer. Which was one of the reasons that Paolo Ursini hated them as roundly as they hated him.

They were Spanish. The gutter sweepings of the Malaga docks. They were young, strong, lusty. He was older; educated. They had hot-blooded women – and brawls in bars that bordered on the legendary. He had as many books as would fit in a suitcase with his clothes – and the occasional whore when he was desperate. They all came from within ten kilometres of *La Carihuela*'s berth. He came from Turin. They were ill-shaven, untidy, unremittingly sloppy in everything except their seamanship. He was punctilious, perfectly shaven and as neat as a maiden aunt. They ran around the decks above and below with the sureness of monkeys in the forest canopy. He was always unstable and slightly seasick. Even in the engine area which was his domain, he felt slightly out of place, even, on occasion, disturbingly claustrophobic. They seemed oblivious to the rotting-fish stench that pervaded everywhere aboard – especially the makeshift galley. He wore too much Armani cologne and tried not to breathe too deeply. They seemed to subsist on a gut-wrenching combination of seafood, chorizo, saffron and rice. He pined for pizza and pasta. They were *family*; they *belonged* – with each other, with the boat and on the water. He was unattached, footloose; rootless and lonely – the hired gun. He really belonged in a factory with unshakeably earthbound foundations and cavernous workshops boasting the pristine atmosphere of an operating theatre – and no tight spaces or dark shadows – constructing the most intimate sections of Ferrari motorcars with the calm precision of a master surgeon. But jobs in the Ferrari factory were few that year and Paolo had been desperate enough to put himself out to hire even down in Spain. And when even the Seat factory proved impenetrable, he found himself lost and destitute. Then he met one of *La Carihuela*'s bankers in a Malaga bar and idly accepted his offer. Needs must, when the Devil drives.

But this was all merely the beginning of Paolo's problems. For *La Carihuela*'s crew saw their mission in life as an epic struggle to wrest the greatest fruits from the most dangerous deeps and grow into comfortable middle-aged domesticity on the proceeds, while Paolo Ursini saw this simply as a relentless attempt to destroy all his good hard work aboard her. With no benefit to himself, either. Quite the reverse, in fact, if his experience of the voyage so far was anything to go by. Certainly there wasn't any gratitude offered when the complex of systems remained miraculously functional, but the insults when it failed went all too rapidly from gratuitous to libellous.

And even this by no means plumbed the depths of the mistrust the engineer held for the rest of the men aboard. For a start, Captain Bosola was set on running the venerable engines to ruin, always in a hurry to seek out the next catch – usually to be found lurking under the nearest storm, or deep within the most forbidden and fiercely guarded foreign territorial waters. Then the wild young captain insisted on bringing the whole floating disaster to places where the weather alone tested heating, lighting, water- and waste-disposal well beyond their limits. Furthermore, the mate and his barbarian acolytes were determined to destroy the cranes and winch motors that pulled the huge nets in and out – and the servos that raised and lowered the aft section and runways when they did so. Finally, the whole bloody lot of them were determined to get so many catches aboard that catch control, from the chute-hatches, belts and tables in the fish room to the refrigeration units in the chilling holds, was simply permanently overloaded. Inevitably, there was always something going wrong somewhere. Usually in some dark and disgusting constricted space full of wild shadows and even wilder stenches. It was almost enough to send a man mad.

What in God's name will go wrong next? Engineer Ursini wondered, crouching over the labouring motors, trying not to smack the back of his seal-smooth head on the deck immediately above and trying not to vomit into his oil-tray below. The relentless see-sawing motion had begun to ease for the first time since the Icelandic gunboats had fallen below the horizon astern some twenty-four hours since. That promise of respite had given him the opportunity to dash down here and check his charges – a kind of insurance against the next inevitable mechanical failure. As he worked, so the relentless motion seemed to ease a little further. But perhaps that was only the steadying effect of the nets that had gone over the stern at the first sign of the storm beginning to ease. The distant rumbling roar of the wind had seemed to moderate a tone or two, however – so perhaps it was more than the effect of the nets after all. Perhaps they really were heading for a little calm weather, he thought.

But no sooner had the hope occurred to him than he heard another stirring of thunder much more close at hand, the sound of half a dozen bloody great Spaniards rushing aft with one accord. That would only mean that the mate and his men were stirring themselves – unnaturally full of animal energy from their unusual six hours' storm-bound slumber – and were getting the bulging nets back aboard once again.

Ursini looked around the cramped little engine room one last time and, with a shudder of soul-deep revulsion, began to unfold himself. If the crew were back on deck and the nets were coming in, then it would likely be the winches that would break down next. They were designed to handle catches of anchovy, not cod and redfish. He eased himself out through the tiny, crazily tilting doorframe with its lashed-back door and hesitated for a moment, taking an instant to stretch his cramped body and to straighten the creases on his perfectly pressed overalls while waiting for his legs to adjust. Once he got up above deck-level, he would be caught up in the mad whirl of activity and he knew from bitter experience that if legs or stomach let him down he could expect a lot more derision than help.

When he could trust himself, he went on upwards, using the wildly leaping companionway as a final test of his fitness for the deck. As he did so, he was unceremoniously barged aside by a human avalanche that resolved itself into two soaking sailors dashing down towards the fish room. At least they didn't knock him over. With mounting confidence and gathering irritation, he pulled himself into the deckhouse proper, then out aft, into the covered runway that led from port to starboard behind the bridge-house itself. Here he crossed to the carefully organized peg on which he kept his gear, frowning with irritation when he saw that it had been carelessly disturbed. Carelessly – or more likely calculatedly. He stooped and collected his wide-strewn sea-boots and waterproof trousers, checked them for unpleasant surprises then pulled them on. Adjusting the rubber braces, he slipped the rest of his wet-weather gear over his head, tightened his safety harness, adjusted his life preserver and took his lifeline clip in hand before staggering uphill towards the midships doorway that led out on to the deck.

By the time he reached it he was slithering down a slope that pitched him unceremoniously out on to the weather deck itself.

As none of the gantries, cranes or winches seemed to be breaking down immediately, the engineer had an opportunity to look around. Because of the almost shocking impact of the icy blast, his head was cleared for a moment to allow him to do so. And because he was not a widely experienced sailor he was struck by what he saw, for it had an air of novelty to him, and an unnatural vividness that burned into his mind before his eyes exploded into tears.

The last of the rain had cleared away downwind ahead, and the sun was just beginning to glitter blindingly off the tops of the waves behind. And, just as Ursini's legs became used to holding him steady on the down-slope, the next wave powered in under *La Carihuela*'s counter and her whole stern shot ten metres up into the air, sluggishly to be sure, with much howling and clattering from the over-laden winches. But up she went, to settle on the crest of the wave for a moment and show the staggering engineer a vista of surprising calm behind them. And beyond the long trough of calm, something else that no one seemed to notice, fixated as they were with the way the catch was coming in. Something the engineer did not begin to comprehend.

'Stern ramp down,' called the hirsute gorilla of a mate as the crest of the wave washed by. The stern began to fall away again, and Ursini's gaze dropped to where the whole aft wall of the main deck began to slide open in mute welcome for the huge bulging net of the main catch heaving massively out of the water in their wake. At least the sea behind it looked calm enough, thought the engineer in his blissful ignorance.

But then the starboard winch began to scream. The huge wet warp wrapped around it was starting to slip. The drum itself juddered noisily to a grinding halt – just at the worst possible moment. 'Where's the bleeding engineer?' bellowed the mate, swinging round like an enraged silverback.

'Here!' called Ursini and dashed forward on to the pitching, spray slippery deck.

'Late and useless as usual,' spat the mate. 'Quick, boys, get the starboard warp up on to the crane and hold it there. Didn't you hear me, Carlos? Drop the stern ramp and get this lot aboard *now*!'

The mate ran out into the middle of the deck, swinging a grappling hook, his gaze fixed fiercely on the whale-sized bulge of the net as it heaved hesitantly out of the oily green deep. In spite of his simian sure-footedness, a monkey-tail of safety line whipped out behind him, just in case. The engineer froze, riven with shock. He had forgotten to attach his own line. He half turned, seeking the nearest attachment point. The wave slid out from under the trawler altogether and she sank back into the following trough. The catch heaved up as though it was alive – as a single entity instead of half a million netted together. The mate's grappling hook bit into its side and the sailor turned like something out of *Tarzan*, tossing the line to the winch-man to attach to the port-side crane. The trough bottomed out and the back of the trawler settled beneath the surface. Green water swept upwards, past the screaming winch, towards the foot of the cranes midships.

The men in the fish room below popped the cover on the huge chute leading down to the belts and gutting tables.

Ursini's feet slid out from under him and he fell flat on his back, striking his head on the deck with sickening force. A howl of derision went up from the others, but it was drowned by the sudden, overwhelming screaming of the emergency siren. *La Carihuela* herself was mocking the useless fish-flopping of the helpless engineer while he swirled across the deck as though the gathering water would wash him down on to the belts and tables to be gutted and frozen with the rest.

Really beginning to panic now, Engineer Ursini grabbed at the nearest solid-seeming deck furniture. It was the broken winch. No sooner had his hands closed on it, however, than it began to spin wildly in reverse as a kilometre of warp whipped wildly free. Lucky not to lose his hands, he was hurled sideways into the gathering waves that seemed, suddenly, unaccountably, to be sweeping into the midships area.

There was an overwhelming rumbling. For no conscious reason he could work out, Ursini found himself thinking of Etna and Vesuvius, as though this were some kind of volcanic eruption and nothing to do with water at all. The struggling engineer found himself on his back, half floating, with a horrifying sensation that he was simply being swept overboard. His fingers scrabbling automatically for the inflating toggle of his life preserver, he looked up, and like the trawler itself, he screamed. Then for the next few terrible moments – moments that changed forever his ideas of natural reality – he was the only one of *La Carihuela*'s crew who really had half an idea of what was happening.

As the huge rogue wave swept in, the turbulence beneath it simply sucked the bulging net back down, gulping away fifty metres of fish-packed netting with several kilometres' worth of warp, sweeps, headlines and ground ropes trailing behind, returning the catch to the depths it came from in little less than moments. Tugging down the rear end of the trawler as the winches, drums, cranes and gantries took the terrible strain – and buckled beneath it. The only winch that did not rip straight out was the one that was broken – it simply spewed the warp away like the string from a huge spinning top. The cranes above were not so fortunate. They toppled like trees beneath the woodsman's axe and crashed along the already sinking deck. They tangled against each other, forming a skeletal wall reaching right across the deck screaming back to smash the gape of the stern-ramp wider still. They hesitated there for the merest moment to jerk the whole stern of the trawler down by another few fatal metres then vanished into the black depths with the rest of the netting, just as that massive wall of water stepped aboard.

Paolo Ursini was lifted almost gently on to the massive bosom of the thing and swung around as his feet left the vanishing deck and the inflated collar of the preserver held his head at the surface for the moment. He saw the wave sweep along the afterdeck, some infinitesimally microscopic particle of it flooding down the hatch and filling the fish-room in the nanosecond before it took off the bridge-house altogether like a guillotine dealing with an old French aristocrat. The bridge-house seemed to tumble forward, falling in a weird parabola over the downward angle of the bows as the beheaded boat went down, spraying out great pulses of air bubbles instead of streams of blood.

It went under so fast that the mate and his men on deck were still alive and screaming for the whole terrible ride down into the dark – all four of them clawing at the wildly rushing water as though they could somehow pull them-selves back. Faces staring upwards, eyes rolling and mouths wide, their preservers inflated like Paolo's, straining help-lessly at the ends of their hull-secured lifelines, coming and going through billowing clouds of teasingly free-moving bubbles, like a bunch of well-tethered balloons on a windy day.

The topmost section of the rogue broke over Paolo then, pushing him deep beneath the surface, as though the gods of chance and the ocean had decided he should join his crew-mates after all, and he saw something more strange and wonderful still. For, just as *La Carihuela* slid down into the shadows where even the sunbeams could not pierce, so something huge enough to dwarf her began to rise majes-tically into the light. Something huge enough to dwarf the largest whale that the engineer had ever heard of. Round and black and festooned in some strange type of sea-web, the head of it rose like the face of some legendary monster. When the two shapes came together, Paolo got the strangest impression that the newcomer was eating the trawler. That would be an apt enough fate, after all, considering how

23

many fish *La Carihuela* had carried away to the dinner tables of the world, he thought, dreamily – blissfully unaware of what was actually happening and how terribly close to death he was.

The two of them came together seemingly in utter silence, and a great explosion of bubbles billowed like quicksilver out of the dark. When they dissipated, the trawler was gone forever. The black-faced, wild-haired monster seemed to hesitate, then onwards and upwards it came, pulling out of the shadows behind it a simply enormous body that sported an absolutely gargantuan fin.

Is it coming to eat me now? Paolo wondered, with the readiness of a man who had been terrified by *Jaws*. And only the nearness of death made him view the prospect with such icy calm.

But then his life preserver performed its function and smashed his head up through the surface of the water with utterly brutal force. The wind punched him in the face and woke him up. He found himself halfway down the long black back of the rogue wave, in the middle of the stormy Denmark Strait, utterly alone with a monster which appeared to be about a hundred metres in length and that ate trawlers and their crews. He began to cry with simple terror, and the warmth of his tears on his almost senseless cheeks told him how terribly cold he had become.

Then the automatic beacon on his life preserver sprang into life, its batteries given life by their immersion in salt water. The little light on the top of it began to wink with all the frail intrepidity of a lone star in a lost galaxy. Its automatic distress signal began to call – just as feebly – for aid.

And the first call was instantly answered. Paolo's hand rose to the urgently sounding transciever. His ill-trained fingers, made clumsier still by the cold and the lingering nearness of death, hit the buttons randomly. There was a string of pulses that formed itself into the pattern of a message – an automatic distress signal like his own. Indeed, the confused man for a moment thought it was his own – that he was receiving some weird kind of distress-call echo.

But then his engineer's understanding of basic communications reasserted itself. A transceiver in receive mode cannot really be expected to be picking up its own messages.

Smitten with hope, Paolo began to look around.

And there, surprisingly close at hand, was a life raft.

Four

Impact

You could cut the atmosphere aboard *Quebec* with a knife – almost literally. Captain Robertson had kept the newly commissioned HMCS submarine under the ice almost to the limit of her specifications while he tried to hammer the crew of eight officers and forty other ranks into shape and get to know their vessel's little foibles and failings. And, most of all, to test the newly fitted air-independent system that supposedly isolated the Paxman Valenta diesels and the massive array of batteries that powered them. *Supposedly isolated* were unfortunately turning out to be the mots justes.

Captain Robertson had certainly been wise to stay this side of the Pole, though, rather than risking a direct run home round the top of Greenland and south through Baffin Bay. His masters at Canadian Fleet Atlantic HQ in Halifax – and Commodore Pike in particular among them – had been insistent that he stay within reach of the British Isles until he was absolutely satisfied that he didn't have another *Chicoutimi* here. And, apart from the recent failure of the isolation system, the vessel seemed sound enough. So he was taking her home at last – the long way round.

However, Robertson and his crew had suddenly discovered that his apparently wise decision had an unexpected impact on the voyage. No sooner had the tired, tense submariners brought *Quebec* out from under the ice, heading up to snorting depth for a much-needed breath of fresh air, than they had found the Denmark Strait had other ideas. Instead of allowing them to get either snorkel or search periscope up, the Atlantic had put such stormy turbulence above them that snorting – or even surfacing – proved impossible. And the shaking *Quebec* received in the attempt seemed to have overcome the isolation system and started the batteries to leaking somehow and somewhere as yet undiscovered; and it had backed up the whole waste-disposal system and made the heads all overflow.

The frustrated, bitter, increasingly bloody-minded crew were working therefore in a chemically mephitic fog of ammonia, chlorine and dioxides of carbon and sulphur. The air was scarcely breathable up in the bridge below the tall fin. What it was like down in the engineering sections beggared belief. And they had been suffering this for several days now. Long beyond the life expectancy of the gas masks that they carried. Eyes were streaming. Throats were burning. Stomachs were churning. Tempers were fraying. Mistakes were being made.

'We have to surface immediately, Captain. The crew are really beginning to suffer. It's only a matter of time before something dangerous happens. The storm seems to be clearing now. The surface vessels fore and aft of us are riding easier and running well clear. It's not as if we're under orders to stay secret. If it was calmer we'd be running on the surface in any case.'

'OK, Bob, I take your point. I don't propose to stay down here a moment longer than I need to.'

'Then take her up, Captain. Take her up now!'

As if to emphasize the young first lieutenant's desperate plea, the power flickered. Just for a moment there was darkness and a ghastly silence broken only by the steady, soundless vibration of the motors and the eerie whispering of the water along the single-skinned hull around them. Then the light came back and the whisper of the water was lost amid the sounds of automatic alarms and the urgent, almost febrile clicking of machines restarting and recalibrating. 'Right!' snapped Captain Robertson. 'We're going up. And tell Commander La Barbe I want him or one of his engineers here with some kind of an explanation for that blackout before we hit the surface!'

Quebec's long hull began to angle upwards as the captain's orders were translated into increased power to the propeller, pumping of ballast and realigning of external vanes.

The crewmen overseeing these processes began to call the degrees of angle, their rasping voices alive with gathering excitement.

The depth gauges showed a rapid rise towards the surface and the crewmen observing them began to sing out the diminishing depths in series.

'Thirty metres, Captain . . . Twenty-five . . . Twenty . . .'

'Ready with the search periscope.'

In the midst of them all, the lone voice of the sonar officer suddenly cut through the burgeoning relief. 'Something dead ahead, Captain, I can't quite make it out. Looks like a really tight-packed shoal of fish perhaps . . .'

But his tentative warning was simply overtaken by events – as the great tug *Sissy* had been a few minutes earlier. And events once again took the form of the rogue.

The wave was thirty metres high. It was formed out of the movement of water particles that rose and fell in series, allowing the almost semicircular form of the crest to move forward along the surface while they themselves just went up and down in a semicircular inversion beneath. But because so many of them went up thirty metres into the stormy air, a like number went down the better part of thirty metres into the depths of the icy black ocean. And their movement at the very least created a scarcely imaginable undertow.

It was as though the rapidly surfacing submarine found itself for a few horrific moments under the weight of some gigantic watery steamroller. Her racing propeller was smashed downwards as the fluid through which it was moving simply sank nearly twenty metres in an instant. Then the same invisible, unsuspected force rolled forward along the submarine's entire length pitching it forward with brutal force and sending it tumbling back down into the depths among the quicksilver shoals of redfish in a dark and dangerous reflection of *Sissy* soaring upwards among the gulls.

The bridge and control rooms were instantly thrown into chaos. Men and loose equipment were tossed hither and thither. Anything not bolted down flew up and sailed back down the sudden precipitous slope towards the sinking stern. Chairs and those sitting in them simply took off. Those who managed to stay in situ as everyone else flew backwards were almost immediately pitched forward with equal force. And when that happened, the danger suddenly came not from the loose equipment sliding around the heaving deck but from the solid screens, panels and displays into which heads, faces and torsos were thrown as bodies heaved helplessly forward. Most forcefully amongst these was Lieutenant Pellier, the diffident sonar officer whose forehead all but shattered the display screen of the Thales Type 2040 sonar which had been warning of something unexpected in the deep water immediately ahead.

The lights and power flickered once again. But this time the darkness lingered just long enough to bring a wash of simple terror with it every bit as potent as a wash of abyssal water would have been. And instead of the whisper of the water on the single steely skin there was the screaming of the hull itself as the power of the turbulence sought to rip it all apart. A screaming and a sort of hissing, rippling tapping that worked along it from the bulbous bow.

Captain Robertson was an easy man to underestimate. He was by no means tall. Nor was he as young or as slim as he had once been. His short beard and ruddy cheeks – unusual in a submariner – were more reminiscent of Santa Claus than of Sean Connery. But *Quebec* had something of *Red October*'s functionality if not of her size or naked threat – and her captain was clever, fast and hard. And an outstanding commander in a crisis. He was the first man up, therefore, finding his feet even before the light and power returned. So that when they did, he was still clearly on top of things. 'Continue with the manoeuvre, men,' he ordered evenly, his voice steadier than his feet and the calm of his tone belying the blood that was streaming down his face as he leaned against the solid column of the periscope. 'Report our progress as soon as you can. And I would still like this search periscope up as soon as it's convenient . . .'

The men picked themselves up and returned to their posts. But it would have been too much to expect *Quebec* to have come through such an adventure utterly unscathed. 'There's something wrong with the vanes, Captain. They are not answering properly. I can't get them anywhere near full elevation.'

'What's our angle of ascent?'

'Fifteen degrees maximum.'

'Proceed on that, then. Continue to dump ballast. What's our current depth?'

'Fifty metres, Captain.'

'We must have dropped damn near thirty metres in about ten seconds. No wonder the old girl was creaking and groaning. God alone knows what that must have been like up on the surface. How are we coming up?'

'Slowly, Captain. Fifty metres . . . Forty-five metres . . .'

But at least they *were* beginning to come up again. What was the name of that old book? *Eric, or Little by Little.* Something like that. Little by little certainly seemed to be the way they were coming up now . . .

'Forty metres, Captain . . .'

Captain Robertson wiped his face with his right palm and looked around, smearing thick blood thoughtlessly on his uniform trousers as he rubbed it clean. About half of the bridge watch were back at their posts. Most of the rest were beginning to pick themselves up. One or two would need medical attention, and the machines for which they were responsible would need some attention as well, by the look of things. And the sound of things, given the number of alarms that were sounding once again.

As soon as they surfaced, decided Captain Robertson, he had better get up and into the outside world and put a call through to Commodore Pike at the Canadian Fleet's Atlantic headquarters on the secure cellphone. MARLANT Command were not going to see the funny side of this at all. And if he had to put out a general mayday, then the last few months of his service would be spent facing the enquiry into this mess.

'Thirty-five metres . . .'

The enquiry – or, Heaven forfend – the court martial.

'Thirty metres . . .'

30

The first lieutenant arrived then, shaken and limping but still functional. 'Commander La Barbe sends his apologies, Captain. He cannot leave his machinery control room or spare anyone from the engineering sections at the moment. It will take him some moments to check for further damage after that . . .'

'Twenty metres . . .'

'There is some good news, however,' continued the first lieutenant. 'The waste disposals are no longer blocked. The heads are now clear.'

'Fifteen metres . . .'

'That'll be convenient,' said Captain Robertson, stepping away from the periscope as it hissed into life now that they were coming to the correct depth again. 'Any more shocks like that one and we'll all need the head as a matter of some urgency.'

But no sooner did Captain Robertson speak than the bow of his command smashed into something. The impact was glancing, throwing the forward sections of the submarine abruptly upwards. The bridge watch went down like ninepins once again. The sound of the collision exploded back from the big bulbous bow of her teardrop shape, and Mark Robertson, bouncing off the periscope and opening up the other side of his forehead as he did so, thanked God, MARLANT and Commodore Pike – in that order – that they were running unarmed at the moment. For Heaven alone knew what that unthinkable impact would have done to a full complement of eighteen Gould Mk 48 Mod 4 heavy-weight torpedoes.

This time the lights did not flicker and there was not even the most fleeting loss of power. So that Captain Robertson, as he bounced erect yet again, was able to bellow at the sonar officer, 'Lieutenant Pellier, what in the name of Christ . . .'

But then he saw the state of the officer in question. And the equipment he was in charge of.

'We're taking water in the forward sections, Captain,' called the first lieutenant.

So the hull was ruptured. High-tensile steel ripped open

and elastometric acoustic tiles showering the ocean floor like big black snowflakes, likely as not. 'Very well, Bob. Seal all forward sections off at once, please.' At least Robertson could give the order without a second thought – the torpedo rooms were empty and no one would have any reason to be down in them. And, thank Christ, all of the electrics down there should be on standby or off altogether. But his next command decision might be less easy – for he had to start estimating the need to abandon ship, and the practicalities of doing so under the circumstances. Now that really would be life-and-death, he thought, glancing up into the conning tower above him with its lock-out chamber and escape equipment. The ancient sailor's adage that you only stepped aboard your lifeboat as the waves closed over your command could hardly carry much weight in the submarine service, after all. 'How are we proceeding? What's our depth?'

'Still at fifteen metres, Captain.'

'Angle of the hull is up at twenty degrees, Captain.'

The men had to shout over the sound of the equipment alarms. Robertson glanced over at Lieutenant Pellier. He was beginning to stir but his sonar didn't look as though it would be any more use in the immediate future than it had been in the immediate past.

'Forward sections still taking water, Captain.'

'Thanks, Bob. Keep an eye on that. Any changes in the rate of flow.' Any falling away of that blessed twenty-degree angle. Any further hesitation in their upward motion. Any sign that they were beginning to slip into the black depth beneath . . . Captain Robertson literally held his breath.

'Still taking water for'rard . . .'

'Still at twenty degrees . . .'

'Still at fifteen metres, Captain . . .'

Still he held his breath. The steady throbbing of the diesels was all that kept him from abandoning even then. For it was their steady forward propulsion that would keep *Quebec*'s head up and give her that one last chance of making it to the surface . . .

'Ten metres and rising . . .' shouted the crewman watching the depth gauge, and his voice cracked with relief.

32

The impact of that one blessed cry galvanized Mark Robertson into action once again. 'Get the periscope up immediately, and prepare to surface on my command.' The steel cylinder that had whacked him so hard so recently hissed into blessed life.

Robertson's knees went weak on him then, though he would never know whether this came from relief or latent concussion. But now was not the time for weakness. He tucked the crosspieces of the periscope under his arms therefore, and used the whole thing to hold him solidly upright as he looked up and out through the optical illusion of the prisms into the stormy afternoon apparently immediately ahead.

And the first thing that he saw was a big four-person life raft with the body of a woman lashed to the bright orange bulge of its inflatable side like the corpse of Captain Ahab tangled in the harpoon lines on the great white flank of Moby Dick.

Five

Raft

Robin Mariner stood on *Sissy*'s outer starboard bridge wing, looking back along her wake as the brave little vessel hesitated on the crest of the massive rogue like a suicide on a cliff-top. The last of the storm wind battered both the woman and the tug almost brutally, armed with stinging slingshots of foam. It roared gustily, like an angry monster. The topmost reach of the huge wave hissed like a chorus of serpents. *Sissy* see-sawed, and Robin clung to the after safety rail, with her right hand – making assurance doubly sure – tightly over the clip that secured her lifeline. Every fibre of her seaman's being felt the tug's increasingly dangerous hesitation, her suicidal desire to plunge back forward down the precipitous slope which she had just climbed to within a heartbeat of safety. There was nothing more to be done, however; nothing but to watch and pray.

The back of the wave stretched down and away from Robin's toe-tips like a hillside in the rolling Sussex downlands near her home, it was so huge, so seemingly solid and so green. She half expected to see a little river valley at its foot, shaded with trees, dappled with pools, calling to the freshwater fly-fishermen in her family. But no. Instead there were the next massed ranks of waves, seven to ten metres high from trough to crest, marching in rank after rank out of the heart of the Denmark Strait. All too eager to march right over the top of them if *Sissy* slid suicidally forward now, instead of settling safely back.

And it was in that moment, while everything hung so

literally in the balance, that the inflatable life raft exploded open and rapidly began to inflate.

The life raft sat in a bright orange capsule suspended from a pair of little davits at the outer end of the bridge wing. It was designed to take eight, so it was quite a substantial item. It was self-inflating, made to react to immersion in salt water. No one had ever considered that there would ever be enough salt water to make it inflate this high above the weather deck – unless *Sissy* were sinking, in which case the raft would be needed anyway. But circumstances had transpired to make the safety equipment unutterably dangerous to the men and women it was supposed to be protecting.

The almost indestructible plastic sections burst apart and tumbled away down the wind. Cylinders full of compressed gas began to inflate the tightly folded circular body as though it were some massive carnation coming into blossom. Robin knew what would happen next: inflatable spokes would unfurl and raise the wind- and waterproof canopy, like the wing of a butterfly emerging from its chrysalis. And it was already beginning to take flight. The super-strengthened lines reaching back through the pulleys at the davits' outer ends to the little hand-winches at their feet would hold the whole thing against *Sissy*'s side as it blossomed. In seconds it would go from a neat, tight, aerodynamic capsule maybe a metre and a half in length to a huge round kite with a diameter of more than four metres and a volume of many more.

Still growing rapidly, the life raft leaped off the crest of the wave into the teeth of the wind. Robin felt *Sissy* shudder as the gale took firm hold and began to wrench the tug forward down the precipice of the leading edge and to her doom. Within moments the life raft would be fully inflated and, unless it burst under the strain, the pressure on the finely balanced hull would be irresistible.

Robin was in action without a second thought. Without any thought at all, in fact, other than that she must cast it loose before it pulled them all over the edge. When her safety line brought her up short, she simply punched herself in the midriff, opening the quick-release of her harness. Then she was at the outer edge, her hands busy with the tangled cordage there. But the sudden movement of the still-swelling life raft, the fact that it had gone up instead of down, the fact that it was flying now, straining at its tether like a wild thing, all conspired to make an impenetrable mess of all the carefully designed lowering and release systems. The line through the forward davit was hopelessly snarled. The line through the aft one whipped about like an irritated anaconda while the winch-handle span like a windmill.

Robin whirled and ran back along the bridge wing. On the outer wall of the bridge-house, just outside the bulk-head door into the bridge itself, there was an emergency point that contained in its glass-fronted box, among other things, an axe. Robin's education had hardly been classical in nature, but she knew as well as Alexander the Great how to deal with Gordian knots. She hit the release, tore the red-headed weapon free and turned again in an instant, so caught up in the action that she didn't even consider telling Richard or Tom Hollander what was going on.

Robin swung the axe high as she reached the tangle of cordage. It was at the winch point at the davit's base, fortu-nately, not out at its outer pulley end. Her attention was focused exclusively on the bright orange mare's nest. She didn't even spare a glance to the fully inflated life raft, which hung above her like a dangerous orange moon. She brought the blade down with the accuracy of a medieval executioner and the knot simply shattered, as though the bright orange fibres were made of spun sugar or glass. The life raft tore away, ripping the short-cut line out of the forward davit in a nanosecond, moving with such over-whelming speed that the line through the after davit leaped up into the air. The bright orange length of it, out through the pulley already, reared back inboard and wrapped itself round Robin. Fortunately for her, it coiled itself around her hips, buttocks and upper thighs where her body was at its strongest and most supple. A little higher and it would have broken her back. Higher still and it would have snapped her neck. Any lower and her legs would have gone, like a couple of brittle breadsticks. But as it was, the intrepid woman had an instantaneous impression that someone of gigantic power had simply booted her in the behind. And up she sailed like a rugby ball heading for a conversion as *Sissy*, behind and below her, settled safely on to the long back of the wave.

The life raft welcomed Robin aboard with a slap in the face that broke her nose and loosened a couple of teeth. And switched out her consciousness like a power cut. The fully inflated side, further puffed out by the wind, was more like a brick than a balloon. And the weight of the insensible woman strapped in a cat's cradle of cordage to the outside of the waterproof canopy put paid to any notions the raft might have had to emulating a kite any more. The whole lot slammed down on to the crest of the wave so recently vacated by *Sissy* with enough force to compound the damage to Robin's face and deepen her unconsciousness to near oblivion. But where the tug had four fully-pitched propellers, a weighty hull and superstructure – not to mention the law of gravity – all pulling her back and down, Robin's vessel did not. If it could not be a kite, the raft seemingly decided that it would be a surfboard. Though there was – blessedly – no actual surf as yet, the bright little vessel settled on the crest of the wave, swung round so that the windproof canopy could take the wind like a sail, and surged away forward into the stormy North Atlantic.

As it did, so, however, several other things happened. The windproof sail of the inflated tent, as it caught the moderating gale, swung round so that the weight of the deeply insensible woman settled on its forward side – well protected from the breeze and the foam it carried. Chance dictated that Robin was lying half across the entrance to the solid tent-section, so her weight and position meant that the dangerous over-inflation of the raft itself was lessened. And so, therefore, was its uncontrolled, wind-fuelled buoyancy. The tent-side sank back and some of Robin's weight was taken by the side of the inflated raft which stood high and solid, like a pile of huge fully inflated red inner tubes sitting exactly on top of each other. Still face down, Robin's body folded until she was almost kneeling on the topmost tube. It was by no means comfortable – but at least she wouldn't choke or strangle now. Though she still stood a very good chance indeed of drowning or dying of exposure.

For a few more moments the raft bobbed on the very storm-torn crest, like a cork caught in a mill-race, powering forward at an incredible speed. Then it settled back, almost regretfully, and the peak of the wave slipped slowly forward from under it, as the foundations of the watery mountain began to shake the submarine *Quebec* nearly fifty metres below. The little vessel's forward speed moderated, but, still in the grip of the wind, it headed westwards almost as swiftly as the submarine. It settled more sedately into the water. And its automatic distress signal started its urgent, vital broadcast.

But no sooner did it do so than very much more powerful distress calls choked the airwaves and drowned the frail little signal out. *La Carihuela*, a couple of hundred metres west, and twenty metres down below the leading edge of the wave, her nets out, her stern open and her defences down, was stamped helplessly under by the monster upon whose shoulders Robin bobbed. And as the Spanish trawler went, she let out one brief but overpowering cry – like Carmen, as jealous Don Jose's knife slides home in her heart.

The back of the wave, as smooth as a great green dolphin, suddenly erupted in a huge hill of foam, as though some new volcanic island was being born out of the depths so far below. The life raft's steady progress faltered. It slid back a little eastwards and north towards the distant Greenland coast as cross-waves surfed towards her. The guysering of *La Carihuela*'s life went on and on relentlessly, as every tiny bubble of air was crushed out of every space – and soul – within her; and then it began to settle.

As it did so, the head and shoulders of a lone man in a life jacket burst up like the last, most substantial bubble of all. The sleek head of the Italian engineer looked around, disorientated by lingering terror and by the vastness at whose heart he now found himself adrift. Then he saw the life raft and began to make his clumsy way towards it. And while he did so, as though it had finished its God-given task now too, the wind stopped gusting abruptly and the seas began

38

to moderate. By the time that something akin to calm returned the wave itself was long gone, vanished silently beneath the last of the storm that caused it, away beyond Cape Farewell.

And up into that sudden silence between the lone survivor and the life raft thrust *Quebec*'s periscope. It cut through the water like a shark's fin, kicking up a tiny bow wave and spitting spray up into the glare, heading straight for the slowly spinning life raft with the unconscious Robin kneeling face down, lashed to its side. No sooner did it appear than Paolo Ursini started shouting at it, as though it could hear as well as see. He redoubled his efforts and thrashed across the heaving water towards the convergence of the two things that looked so much like salvation to him. For how could he begin to imagine how much damage his long-dead companions and their long-lost boat had done?

Six

Rescue

Captain Mark Robertson brought *Quebec* to the surface with all the delicacy that his vast experience and the restrictive situation allowed. For, in spite of the sorry state of his vessel, he had absolutely no intention of letting any unconsidered or abrupt action by his crew or his command add to the very clear and potent danger that the woman on the life raft faced. Delicacy in any case would have been the order of the day – given what the battered and shaken submarine had already been through on this watch alone. And that, as it turned out, was providential.

Quebec came up straight ahead, with her propeller turning at little more than idle. The eye of the periscope remained fixed firmly on the bright blood-orange life raft as the fore-deck broke water and began to shrug the Atlantic billows aside like the head of a breaching whale. The life raft slid sideways as the round snout surfaced, pushed sluggishly away by the outwash. Mark swung the periscope round to the right, trying to keep the bright raft in sight as the forward motion of the submarine, slow though it was, whirled the circular coracle down the side below the rising fin. But it was a hopeless task, of course.

'Rescue party up and out,' he called, his voice echoing through the quiet of his ship as he talked to several men at once. 'Bob, can you lead that? Take five men with you and your best medical book. Through the after hatch, I think. Sparks, get me base at your earliest convenience. Helm, how's she handling?'

'Vanes still wedged tight, Captain. I don't know what in hell's the matter . . .'

'Very well, stop all. Let's see how she sits. Chief, can you send a team to look at the vane-control servos . . .'

'I've checked the schematics on the diagnostic computer program, Captain,' came Chief La Barbe's reply. 'There appears to be no mechanical or electrical malfunction . . . .'

'I've heard that one before,' breathed Mark, swinging the periscope in a full circle, skipping nimbly round the deck as his feet followed his head and shoulders. 'Son of a bitch!' he said.

The language was unusually salty for him and several of the crew looked askance. 'Bob! Can you hear me? Damned if there isn't another one!'

'Another life raft, Captain?' came the first officer's voice through the intercom.

'No. Just a man in the water. Looks all-in. Must be colder than a witch's . . .'

'External temperature reading one degree Celsius, Captain.'

'Make this guy your first priority then, Bob. He'll be dead of exposure in a very short time indeed. Helm, propulsion, we need to come up to a quarter revs and prepare to swing twenty degrees left. Bob, I'm swinging round closer to this guy but if push comes to shove you'll have to get out the inflatable – or send someone in for a swim.'

'Right, Captain. Opening the hatch now. We'll be up and out in a . . . Jesus Christ, what the f . . . —'

Quebec's first officer, Bob Hudson, stood at the head of a vertical ladder, at the mouth of the after hatch. He had just swung the hatch cover back and was preparing to step up on to the deck in short order with hardly a second glance. The captain's command in any case had caused him to glance down to the bundle at the foot of the ladder, which was where the deflated inflatable was stowed. But now he looked up, in mid-conversation, to see that the bright blue ozone-smelling beauty of the sky was barred with a black grille.

41

Lines of blackness crissed and crossed at right angles making squares of sky about thirty centimetres from side to side, edged in steely black.

The submarine's hull began to tremble as helm and propulsion obeyed their captain's order.

Bob gaped. 'Just what in heaven's name is that?' he asked. But his voice was far too quiet even for the five men in his team to hear.

As if in answer, the squares vibrated into life and their stirring caused a big dead cod fish a good deal more than a metre long to tumble in on Bob's head, then slither on down the shaft like a flexible torpedo.

'It's a net! Captain! We're wrapped in a fishing net here! Jesus . . .'

Bob was up on the top rung in a twinkling, his hands thrust up to test the strength and thickness of the netting across the hatchway. What his nimble fingers told him was very bad news indeed. This stuff was state-of-the-art polypropylene, thicker than his thumb and stronger than steel. Indeed, it resembled dull steel for it was grey. Almost exactly the same grey as *Quebec*'s hull paint, in fact. 'Dumas,' he called down to the crewman at the foot of the ladder, 'get me some bolt cutters. Quick! And Faure, get that fish down to the galley.'

While he waited, seething with frustration and all too well aware that there were at least two people dying just outside, Bob squinted up and tried to work out the best way to clear the hatch. The crosspieces between the strands were too thick for anything other than oxy equipment or power saws to cut. He would need pretty strong bolt cutters even to sever the individual stings, he thought. But they'd certainly need to do something for there was no way anyone could ease though a mesh designed to trap a North Atlantic cod.

Up in the command area, Mark Robertson was back on the periscope, but for once that fine instrument let him down. To begin with, it *was* just slim enough to penetrate the weave of the netting. Secondly, as he had discovered while watching the life raft – but without quite grasping the significance – it did not show him certain areas of his command with any clarity. It was, of course, designed to scan the mid-distances of torpedo range, not the immediate proximity of hull and decking. Even the foredeck, sitting low in the water and restlessly awash, remained effectively hidden, for the sun was settling lower now, and it glittered off the water in front of *Quebec* with all the blinding dazzle it had used to hide the rogue wave creeping up behind *Sissy*.

Such was the disposition of the net that was visible behind the fin – just visible, grey on grey – that it looked to the frowning captain that he might be lucky here and have just picked up one part of a trawler's discarded net. That it might just be draped across the after hatch leaving the rest of *Quebec* uncovered, like a saddle cloth across the back of a thoroughbred.

The next logical thing for Mark to do, however, was to go up into the little open cockpit atop the fin and take a good look for himself. To make doubly sure. Even in the face of the fact that he could see nothing too badly wrong. And that, even through the roller-coaster ride of the wave and the collision, none of his experiences or equipment had given even the slightest hint that *Quebec* might be almost entirely shrouded in *La Carihuela*'s net.

But even as Mark tensed himself to follow this most sensible course of action, the radio officer called, 'I have the admiral for you, Captain.' So Mark went down to make his report instead. Which is what he was still doing when disaster after disaster struck in such swift and devastating succession. 'Admiral, I have to report that *Quebec*'s current disposition is as follows. We are proceeding through secure sea area Tango Zero at one quarter revs, making less than one knot as we turn through twenty degrees on to a heading of 280 degrees magnetic. There are two people in the water, neither of whom are from this command, and we are in process of effecting a rescue . . .'

Dumas brought the bolt cutters just after Faure returned with the chief's heartfelt thanks and compliments. Bob soon had the first strand of the netting firmly between their jaws. A grunt of effort brought the blades together and the polypropylene strand snapped apart. A second shared its fate pretty quickly – for the cutters were heavy and Bob found it hard to be working above his head. Two strands were hardly enough to allow an easy exit, however, but Bob was as well aware as his captain of the humanitarian mission they had undertaken here. There were black spots and bright flashes obscuring his view by the time the third strand parted. He passed the cutters down to Dumas and pulled himself out on to the deck.

Before Bob had time even to look around, the stranger hit him. The stranger was a slight man bulked out by survival gear and a life jacket, clearly the lone survivor the captain had spotted through the periscope. But that only became obvious to the lieutenant later, after the shock of their meeting had worn off. At that moment, Bob had an instantaneous vision lent overwhelming power by simple shock of a completely bald head and blazing brown eyes that glared at him with almost lunatic intensity. The stranger appeared so unexpectedly and devastatingly that Bob was knocked backwards. The two men fell together on to the netting on the deck. That netting told Bob at least how the stranger had pulled himself aboard. And that realization was all the information he was going to get for the moment, clearly, for the stranger went out as they hit the deck just as though he had been coshed with a baseball bat.

Bob rolled the corpse-like body over to the hatchway as Dumas snipped yet another strand and opened the whole thing wide. Bob slid him in and he went on down, scarcely more safely than the cod fish. 'Keep cutting, Dumas,' he ordered. 'We may need to get another one like that aboard. Tell the captain we need to reverse the heading now if we're going to pick up the woman on the life raft.'

Then the young first officer pulled himself erect and looked away starboard to the north. The life raft was actually surprisingly close at hand. The apparently lifeless body held at its side by a tangle of lines was on the near side. There was no doubt in Bob's mind, as there had been no doubt in his captain's, that the figure was that of a woman. And this certainty was nothing to do with the traditional lack of female company that fooled the eyes of sailors in legend. Fooled them so that the manatee, ugliest of creatures, became the basis of the legend of beautiful mermaids. For there were four woman aboard *Quebec*. Though none of them, to be fair, possessed such temptingly full hindquarters as Robin displayed in the wet-weather gear made almost skin-tight by the tension of the ropes that held her in place. Nor indeed, now he came to notice it, did any of the women aboard boast such a dazzling glory of guinea-gold ringlets. Only seaman Faure, indeed, had anything like that dazzling head of hair – a throwback to some long-dead Viking ancestor come ravishing into Vinland with Eric the Red, no doubt.

'Have we a line?' Bob called down to Dumas. 'Given a weight or a grappling hook I think I could catch her and reel her in pretty quickly.'

'Faure has a line down below,' answered Dumas, breathlessly, dropping the heavy bolt cutters. 'And I noticed a grappling hook in stores when I got the bolt cutters.'

'OK,' decided the first lieutenant. 'Let's go with that.'

'If,' continued Dumas, whose forebears were black-haired, black-eyed Provençal and noted for their dark views on life and so forth, 'you *want* to use a grappling hook to secure an inflatable life raft . . .'

But by this time Bob's concentration had wandered very actively away. For he had at last looked around, and he had seen what Mark Robertson had not. The net which lay over the after hatch was not by any means an isolated phenomenon, like the saddle cloth lying across the back of a horse. The whole of the after area of the submarine was festooned with the grey web. And so, as Bob turned to look, was the fin itself. The whole of the ten-metre tower was draped with netting as though it were a fly in the grasp of some unimaginable spider. Through it thrust the suddenly frail-looking uprights of the periscope, the communications mast, the snorkel and the rest.

Mind reeling with the implications of what he was seeing, the first officer reached for the walkie-talkie at his belt to report his all too disturbing observations to his captain. And as he did so, the vessel, on his order, reversed her heading and began to swing north towards the life raft and Greenland beyond. But the walkie-talkie was not there – knocked loose either while he was working with the bolt cutters or by the falling cod fish. He swung back, mouth open to call to Dumas or Faure, when both of them came up out of the hatch. Faure held the line and Dumas held the grappling hook. 'Here you are,' said Dumas. 'Just what you need for pulling a balloon aboard.'

Bob took the line and the hook at once. It simply did not occur to him that the situation was potentially fatal. He would report to the captain as soon as possible. In the meantime, if the woman on the life raft wasn't dead already, she would be dead all too soon if he didn't do something about it pretty quickly. His first cast reached the life raft and caught in the very apex of the inflated tent immediately above the woman's golden curls. Bob tugged gently, then more firmly. The raft began to drift towards the submarine and Bob got the confidence to pull even harder still. But that proved a mistake, for the sharp hook simply tore the top of the little tent away, and, with it, the life raft's automatic emergency beacon. Luckily, it slid off without puncturing the sides, but the inflatable spokes that held the tent erect slowly began to droop and the lifeless body topped decorously forward like a tree being felled in slow motion.

Bob pulled the grappling hook back aboard as quickly as he could, freed the hooks from the ripped canvas and threw the beacon into the water without a second thought. Then he cast again. This time he managed to snag the tangled lines beside the almost horizontal woman. But as soon as he began to pull, a fearsome hissing told him that he had managed to puncture the topmost tyre of the side. He pulled the life raft towards the submarine, all too vividly aware that the section immediately beneath the comatose woman was deflating all too rapidly and there was a real – and increasing – danger that she would slide into the water. And from the looks of her, if that happened, she would soon be as dead as the codfish in the galley – if she wasn't dead already. But finally, as he pulled the last of the line aboard, he felt the weight of the damaged raft come heavily on to the rope. 'Dumas,' he called, 'Faure, see if you can get her free. I'll hold her steady against the side.'

It took all of Bob's strength to do so, for the deflating life raft was a potent sea anchor – as it had been an all too lively kite. The collapsing vessel pulled against the forward motion and the steady turn of the submarine, almost pulling Bob into the rhythmically heaving water. Dumas and Faure used the netting as the other survivor must have done – but to let them down the side rather than to pull them up in the first instance. Then, as the first lieutenant really thought his arms were giving out, they had her. Whooping with Gallic victory they pulled her free and hefted her back up the side. 'You can let the line go now, sir,' called Faure. 'We have her safe aboard.'

Bob was glad to do what he was told, and he hesitated once his hands were empty, stretching his strain-stiffened shoulders as Dumas went down first and Faure lowered the still, corpse-like body down to him. Then Faure himself stepped down into the hatch. He paused there, looking up at the young officer. 'Well done,' he said. 'You have saved two lives today.'

But just at the moment that Faure paused to congratulate the first officer, the trawls at last wrapped themselves around *Quebec*'s propeller. In an instant, the whirling single screw had gathered all the slack around itself. But the chief, inspecting the Vane servos, was too slow to cut power and disengage the propeller before disaster struck.

The whole net section slid back as the lines tightened so fatally. The ropes of the net's weave screamed with tension. Like the blade of a blunt guillotine, the strands round Faure slid inexorably towards the stern. The rope caught him imme-diately under the rib cage, and there was nothing in his torso but his spine to stop its sudden slide. The edge of the hatch was scarcely sharper – but the force they exerted between them was that of a pair of bolt cutters a thousand times larger than the ones Hudson had just used. Faure let out a kind of whistling wheeze. He didn't even have time to scream – though the whole of the submarine seemed to be screaming now. His head and shoulders simply leaped upwards as though

47

he were jumping up out of the hatch. But his hips and legs fell down on the unconscious woman below. In between, there was a huge explosion of blood and mangled organs as though the unfortunate submariner had swallowed a live grenade. Bob saw all too much of it, for the net that he was standing on jerked backwards with the rest. He was hurled, face down and puking helplessly, across the deck until he was looking down the hole where Faure's legs and much of his blood had fallen. But there was a new net shrink-wrapped around the whole hull, taut as a vacuum pack and even stronger than steel across the gape of the hatchway. And, in the instant that he found himself looking down at Dumas's stark white face, the power and electrics went as the main shaft shattered with the strain and the propeller snapped to a halt. The way came off *Quebec* at once and she began to settle instantly.

Something massive fell on to the deck beside the sprawling man, clanged and clattered and rolled away. Out of the corner of his eye he recognized the communications mast beheaded from the top of the conning tower. The thought of it made him think of Faure once again and his stomach heaved helplessly. Something else fell down in exactly the same spot and rolled away in series. The snorkel. The periscope would be next, he thought almost dreamily. Christ, what a total mess this was!

'Shut the hatch, Dumas,' yelled First Lieutenant Robert Hudson with the kind of bravery that wins posthumous medals. 'Dumas, for God's sake shut the hatch!' And the last thing that he saw before the first wave took him and washed the puke away at least was the crewman obeying his order faster and more efficiently than he had ever done before.

Then the periscope indeed came down on the deck beside him, chopped off by the power of the tightening net, and the brave young officer rolled away from the sinking vessel into the all too immediate sea. He hung there for a moment, terrifyingly aware of the vastness of the ocean in which he was so suddenly so alone. His instinct for self-preservation suggested with almost overwhelming power that he should pull himself back aboard like the first survivor had done.

48

That he should clamber up the netting across the deck and up the fin like a kid on a climbing frame until the men trapped aboard worked out a way to bring him in. But his position so close and so low in the water simply emphasized the way *Quebec* was beginning to sink without power to move her forward and keep her pumps working. The thought of being trapped aboard the net-wrapped, dark and power-less, escape-proof vessel during the next few hours struck him with a shocking physical force, like the attack of a hungry shark. In an instant his imagination leaped back aboard the stricken vessel and foresaw its drawn-out future in a second or two of shocking empathy. He imagined every horror as she slowly settled to the bottom of the abyssal ocean.

The men and women aboard her would become the centre of a grim race between the leaking water, the freezing temper-atures and the thickening air. Would they suffocate or freeze before they drowned? Would his friends and shipmates run mad in the claustrophobic darkness, helpless and far beyond hope of rescue? Would they raid the galley looking for suici-dally sharp knives? Would they break open the arms lockers looking for guns? What in God's name would they do to themselves? What would they do to each other? As disci-pline, control – humanity, even – leaked away with the last of their hope. The thought of it simply made his blood run cold. A quick, clean death in the upper ocean suddenly seemed almost tempting and he was abruptly torn with bitter regret that he had taken the man and the woman aboard and robbed them of the lesser of two such terrible evils. He let the air out of his lungs and prepared to take the easier option at once.

But then the half-deflated life raft nudged him in the back of the head and offered him a third alternative after all.

Seven

Driven

Tom Hollander had met some focused and driven people since he had assumed command of *Sissy*. But he had never met anyone quite like Richard Mariner. 'We follow the wave,' grated Richard as the enormity of Robin's disappearance began to hit them all. 'And we go to the top of the green.'

'That's not standard "man overboard" procedure . . .'

Tom was thinking in terms of Williamson turns, lifeboats out, calling for aerial support. He had already called for drysuits in case anyone had to go overboard, and there was a team on the foredeck getting the Zodiac dinghy ready for just such a jaunt.

'Present heading,' repeated Richard. 'Full speed. And I do mean it when I say top of the green. You can get thirty knots out of *Sissy* before she goes into the red if you drive her hard enough. At least you can according to her paper specifications, even with a seventy-five per cent setting such as you're running now. Go for it, man! Sparks, monitor all the emergency wavebands. Goes without saying. Keep your ears sharp. Tom, I want to show you something . . .'

Tom nodded at the helmsman, shrugged at the radio operator and followed Richard out on to the bridge wing. He was wondering how his chief engineer was going to react to having his precious motors treated in this fashion – and, to be frank, whether his owner was beginning to crack under the shock of his wife's disappearance. But no. He was about to be educated, though he didn't know it yet.

Tom had always considered himself an observant and

50

insightful man. He had a good shiphandler's eye for detail and an intelligent person's ability to interpret what he saw. But if he had ever considered himself a seafaring Sherlock Holmes, he discovered all to swiftly and graphically that he would be lucky to equal Dr Watson.

'What do you see?' asked Richard as they stepped out on to the blustery bridge wing.

'I see what you see, Richard,' Tom answered confidently and with calculated brutality. 'Robin lost overboard. Now we're wasting time. We should be performing standard search and rescue . . .'

'Bear with me, Tom. I'm confident that we're heading in the right direction and coming up to our optimum speed. I think I know what happened and if I'm right, Sparks will get a distress call any moment now that will allow us to refine our heading even if we can't triangulate. The only thing I'm not sure of is your support. I really do know what I'm doing. But if I have to prove it to you then that will be time well spent. Now, apart from Robin's absence, what do you see?'

Such was the intensity of Richard's speech and manner, Tom could not resist. He looked around the bridge wing, eyes narrow and mind most vividly alive. He stood with his back to the bridge door as he did this, sending his gaze out northerly towards the Greenland horizon. So he did not see the vital clue. 'Life raft's gone,' he said. 'She'll be lucky to have got herself aboard that if that's what you're thinking. But it does look as though she jumped – her lifeline is here and the harness has been released. Not broken. See? Released. You think she panicked somehow? Maybe when we were sitting right on top of the wave. Yes. That'd make sense, wouldn't it? There was a moment there when even *I* thought we were going to fall back under and get swallowed right up. Yes. OK. I see that. You think she panicked, freed the life raft, hit her safety line release and jumped. But why would that have taken her forward instead of back?'

The answer slapped him in the face as he turned to glance back along their wake towards the Denmark Strait. Then it died fitfully away to be replaced by a steadily gathering headwind that cooled the back of his neck. But he was too preoccupied to understand it all.

'You've got it wrong, Richard,' he concluded. 'She's somewhere out there in our wake, whether she's in the raft or not.'

'No,' said Richard quietly. 'You've got it wrong. Let me tell you what really happened . . .'

Five minutes later, Tom was convinced. In the interim he had received an educational master class in such matters as Robin Mariner's unflappable, quick-thinking intrepidity. In the importance of missing axes. In the manner in which said axes had been applied to knots that were beyond the reach of a person wearing a safety line and harness. Of the reason why the shattered knot existed in the first place – and the upward force that had raised the winch end of the forward davit a good thirty centimetres higher than its after mate, in spite of the fact that it was made of sound, strong steel. And how it had been bent not just upwards – but forwards as well. How much line was still aboard from the twisted forward davit. How little from the sound, steady aft davit. How inflatable rafts inflate. The likely effect of them doing so in a gale at the top of a thirty-metre rogue wave. How this was a very logical explanation for the damage to the davit they had seen. Of the true significance of the very moment himself Tom had mentioned when the ship had suddenly seemed about to fall forward, but had settled back safely instead. Just as though an airborne drogue pulling them powerfully down the wind had been released to run free and save them.

'She must have gone overboard with it,' Tom breathed as they stepped back on to the bridge.'

'She's as quick and steady on her feet as a cat,' said Richard. 'She's not likely to have slipped. And she won't have jumped. So the long line must have taken her. The one that wasn't tangled up and chopped free. It must have wrapped itself around her and jerked her overboard.'

'I accept that . . .'

'Then she is at the very least attached to an inflated life

52

raft, isn't she? With any luck at all she'll have pulled herself aboard.'

'So we just need her emergency signal and we've got her . . .'

Tom made it sound so easy, in the same way as Richard had made it all sound so inevitable. Neither man at this stage wanted to calculate the odds against Robin's survival even if they were right in every detail. But even so, Tom was quick to send a man out on to each of the bridge wings with a walkie-talkie and powerful binoculars. Logic was all very well. Radar and radios were also fine in their way. But under the circumstances a couple of pairs of keen eyes would likely serve them best. No sooner had the lookouts exited than the drysuits came up from below and during the next few minutes, on top of everything else, Richard and Tom changed into them as they commanded the bridge.

'We just need the signal now,' repeated Tom when the men were gone on watch, as he stepped into the drysuit's trouser section.

And as he spoke, the radio screamed.

The radio officer leaped up out of his seat, tore off his headphones and gave everyone on the bridge an advanced education in Afrikaans invective.

'What was that?' demanded Richard at once, fine-drawn, indescribably tense, hopping on one leg as he too stepped into the protective gear.

'It's a mayday,' replied the radio officer. 'All channels. Full power and nearby.' He looked across at Richard as he answered. 'Dead ahead, I'd say.'

'But it's not our life raft, is it?' asked Tom, who was standing by the helmsman as he drove the ship as ordered with every ounce of power that was safe. Looking at the power settings and waiting for the chief to call as he pulled the unwieldy trousers up round his lean waist.

'No, Captain. I don't know precisely what it is. But no way is it our raft. Hey! Now what . . .'

'Now what?' Tom was becoming almost punch-drunk as one thing followed another in such disorientating series.

'It's stopped. Just like that. The full works one minute, dead air the next. Scary.'

'We need to be there,' said Richard. 'Whatever that was, it sounds like it was big and brutal. I'd say our rogue wave just caught some poor bastard with his defences down. Wasn't there a trawler or something showing on the radar pretty well dead ahead of us just before the rogue hit? Is that still reading there?'

'Nothing reading dead ahead,' answered the first officer from his position by the radar. 'Nothing above the water, anyway. And that's all we could see with this.'

'Still, better push in for a closer look,' said Richard.

'That makes sense,' admitted Tom. 'But whatever sent that signal it wasn't your wife or our life raft.'

'I know that. Sparks! Get those headphones on and keep searching through those emergency wavebands.'

'Aye aye. But I'll have to turn the volume up. That last lot's sent me nearly deaf. Jesus! I haven't heard a noise as loud as that since the Stones played Sun City!'

As *Sissy* drove westward at full speed, Richard shrugged the top section of the drysuit over the breadth of his shoulders and prowled round the bridge, zipping zippers, tightening straps and going through the logic of his explanation time and again. He felt in his bones – in his water as the Irish say – that he was right and Robin was somewhere dead ahead. And yet, if he was wrong, then he was powering away from her at full speed. Putting one nautical mile between them every two minutes. And two minutes was about all she could be expected to last if she was in the freezing water anyway. Two minutes or four – maybe six at the outside – before exposure stole her away from him at last. The thought of her alone out there, of her blonde hair like a tiny beacon tossing on the lonely immensity of the ocean, was almost more than he could bear.

Abruptly, it *was* more than he could bear.

He drew breath to capitulate. To tell Tom he was free to do whatever he wanted; whatever correct procedure might dictate. At the least, following proper sea-lore would have the benefit of reducing the burden of responsibility. To have obeyed the timeless laws of the sea like countless sailors before him and then to have got it wrong was almost acceptable. A responsibility shared with sailors back before the beginnings of history whose accumulated wisdom was never quite a match for the hunger of the sea. But to have made the decision himself and alone; to have forced the ship and crew to his will, to have driven them all westwards at the top of the green, to have got it wrong and left her to die alone somewhere far in his foaming wake . . .

The thought was more than he could bear.

'Tom . . .' he said. But the emotion that the uncharacteristic uncertainty had released within him made his voice turn thick and rusty. The monosyllable was lost beneath the racing of the engines, the gusting of the wind, the relentless battering of the waves that *Sissy* was stamping down. He cleared his throat, ready to try again.

Eight

Contact

'Got a contact!' shouted Sparks as Richard called to Tom again. 'Loud and clear and dead ahead! Two signals. Much less power than the last lot. Smaller. Maybe a lifebelt maybe a life raft. Maybe one of each.'

'Let's go and see, shall we?' Tom flung over his shoulder at Richard, a look of simple awe on his weather-beaten face. 'We're all dressed up, after all. We ought to have somewhere to go . . .'

'Hey!' chimed in the voice of the first officer once again. 'There's something reading on the radar dead ahead.'

'Life raft?' demanded Tom, almost fizzing with excitement now.

'Could be. It's small enough. But it's sending quite a signal. More like metal than rubber I'd say. But what in God's name could something that small be doing all the way out here unless it was a life raft?'

Then he answered his own question as the rest of *Quebec* heaved herself up above the ocean's surface and into his radar range. 'Shit! It's a sodding submarine! A bloody great submarine just surfaced dead ahead of us.' As if to emphasize the first officer's words, the automatic collision alarm on the radar started to sound.

'How far?' demanded Tom and Richard both at once, for the alarm meant that the vessel was dead ahead and very close.

'Five miles.'

'Three minutes at this speed,' calculated Richard, suddenly grateful for Tom's forethought. If they were just sending down for the drysuits now they would never get over the side in time.

'Why can't we see her?' demanded Tom. 'Watch? What are you doing out there?'

'Got her!' called in both lookouts at once. But the man on the starboard wing continued speaking, his voice coming out of the bridge speakers even though he was close enough to have communicated with a shout. 'There's something wrong, though. Her outline's not right. It's almost like these field glasses are out of focus – but they're not.'

'Hey,' chimed in his companion on the port wing. 'I can see a life raft. I don't know if it's ours . . . No, it's gone behind the sub. Wait! There's someone in the water this side of her.'

'What in God's name is going on?' demanded Tom of no one in particular. The succession of events was threatening to overwhelm him once again. 'Sparks. We have eye contact with the life raft now, I guess, so we don't need you monitoring the emergency bands any more. See if you can hail that sub and find out what on earth he's doing, will you?'

'Fall off a couple of points to port and throttle back,' said Richard quietly to the helmsman. 'We'll be there in a couple of minutes and we don't want to run them all down.'

'Watch? What can you see?' demanded Tom.

'Looks like the sub's turning to pick up the guy in the water. Yup. He's pulling himself aboard. Right. At last. Here comes someone out of the after hatch. Wonder why it took them so long?'

Richard, burning with frustration and uncertainty, had nothing to occupy his hands now that all the zips and straps on his drysuit were done up tight. So he pulled a pair of binoculars from their holster on the side of the captain's chair. He slammed them to his eyes and focused them through the clearview, using the manual override to cancel the infrared beam of the automatic which would otherwise have focused them on the bridge windows immediately in front of him. Though, given that he was wearing thick gloves as part of the all-in-one drysuit, this took more than a little expertise.

'Sparks. Any contact?' asked Tom.

'Nothing. If I was the sub's captain I'd be calling home on a secure line first thing I did when I surfaced . . .'

'Yeah. I guess,' agreed Tom. 'Fall off another point to port, helm. And half power to the motors. I want to be able to stop on a penny when we get there.'

'You may want to stop a little while earlier than that,' said Richard suddenly. 'That submarine is wrapped in fishing nets. Stem to stern and truck to keel by the look of things. I hope the captain has the wit to stop his engines before anything gets tangled in his propeller.'

'First survivor down the hatch,' called the port wing watch.

'Starboard watch, can you see what's happening with the life raft?' demanded Tom.

'Nothing, Captain. The sub's in the way. And it seems to be swinging to starboard now in any case.'

'How long till we get there?' Richard asked the first officer.

'At this speed, still five minutes.'

'That's what I thought. Sparks, can't you raise him? I don't think he realizes how much trouble he's in . . .'

But the submarine remained stubbornly silent as *Sissy* raced towards her, the tug's wild dash westward moderated only by the wisdom and experience of the men on the bridge who were rightly fearful of colliding with something – or someone – in the water. Three pairs of sharp eyes kept watch through three pairs of state-of-the-art binoculars, but after the tussle between the man who had pulled himself aboard and the officer on the afterdeck, their vision was obscured by the turning submarine. And, abruptly, their focus was torn away from the afterdeck and up to the top of the conning tower. From their position, the disastrous entangling of *Quebec*'s propeller in the net's long cables became obvious not in the sounds – which they could not hear – or in the destruction of poor Faure – which they could not see – but in the beheading of the conning tower. For, abruptly, under their stunned and disbelieving gaze, the slender uprights of the communications mast, the snorkel and the periscope all fell backwards like the tallest flowers in the field cut down by wanton fate. The whole skin of the submarine seemed to blur out of focus, then settle once again. And her forward motion faltered. Her starboard swing towards the life raft stopped. Her confident riding of the billows ceased. She slowed, steadied and settled all at once.

And Tom, the tugboat man, spoke for them all. 'Oh shit. She's in trouble.'

'Bad trouble,' agreed Richard. 'Helm, take us in as fast as you can. Tom, I think we'd better get ready to get our feet wet.'

By the time *Sissy* pulled up alongside *Quebec* there was a team in drysuits and survival gear on the tug's foredeck. They had prepared the ship's twelve-man Zodiac to go over the side and were ready to go down in it. They were ready to put on diving equipment and go into the water itself, but that level of preparation would take too long, so they had drawn the line here for the time being. There was a team waiting to go out on the afterdeck and get the towing cables rigged – but they too held back for the moment while the team on the Zodiac completed the first recon.

Richard was there as a matter of course. And so was Tom, confident that his first officer could command *Sissy* well enough in their absence. Both of them had waterproof walkie -talkies among the equipment at their belts. These were the only radios likely to be used in the immediate future, because the frail signals from the lifebelt and the life raft had both ceased at about the same time as the submarine's communications mast had fallen. And that in turn had cut the sub off from the outside world – unless someone could go up and crouch in the lightly netted conning-tower cockpit and try calling out with a mobile phone.

Though that was not as silly as it sounded, thought Richard grimly. It was exactly how the captain of the waterlogged and powerless *Chicoutemi* had contacted Fleet Command in Canada when a rogue wave swamped her off the Scottish coast five years and more ago. And it had worked well enough, too, until the cellphone's battery ran out. But these thoughts were only a way of occupying his frantic mind as he searched the nearby water for some sign of Robin.

59

The submarine was nearby and surprisingly massive. Her long grey hull – grey webbed over grey paintwork – was imposing even though she was riding low in the water, her foredeck and after sections awash. Up on the bridge wings the lookouts could see over everything except her conning tower but down here she blocked out half the ocean. 'Let's get the Zodiac in the water and go for a closer look,' demanded Richard, his patience running out at last.

No sooner had he spoken than Tom's walkie-talkie buzzed. He put it to his ear. 'The lookouts say there's what's left of a life raft round on the other side. It's awash and mostly deflated. But there could be someone in it.'

'Let's go!' said Richard again and within a very few minutes the Zodiac was powering across the restless ocean, round the low fin of the submarine's sinking tail. As they sped over the sub's propeller towards the life raft, Richard looked down and winced. The grey strands of the trawl lines seemed to have fused around the great bullet-shaped screw. Set, as though molten steel had been poured over the propulsion unit and then plunged in liquid nitrogen to set in a solid, unbreakable carapace.

But then Richard's attention was distracted by a shout. The life raft was in sight at last – and surprisingly close at hand. He pushed into the bow-seat, where the hard plastic sides met in a blunt point above the super-strengthened plastic of the hull itself. The crewman in control of the big Johnson Seahorse outboards gunned them to full power and the twelve-man vessel skimmed in at full speed.

The life raft was in a sorry state. The tent section was torn and deflated. The top level of the three-part hull was flaccid. The waves washed over it as the weight of the waterlogged canvas and whoever – whatever – lay aboard pulled it dangerously down. But then Richard's heart leaped agonizingly. In the water just beside the life raft, tangled in the lines just as he said she would be, there was Robin. He knew instinctively because of the brightness of the sea-washed curls. He reached forward, reckless of the danger, to grab her at once. She was floating face down and that was terrifyingly bad. No one aboard the Zodiac said anything as the sleek black vessel powered in. Richard leant further out, straining as the two men nearest held him on his seat by main force. The wash of their arrival lifted the life raft and pushed it away, taking the bright-haired body with it. Then his fingers brushed her shoulder. He grasped and pulled, hope welling to replace the pain of terror in his chest. He pulled, rearing back, to lift her into the Zodiac.

And she came, but all too easily. Came up and out of the water in his arms. A torso only, chopped off roughly at the waist. 'NO!' he screamed, overcome at last. 'ROBIN, NO!'

But Tom was there, and this time he saw more than Richard did. 'Richard! It's all right. This isn't Robin; it's some other guy. Some man with yellow hair, that's all. This isn't Robin! Do you understand?'

Richard mechanically put the dead man down and what was left of submariner Faure lay on the Zodiac's slatted deck like the victim of a shark attack.

But the shock and horror made Richard almost febrile. No sooner had he put the torso down than he swung round to the life raft once again. For there, below the deflated tent, lay the outline of a body – as unmistakable as someone sleeping beneath a sheet. Richard hurled himself forward once again, catching at the tangle of ropes. He pulled the half-deflated life raft against the Zodiac's tough bow with superhuman strength. 'Get her out,' he shouted. 'Someone get her out!'

And, obedient to his command, Tom and one of the crewmen pulled the flaccid, fainting body aboard. But once again Richard was disappointed. Instead of Robin, they had rescued a man in his late thirties, his unconscious face white as marble, marked with horror and caked about the chin with vomit.

Richard snapped then. He had been so absolutely certain. Now it seemed he was so terribly mistaken. His nightmare had come true. None of this was anything to do with Robin. She was somewhere back in the Denmark Strait, dead of exposure and hating him for failing her in the end. He took the young man by his shoulders and shook him, as a terrier shakes a rat. The marble paleness folded into a frown of gathering consciousness. The dark-ringed eyes fluttered open.

'Where is she?' demanded Richard. 'Where's the woman from the life raft?'

Bob Hudson blinked, twice, as his mind came briefly back on line.

'Where is the woman from the life raft?' asked the wild-eyed stranger once again.

'I put her aboard *Quebec*,' Bob answered quite distinctly.

'You put her where?' The wild-eyed face was transformed with hope.

Bob's head rolled over until he was pointing, French fashion, with his chin. And his chin was pointing over his right shoulder at the net-wrapped, hull-holed, slowly sinking submarine. 'God help me,' he whispered. 'I put her aboard *her* . . .'

Then his eyes rolled up, he shuddered once and fell back. He was so utterly dead to the world that Richard thought he had actually died until he felt the fleeting flicker of a pulse at his icy throat. Then he left him lying beside the top half of his shipmate in the bottom of the Zodiac and turned to look at the sinking submarine, his haggard face full of the grimmest speculation.

Nine

Catch

The storm had moderated to a dead calm. The sea was settling too, although a swell still ran south-westwards down to Cape Farewell peaking at more than a metre. A swell steepened and sharpened by the counter-flow of the northernmost reach of the Gulf Stream, which was running lazily counter, bringing warmer water with it. Warmer water that betrayed its presence to Richard's wise eyes in the slightest of steamy hazes as well as in the sharpening waves. But not even Richard, yet, could see the more sinister significance that the warmer water might bring to their situation here.

The sun was setting westward towards Canada dead ahead in a cloudless prairie sky, while dead astern in the evening-blue east above the Denmark Strait it was beginning to promise a star or two. There should have been a timeless silence broken only by occasional lapping and hissing from the sea below and the calls of gulls above as they gathered for their evening feed on the fishy riches coming up from the hot, rich south.

Richard, his legs widely astride as he rode *Quebec*'s narrow foredeck, bellowed over the industrial clangour of *Sissy* hard at work. 'How's it coming, Chief? Over.' The taller waves were breaking over his boot-toes now. And, in a kind of Catch-22, just as the slowing of *Sissy*'s wild drive down here had meant that the last five minutes before her arrival seemed to stretch out longer and longer, so the moderating seas simply served to emphasize how the stricken submarine was steadily settling lower and lower in the water. Even the smaller waves had started washing over her now. The teams they had sent swarming all over her, clinging to the nets like families of spiders, were beginning to complain of cold and wet and grow nervous of the rising water level.

But at least they had established, by tapping, that there was life somewhere within the hull – though more formal and complex communication was currently awaiting Sparks and his team on top of the conning tower.

'What? Over,' came the chief's reply, almost lost in the rhythmic hammering and clanging all around him. He sounded to Richard like a blacksmith whispering in his smithy.

Even though both men were using walkie-talkies, and were on vessels sitting as close together as seemed safe under the circumstances, they still had to yell loudly and listen carefully.

'Tom wants to know how long now? Over.'

'Tell him ten minutes; fifteen tops. Unless he keeps calling in and slowing us down, of course. Chief Engineer out.'

'Thanks, Chief. Out. Ten minutes, Tom. Then I guess another five to get it in the Zodiac and another five to get it here. I know we're nearly ready to receive it but it'll still take us a good fifteen minutes, on top of everything else, to get it in place. And that's if all goes well. Say forty minutes, to be on the safe side, before we transfer the messenger. An hour before the tow-line comes aboard, if everything goes according to plan. Eighty to ninety minutes before we can start the tow. A couple of hours before we get up enough speed to make much difference. Assuming that the whole Heath Robinson contraption holds together in the first place, of course. That'll be after sunset. Darkness will slow things down into the bargain, I should think.'

'I think you're right. One way or another, it'll be close.' Tom turned and looked up at the conning tower standing shrouded in heavy grey netting up above them. 'How's Sparks doing up there? I could really use some good news right about now.'

'Tell me about it!' Richard put the walkie-talkie to his lips and thumbed the Transmit button. But then he hesitated, sidetracked and released the button after all. Something worrying was stirring at the back of his mind as he gazed away into the pink haze of the evening dead ahead and the waves as sharp as sharks' fins moving through it. But still he did not connect the haze with anything relevant to their current situation.

Instead, Richard's dark thoughts took another turn instead. For Tom was right – not only in what he had said but in what he'd left unsaid. They were in the middle of a situation here with enough legal ramifications to feed a parliament of lawyers. They should not bring a line aboard without permission of the owners – to wit the Canadian Admiralty, or whatever they called themselves. The Canadians' most immediate and accessible representative was the captain and they really needed to talk to him before they proceeded. And he in turn should check with his superiors. Someone should be talking Lloyds' Open Form, or daily rate for the salvage of the submarine. Or something else that gave *Sissy* some kind of recovery rights over the expensive hull that they were rescuing and gave them some kind of insurance for the risks that they were running.

But of course, reasoned Richard grimly, if they were forced to wait much longer for a decision from on high, the stricken vessel would settle so low in the water that they would never be able to retrieve her in any case. Then they would not only lose all that money but – far more importantly – all those lives. And, like a stranger stopping at a traffic accident, they were assuming a whole range of legal duties. Certainly under English law – with which Richard was all too intimately acquainted these days – now that they had stepped aboard the stricken vessel they had assumed legal responsibility for all those endangered lives. Unless they could prove that they were doing everything that was reasonable in the circumstances, then they would be facing lawsuit after lawsuit from the relatives of anyone who died from here on in.

Worse than that, in the absence of any help and advice – or

65

knowledge about the construction of the submarine – the best they could come up with was a kind of makeshift cradle to feed the tow rope though the netting itself and keep the sub afloat that way. Until they could get the officer they had rescued themselves back into the land of the living, that was the only hope that they could see.

This plan, however, did mean that they were having to be very careful which bits of the net they cut away. It would be absolutely fatal to get the towline aboard and properly secured, then to set *Sissy* moving slow ahead merely to pull the nets off *Quebec* as though they were skinning an eel – and watch helplessly as the sub went down anyway.

With Robin aboard, alongside all the rest.

And that was something Richard was simply not going to allow to happen.

Tom called down the deck to the two teams with bolt cutters, 'The chief says ten more minutes to finish the cradle so we reckon maybe fifteen to get it over here. Will you be ready then?'

'We're ready now, Captain,' answered one of the teams.

'As ready as we'll ever be . . .' added the other.

While *Sissy* was a focus of activity, bustle, light and noise, the submarine was still sitting dead in the water, as motionless as a hunting crocodile. They had managed no meaningful communication with her and had no idea how things inside the net-wrapped hull actually were. They did not know who was alive and who was dead. Whether the crew had anyone left in charge. Whether there were any plans afoot to get the crippled vessel back under functioning control. It seemed plain to all of them that the primary power systems must have gone down with the destruction of the motors, but there should have been emergency backup from the huge batteries that occupied most of the bottom of the hull. There should have been temporary power enough to support communications, pumps, some sign of life. But there was nothing, other than the tapping that the teams had heard in reply to their own. But nothing more than the most basic communication had been achieved so far.

So Richard had suggested to Tom that they should send *Sissy*'s radio officer up the fin with a team of engineers and a power source of their own. Just to see if they could maybe patch into the wires on the stump of the communications mast and send a message down. Otherwise they were going to have to rely on tapping Morse code on the submarine's hull and hoping someone would start tapping Morse code back. At least, now the seas were moderating, that was becoming a feasible possibility. And it would remain so until the hull itself settled under the water.

On that less than cheery thought, Richard recalled what he was supposed to be doing here. He depressed the Transmit button once again. 'Sparks! The captain wants a progress report. Over.'

'We'd make more progress if we could cut the top off this net and use the cockpit as a base. Then we could get a generator up here instead of a battery maybe. Perhaps we could even find a way of opening the hatch and getting inside, you know? Over.'

'We've discussed that. We'll keep it under advisement. But our main priority at the moment has to be to keep her afloat at all costs. That's our focus down here. In the meantime, do what you can with what you've got from where you are. Over.'

'OK. We see the logic. But there's not a lot to report at this precise moment in time. This is quite a mess up here. Over.'

But Richard wasn't listening any more. The Zodiac was on its way over from *Sissy* with the big curving metal cradle aboard. That was a good step forward. The teams further down the foredeck had cut holes in the netting to accommodate the curved steel gutter the chief had just designed and made. They were planning on finding enough slack in the netting to feed the thing through, then lie it down on its side with the curve of the gutter facing towards the fin and the open ends towards *Sissy*. Then, when it

67

was securely in place, they would feed a light messenger though it, take the end of this back to *Sissy* and, feeding out from one huge winch, gather it in at the other until they had pulled the tug's huge 80mm woven monofilament towing line aboard. Not just aboard, in fact, but round through the steel channel in the netting and back to the second winch on *Sissy*. This huge loop would sit in the cradle – hopefully without chafing. When *Sissy* began the tow, the cradle would pass the pressure evenly to the netting and all the strain would be distributed around the web-wrapped hull allowing them to move the vessel forward without tearing the netting open – or pulling it right off.

Once the sub was safely and steadily afloat, the rescuers could proceed to Phase Two of their plan. When they had decided what, precisely, Phase Two was going to be.

Tom's experience in towing – supported by Richard's in general shiphandling – suggested that once her hull was moving, the submarine would gain sufficient buoyancy to keep her on the surface, using exactly the same physical laws that keep kites aloft in steady winds. Just so long as none of the other more negative variables – such as any damage to the battered hull – was compounded by what they were doing. If they had a Phase Two to their plan, then that was it. Once the submarine was securely afloat, someone was going to have to get in a diving suit and check the hull for damaged areas where the forward motion might raise the water pressure and exacerbate any leaks.

But as the Zodiac bumped against the submarine's hull and the chief began to unload the big steel cradle he had made, the game underwent a radical change. For the first man off and on to the deck was the submarine officer from the life raft. Because he recognized Richard as the man who rescued him, the pale young survivor crossed to him at once. 'Bob Hudson,' he introduced himself. 'First Officer of the *Quebec*. I think I owe you a considerable vote of thanks.'

'Call it even,' answered Richard. 'That was my wife you saved and put safely aboard. Did she seem all right to you?'

'She seemed OK. She stirred as we transferred her and opened her eyes. But it's good of you to say I saved her. You're going to save her all over again yourself by the look of things.'

'Looks like it,' agreed Richard shortly. He had no intention of being rude, but his mind was whirling with the implications of Bob Hudson's arrival. Even though he was first officer, Bob would not be able to take any of the captain's decisions about rescue and salvage unless the captain himself was dead. So his presence didn't loosen things up on that level. On the other hand, here was someone who would have a good idea of what was going on within the all too secretive hull. Who might very easily be able to explain conundrums that had puzzled them all so far. And if he could do that, then he might well be able to advance the rescue very rapidly indeed.

Typically, Richard went straight to the heart of things. 'Looks like *Quebec*'s lost all power,' he observed. 'There's no life in the hull. We've picked up a signal or two by tapping on the hull so we know there are people alive down there. But there's been no spoken contact – by shouting or using the radio. And no one's tried to open the hatches and talk to us.'

'Power and light went down when the screw got caught in the nets. I saw it happen just before . . . Well, you saw poor old Faure . . . No; I was looking down the hatch when it all went dark. I can't say I'm surprised. The system wasn't running right. The chief's main gripe was the way the power system kept giving him grief. It was a new system, isolated for work under the ice, but like most of these things it was borderline experimental, always running just a little bit beyond its design specifications. Never really reliable. Like those Formula One racing cars that keep breaking down in a way your average family roadster never should.'

'Well, I can see how propulsion would have gone down when the screw got tangled up, but they should have had emergency power from the batteries at once, surely. And then they should have been able to isolate the power systems, shouldn't they? Keep the alternators charging up the batteries even if the shaft's not turning. Running the thing in neutral, so to speak. They should have been able to get things back on line by now, surely.'

'Yes. You'd think so. That's all part of the design, of course.'

'And in any case, even with all that down, the fail-safe or default should ensure that the emergency battery power comes on automatically,' insisted Richard.

'Jesus, yes! I mean, without even auxiliary power, they really would be stuck. No bilge pumps to clear the water out of her. No air-con pumps to circulate the atmosphere. Not even any power to the hatch auxiliaries. God! Do you think that's what's happened? With backup power down they wouldn't even be able to open and close the hatchways.'

'But you said you saw the after hatch close *after* the power went down.'

'That's right. That's the fail-safe. Power down: hatches close. Hatch auxiliary motors shut off. Safety bolts go home.'

'Trapping everyone aboard? That doesn't seem like very good design . . .'

'The escape route is through the conning tower and up the fin. The hatches there should still operate, even without power.'

'Then why hasn't anyone come up that way to contact us, I wonder.'

Bob Hudson glanced up at the top of the fin. 'Well, I'm not what you'd call a betting man,' he said slowly. 'But I'd lay pretty good odds that when the periscope and every-thing else up there was chopped off, cut down and ripped out by the roots it somehow smashed up a lot of the stuff on the inside of the fin as well. And I mean, if the escape pod in there has been knocked askew, or the passages and shafts in there are blocked off or twisted up, then there really is no way out. Especially if they haven't got light and power to see and solve their problems.'

'We really do need to get in there and take a look if we possibly can,' mused Richard, speaking as much to himself as to Bob.

70

'Well, I guess if we're going to try, then now is the time to do it,' agreed Bob. 'It'll be dark soon and that could well make things much more complicated.'

'If power's down then it's going to be dark in there in any case,' said Richard grimly. 'But you're right. Let's go up and talk to Sparks.'

At the base of the fin Richard thumbed the Transmit on his walkie-talkie once again. 'Tom? It's Richard, Over.'

'Yes, Richard?'

'Just checking in. *Quebec*'s First Officer and I are going up to see if we can release the main escape hatch and get a look inside. Bob knows where the emergency catch is located and says the system is fail-safe to open. There may be damage to the internal structure of the conning tower that we should know about as soon as possible. Over.'

'Sorry, Richard, that'll have to wait. Time's caught up with you. I'm clearing everyone off *Quebec* now except for a small team to oversee the tow. I'm just about to run the messenger back and take up the tow. I don't want anyone aboard *Quebec* who doesn't have to be here until we see what happens as the tow gets under way. Over.'

Richard went as cold as if he had been plunged into the icy sea. The thought of going back aboard *Sissy* now that he knew Robin was on *Quebec* and needing his help simply robbed him of breath. He paused for a moment, as the loud-hailers aboard the tug boomed out with the captain's order to return. He breathed in deeply as the crewmen hurried past him, slopping through water already ankle deep, all too keen to get safely off and away. He noted almost idly, such was his preoccupation, that Sparks and his little crew were returning empty-handed. In too much of a hurry to bring the bulky battery, electrical equipment and bolt-cutters with them. Tom was going to be a very unhappy man when he found out about that.

'Point taken, Tom. But Bob and I will attach ourselves to the tow party on the bow, if that's all right with you. Then we'll be in a good position to take any emergency action if we need to. Over.'

'OK Richard.' Tom's voice was dry and almost disap-

71

proving. He was clearly less than happy already. At the very least he suspected Richard had unspoken motives for his near-refusal to follow the captain's orders. 'It's your call. This time. See you back on *Sissy* later. If everything goes according to plan. Captain out.'

Ten

Calm

Richard and Bob stood a little back from the team Tom had ordered to stay aboard and oversee matters until *Quebec* got under way. *Sissy*'s crewmen accepted the messenger line from the crew of the Zodiac and fed it through the curved gutter that lay wedged tightly beneath the net wrapped around the foredeck, the forward curve wedged tightly against a little protuberance standing solidly out of the foredeck itself.

Feeding the messenger through was less easy than it looked. Although the messenger was light and all the men had to do was to put their hands through the squares of net as they passed it from one side of the deck to the other, the gutter itself was under water now and only the very top of the feature it was wedged against stood solidly above the water level.

The team was cold and soaked and a great deal less than contented with their lot by the time they passed the end back to the crew of the Zodiac. Then all of them stood silently, uncertainly, watching the Zodiac pull the messenger back to the brightly lit stern of the tug. As soon as it was aboard, the tug's motors gave an extra cough and *Sissy* started moving slowly away.

Richard at once became caught up in the simple seamanship of the process. Bob, too, was fascinated and they fell into an almost monosyllabic conversation which – at the very least – served to cover their gathering nervousness. *Quebec* remained effectively at rest while the Zodiac was pulling the messenger back to her larger mother ship, but once the big

73

tug had it and the massive winches were employed, the net beneath their feet began to stir and tauten.

'Watch your footing,' said Richard, redundantly.

'Why is he beginning to pull away?' Bob replied irrelevantly.

'I'd guess that if he doesn't, then the simple physics of threading the big towline through the cradle will pull both the vessels together. Once you're afloat there's nothing much to stand between you and Newton's laws of motion.'

'So for every action there's an equal and opposite reaction. Yes, I see.'

The cradle screamed as the strain moved it forward a couple of centimetres across the metal of *Quebec*'s foredeck, settling it more tightly against the upright under the steady pull of *Sissy*'s simple refusal to drift back and close the gap the rope was being pulled across. It was a strange sound for it came through almost a metre of restless water. The net flexed further. The churning water behind *Sissy*'s high, square stern gathered into foaming hillocks. The big red towline splashed down into the water beside them and began to snake towards them like an enormous serpent hunting the little messenger as it fled before it. The cradle screamed another centimetre or two forward, but the sound and movement were different – for it was only the outer ends that flexed. The net itself flexed further, like the fur on a shivering animal.

'You want to go and check things further back?' asked Richard. 'See how well the net's holding in place towards the stern.'

'Yeah. I guess,' answered Bob uncertainly. But he took the length of safety line that Richard handed him as he spoke.

And when Richard turned and started slopping back along the submarine's length, he was quick to follow. They stopped at the conning tower and looked upwards. In the brightness of the sunset, they could see the drum-skin tautness of the net against the massive fin seem to flex and billow as the towline heaved itself up out of the water, following the messenger into the guttering like a ferret following a rabbit down a hole. On the last of the fore-deck they paused, then used the line Richard had brought to tie themselves together like mountaineers tackling a particularly dangerous ascent.

Richard actually took hold of the net on the side of the conning tower and used the vertical web to hold himself erect as he went round on to the afterdeck, pulling the much less confident Bob behind him. Here at first things were easier, for the deck behind the fin was flatter, squarer, wider. But then, from about three-quarters of the way down, the final quarter of the submarine sloped away down to the tangled propeller and the steering gear around it. Richard was almost up to his waist in water – and very glad of his drysuit – when he at last reached the upright fin and peered down past the after aquaplane to check on the state of the screw. The light was dying rapidly now and the whole area aft of the main fin was ghosted with shadows, just as it was chillier in its feel and haunted with strange stirrings and sea sounds. But there was enough light to see the tangle around the screw and feel with his feet how the net was solidly anchored here – as though it was a pattern on the icy hull. And he was able to make Bob up on the last square section of the afterdeck hear him when he called up the length of the safety line, 'It's all solid here. This lot's never going to tear loose.'

And no sooner had he spoken than, as though to prove his words were true, the first counter-wave slapped up into his chest. He looked down, frowning with concentration as this first wave was followed by another, and a third. And then the water settled until a line of ripples started spreading away on either side into the restless sea behind him. His breastbone was creating a bow wave just about level with his heart. And he heard Bob begin to cheer as he too understood what was going on. *Quebec* was begin-ning to move.

In the last of the light, Richard hesitated at the base of *Quebec*'s fin once again, with Bob Hudson standing at his shoulder. Both men were looking up at the ragged outline of the tower-top. Richard had hesitated in the first instance, remembering, suddenly and apropos of nothing at all, the equipment that the radio officer and his team had left up there in their hurry to return to *Sissy*. He and Bob might as well shin up and get what they could, he thought. The electrical stuff at the very least should not be left out here where it could get wet. As he hesitated, his walkie-talkie buzzed. It was Tom. 'You want me to send the Zodiac back for you? Or are you going to stay with the team on the deck overseeing the tow until the end of the watch?'

'I don't want to come back over quite yet. I'll call in again in half an hour or so. Are you going to leave men here all night?'

'I haven't decided yet. We'll see how things go as I come up to towing speed. We're hardly making any progress at all at the moment. I will need to talk things over with you, though.'

'I bet you will! We have to decide where we're actually going to tow this thing *to*! Over.'

'That's easy, Richard. I'll tow it to the man who's paying. Over.'

'Or to wherever the man who's paying wants it taken. I know. Over.'

'So, all we need to do now . . .'

' . . . Is find out who the hell *is* paying. Out.'

The climb up the fin was not as difficult as Richard had feared it might be. The netting was tight against the sub's side but there was still purchase for fingers and toes, especially where the nets were pressed up against each other instead of the conning tower. It was hardly more difficult than climbing a long ladder. And if you didn't look down, not too vertiginous either.

The top of the fin was surprisingly wide and seemed better lit than the main hull some three metres below. The pair then had gone up the forward edge where the hand- and foot-holds were easiest, and so the first thing they

76

discovered was that the radio officer might well be riding for a greater fall than even Richard had suspected. The net had been cut in the very place that Tom had forbidden. It was held in place by the backward-sloping metal that had once contained a glass windscreen – now shattered and gone. Behind this, enough of the strands had been cut to allow easy access to the safe, secure, steady and most of all dry little cockpit. Here, clearly, the radio officer and his team had gathered to work on the dead radio lines reaching down into the shadowed mystery of the conning tower below. The missing equipment was piled on the sole of the cockpit. There was quite a bit of it, though it made a neat little tower and left the majority of the area free.

Richard was in the lead so he shinned over the edge and dropped into the cockpit first. He crossed to the equipment at once and by the time Bob joined him he had pulled out a huge flashlight and was shining it around. The first thing he did was to shine it down to see if he could make out whether *Quebec* was moving rapidly enough to be coming back up to the surface once again. If it was, then there was the possibility of getting her people out through the deck hatches once power was restored. But no: the waves were still breaking over her. Power or no power, the instant a deck hatch opened, the Atlantic would pour in and fill the submarine long before anyone could escape. Richard paused for an instant, fascinated as always by the physics he was dealing with. The water level was only a few centimetres above the hatch level. But it was the water level of the whole Atlantic Ocean, North and South: from Cape Farewell to Hope Bay. From Greenland to Antarctica. And those few tiny centimetres represented sufficient volume to fill a million or so *Quebec*s.

And then as always, Richard's grasshopper mind skipped once again to an arcane piece of knowledge only very distantly related to his original thought. What was it that film producers Lew Grade or Dino de Laurentiis had said of the movie *Raise the Titanic*? 'Raise the *Titanic*? It would have been cheaper to lower the Atlantic . . .' An observation unfortunately accurate now. If they couldn't raise *Quebec* by twenty centimetres or so, then they would indeed begin to lower the Atlantic the moment they opened the hatches.

But, now he thought of it, there was something else that had been niggling at the back of his mind. Now what was that? ... ... ?

'Have you tried the hatch?' asked Bob with unconscious relevance as he too scrambled into the cockpit.

'No,' answered Richard, abruptly swinging the bright beam of the powerful torch inboard. 'Where is it?'

'Here.' Bob was on one knee, his fingers threading themselves through a deceptively tiny handle in the deck. It flipped up, lifting a larger section which in turn revealed a larger handle immediately beneath. 'Stand back,' ordered Bob and Richard saw in the brightness of the beam the black lines that defined the edges of a hatch. Bob took the second handle and began to turn it. There was a hiss of releasing pressure and the hatch lifted up.

The first thing Richard was aware of was the stench. It was a deeply disturbing – distressing – amalgam of human waste and sickness, chemical effluent, engine oil, smoke and fire. But beyond that, there was something else mixed into it as well. Something more difficult to define. Next, he became aware of the absolute blackness within the throat of the hatch itself. The cockpit contained some brightness still from the darkening dome of the stained-glass sky. But that black square contained no light. Seemed to soak up light, indeed, like the uncharted vastnesses of interstellar space. Like black holes. Richard shone the torch beam down as much in a sense of self-protection as in one of natural enquiry. And the bright halogen beam chopped through the shadows to show that Bob's fears had been all too accurate. There were half a dozen vertical rungs below the hatch standing white and regimented in the light. Then the shaft down which they reached twisted out of line. Folded in on itself. Bent. Closed. It would need a closer inspection to be certain, but it looked at first glance to Richard as though they would need some serious kit to get into the submarine that way.

Or, come to that, to get anyone trapped down there out.

But no sooner had the thought come into Richard's head than the whole fabric of the vessel around him seemed to stir. He staggered a little and flashed the torch beam over the side to see if the net was slipping. But no. It all seemed securely in place.

It was only when he glanced back, his quick eyes moving faster than the torch itself, that he understood. For the shaft down into the conning tower was no longer utterly black. There was light down there. Distant and insubstantial, perhaps – a spectral thing rather than a strong beam. But it was there. And, with it, a pulsing grumble of power restored. A sighing hiss of air circulation breathing once more.

And Richard, almost entranced by the complex of experiences and emotions he was feeling, did the most obvious thing of all. 'Hello, *Quebec*!' he called. 'Can anybody down there hear me?' He had no sense of doing anything momentous at that moment. No thought that he might be a messenger of hope in a desperately dangerous situation. 'Hello, *Quebec*,' he called again.

'Hello yourself,' came the distant reply. 'Are you the guy who's been tapping on my hull?'

'One of them,' answered Richard. 'There's quite a few of us out here trying to help you.'

'Well, that's fine and dandy,' came the distant reply. 'And very welcome under the circumstances. Especially if you are Richard Mariner and you have come aboard from *Sissy*.'

There was an infinitesimal pause as Richard assimilated all the implications of the stranger's words, formulated his reply and inserted the next piece of good news of his own, his voice trembling with relief and simple joy. 'I am Richard Mariner and *Sissy* has a line aboard you that seems to be all that's keeping you afloat. I assume you have my wife Robin down there with you. I have your first officer here with me. We're trying to find a way in . . .'

'No!' came the instant reply. 'Whatever else you're doing, you'd best stay out of here! Bob, you hear me, this is Mark and that's an order. You tell them to stay out of *Quebec*! I've a bad situation down here that I want to keep the lid on. And I mean keep the lid on *tight*!'

Eleven

Situation

Mark Robertson was standing at the periscope when the nightmare began. He had been made aware of problems with the early designs of the British *Upholder* class, of which this was the fifth and the last, but much work had been done to overcome them, especially since the Canadian navy had bought them and renamed them the *Victoria* class. The further modifications *Quebec* had undergone to fit her for under-ice work seemed to have reawakened some gremlins, though. There had been loss of power to propulsion several times before. The diesels were like his teenage kids at home: they went through expensive spares like there was no tomorrow and once they were asleep they were the devil's own job to wake up. But nothing he had been briefed about and prepared for had warned him that the unplanned crash-stopping of the screw would short out power, light and life support into the bargain. The systems might overlap; might share some significant elements. But the simple fact was that if the diesels went down, auxiliary power should have guaranteed that everything else stayed on. What *Quebec* was facing now was a situation unlike anything any of them had been led to expect.

But in that horrific moment of revelation when the nets screamed tight against the acoustic tiles of *Quebec*'s outer skin, Mark intuitively knew what was going on. Even as the drive shaft whirled to destruction caught between the power of the spinning motor and the stasis of the tight-bound screw, he knew that he had never been briefed for anything like this. But things all too rapidly became worse than he could ever have suspected – had he been given the leisure to speculate.

The periscope at which he was standing was wrenched away from him as though some giant hand on high had torn it from its fixings. It slid down out of its housing and the crosspiece against which he had been leaning to look upwards crashed to the deck with utter finality. The whole useless tube was only held vaguely erect because it was too long to fall out of the tower completely. Mark staggered forward and came within an ace of falling to his knees. That probably saved him from serious injury, for a storm of metal suddenly cascaded out of the opening up into the conning tower immediately above his normal command position. He only saw the first of it smash down on to the deck before the lights went out, and even in the sudden, shocking darkness the sounds up there continued, as though someone had released King Kong with a jack-hammer in the fin.

There was a huge noise from aft, somewhere between a grinding and a clanking, rising to a penetrating scream. Then there was a detonation. Mark, stunned though he was, was put in mind of a bulldozer full of teenage girls falling off a cliff – that would make a series of noises just like that. The deck shuddered violently, though *Quebec*'s stately progress did not seem to slow at once. The whole of his command gave a kind of a howl and then everything within it closed down, as though it had been the victim of a heart attack or stroke.

Or, given the situation, a victim suffering from both heart attack and stroke at one and the same time.

Then there was silence, except for the gurgling whisper of water all around them. A kind of stasis, as though *Quebec* were an interstellar spaceship drifting down on an undiscovered planet. Like the doomed star freighter *Nostromo* in *Alien*, for instance. And absolute darkness; darkness so complete that for a moment Mark wondered if he had been struck blind.

'Are all of you guys all right?' asked Mark into the lightless, water-whispering void. His voice was rusty and slight – almost a whisper – overcome by the enormity of events.

'OK, Captain,' came the first reply after an instant, in an equally awed whisper.

'I think I may have gone blind,' came another whisper almost at once.

'No,' said Mark with some relief, his voice gathering strength and command again. 'The lights have gone down. That's all.'

'I think I may need to change my shorts,' came a third voice, stronger and full of wry laughter.

'Me too,' came a fourth.

'Don't bother,' came the fifth and last, drawling, chilled, laid-back. 'With the air-con down, no one's ever going to notice.'

There was a little silence after that as they all sat letting the situation sink in. No air-con might be an inconvenience. No power meant no light or heat: that was a great deal worse. No power meant no pumps: and that could be simply fatal. Suddenly the mindless whispering chuckle of the water gained a new and terrible significance. Even Mark, who felt he was handling the burgeoning crisis in the best traditions of his service, began to suspect that the water noises were not just coming from outside *Quebec*. They seemed to be coming from inside her as well.

And, abruptly, it seemed to the stricken captain that the almost balletic movement he could feel, that slow-motion spaceship drifting through the liquid element as though through interstellar space, could just as well be heading downwards as forwards. Ballistic, perhaps, rather than balletic after all. And then he remembered that the after hatch was open while Bob Hudson tried to get the last survivor aboard out of the life raft in the ocean.

The walkie-talkie crashed against Mark's mouth with such force that it split his lip and chipped his tooth. 'Bob!' he snarled, literally spitting blood. 'Bob, are you there? Over?'

There was a brief silence. Then the little instrument came

to life. 'This is Master Seamen Dumas, Captain. It's a mess down here. The lieutenant is still outside, but he ordered me to secure the hatch, which I have done. We saved both of the survivors, Captain, a man and a woman. Both unconscious but stirring. Both in the infirmary now. But we lost Leading Seaman Faure. Well, we lost half of him . . .'

Mark was just about to demand some explanation of the last remark – something that the automatic logs would certainly not cover – but Chief Engineering Officer La Barbe forestalled him. 'Captain, it is Commander La Barbe. Perhaps, when you are at leisure, you would meet me in my office. At your earliest convenience, in fact. Chief Engineering Officer Over.'

Mark frowned, suddenly glad of the blackout. The tone brooked no delay, as they say in old-fashioned stories. And that was very bad indeed. La Barbe certainly preferred to be referred to as Chief; for he was old-fashioned and rather regarded his naval rank as irrelevant to his actual work. So his formal message, ranks and all, was yet another reason to worry. There was a volume of hidden communication in that one short broadcast, and Mark wanted to be certain that he understood every word and nuance of it, *at his earliest convenience*, as Commander La Barbe had said.

'On my way, Chief. Captain Out.' He lifted his thumb off Transmit. 'Has any of you guys got a flashlight handy?'

The quickest-thinking of the control operators reached unerringly through the velvety blackness and pulled a torch out of its clips. He switched it on and Mark was able to pick his way carefully across the command area towards the light. Long before he actually relieved the crewman of the suddenly vital light source, all the others had found theirs too.

As soon as Mark had the torch he felt more secure and in control himself. He swept the beam across the deck, noting ruefully the drunken disposition of the periscope, the pile of indeterminate metalwork on the spot where he normally stood. A pile that looked big enough to have incapacitated him; perhaps to have killed him. The good fortune of his escape buoyed him up. He crossed to his near-death experience at once and shone the beam up the cavernous shaft immediately above. That was where all these deadly bits and pieces had come from, after all. The bright beam should have revealed the regimented perspective of shaft and rungs reaching up towards their vanishing point, which lay, after various trapdoors and safety features, at the hatch in the cockpit. Instead there was a twisted mess of agonized metal closing off the gaping throat as effectively as a hangman's noose.

Mark brought the bright beam down with a shiver of apprehension. 'Sit tight, men,' he ordered. 'And let's ration the light, if you please. One flashlight only for the time being. I'm off to engineering now. I may be some time.'

Mark followed the torch beam along the deck, careful of his footing. It might have been raining ironwork down here as well. But it soon became clear that he could just as well have followed his nose or his ears. For, although the deck was reassuringly clear, there was a sinister smell of burning that got stronger and stronger as he went aft, deeper into the chief's domain.

Here, at first distantly and then more steadily as he proceeded, there were fireflies of brightness that danced up and down, coming and going amid the massive shadows without apparent logic. As he approached, the wraiths steadied into torch beams and the muttering gurgle of watery silence was joined by a mutter of conversation. He began to focus not only on the words but on the people speaking them, as a distraction from his increasing nervousness if nothing else.

'In the early days a crash back would generate more than sixty thousand amperes.' That could only be Lieutenant Chen, La Barbe's right hand. She had gained her engineering qualifications in Vancouver but seemed happy enough in the Atlantic Fleet. Indeed, in the Arctic Fleet. 'Sixty thousand would fry more than an egg, you know?'

'But that was in the early days,' Sub-Lieutenant Gupta answered, every bit as much of a techno nerd as she, and not to be outdone by her knowledge of the motors' history. 'They fixed that.'

'Like they fixed the little fault that opened the torpedo tube slide valves at the same time as the rear doors, allowing free passage into the forward sections to whatever ocean you were under at the time . . .' Chen countered derisively.

'Yes, they fixed that. And it's not relevant here, is it? This is everything *fried*, not flooded.' La Barbe himself tried to pull his warring underlings back to the immediate problem.

'Everything fried when *Chicoutimi* flooded, and she's our sister boat,' observed Chen waspishly.

'Indeed. But there was water involved there too. And less waterproofing than specified in the design. Here it is just the power surge generated by the destruction of the propulsion . . .' insisted La Barbe.

'Is it true that the diesels were actually designed for locomotives?' demanded Gupta suddenly.

'Yes,' answered La Barbe shortly. The question was also irrelevant to the matter in hand.

'They would be better in the French TGV or a Canadian Pacific locomotive,' sniffed Chen.

'Anywhere, in fact, but here!' agreed the captain, entering the conversation at last. 'What have you to tell me that you don't want to say over the walkie-talkie, Chief?'

The three engineering officers looked at one another almost guiltily. At last, as his duty dictated, it was the commander who answered, as though addressing a class at the academy. 'Well, Captain, when the screw stopped spinning the motors were still running. I was not here. I was looking at the aquaplane servos in the bow. No one shut the motor down. No one disengaged the shaft, the motors themselves or the electrical circuits that they feed. The result of course was a catastrophe.

'The screw stopped. The end of the shaft attached to the screw stopped. The motors did not stop. The end of the shaft attached to the motors did not stop. The shaft twisted in the middle like a length of play-dough and tore itself apart. The motors immediately went into uncontrolled overdrive, for there was no resistance now in the broken shaft. The amount of power they were passing into the system jumped incontinently. They burned themselves out almost instantly. But not before the extra charge of their uncontrolled running burned out almost all of the fuses, relays and circuits aboard.

'Thus this process not just caused the motors to overload, but generated such a surge in the electrical system between the motors and the batteries that everything seems to have fried. We are very fortunate indeed not to be facing a major fire . . .'

'Like they did in *Chicoutimi*,' added Chen feelingly. As well she might, thought Mark. For Chen's opposite number, Lieutenant Chris Saunders, had died from smoke inhalation after fighting the fire on *Chicoutimi*.

'OK,' said Mark patiently. 'The question is this: How long will it all take to fix?'

'To fix it all,' answered La Barbe slowly, 'will take a long time . . .'

'Well, let's get started . . .'

'A long time in a dry dock. With a full team of engineers doing an effective electrical refit,' completed La Barbe with just a little more emphasis than was strictly necessary.

'And of course replacing the motors – or the vast majority of the parts . . .' added Chen, her voice prissy and dead.

'Not to mention the screw, the shaft, the gears, the couplings, the . . .' continued Gupta with some relish, every bit as lugubrious as the Provençal Dumas.

Mark just gaped at them, his mind racing. 'Can you fix any of it?' he asked at last. 'Enough to give us back light and heat. And power to the pumps?'

La Barbe looked at his young acolytes. 'If we cannibalize some of the unnecessary circuitry . . .' he began.

'Take it as read that we'll not need to even try restoring propulsion and see what we can take out of those systems . . .' Chen took up the idea and began to run with it.

'Prioritize pumps, then light and heat,' insisted Mark, already looking to the future.

'Air-con and maybe galley . . .' added Gupta, not to be outdone.

'And the infirmary. We'll not get through this without someone somewhere aboard getting hurt or worse,' insisted Mark. 'And communications if it can be done . . .' He realized he hadn't even mentioned the state of the conning tower to the chief. And he opened his mouth to do so now.

Before Mark could say a word, however, his walkie-talkie started calling. 'Captain. Captain, are you receiving me? Over . . .' He didn't recognize the voice, but the tone made his short hairs stir in a way that they hadn't in the crisis so far. There was bad news coming. There was very bad news coming.

'Captain here. Over.'

'Captain, this is Petty Officer Watson in the infirmary. Over.'

'Yes, Watson? Over.'

'Captain, we have a death here. Over.'

'Leading Seaman Faure? I know he was accidentally killed earlier. Over.'

'No, Captain. It's not Faure. And it wasn't an accident. I think we may need some backup. Can you come here at once?'

Mark was in action at once. 'Do what you can, Chief,' he ordered and turned on his heel like a guardsman on sentry duty. Petty Officer 1st Class 'Doc' Watson was the man in charge of the infirmary because he was the most level-headed, down-to-earth unflappable man aboard. No malingerer or shirker could get past him. No wide-boy or double-dealer could get anywhere near his meticulously catalogued supplies. And no physical damage, wound or ailment in the voyage so far had fooled him or found his medical knowledge wanting. When a man like Doc Watson called for backup he got it post-haste.

'Talk me through it, Doc,' said Mark as he retraced his steps towards the crews quarters in the bows. 'Who's your casualty?'

'Ordinary Seaman Annie Blackfeather. Neck broken. Face beaten in.'

88

'God Almighty! Do you know what happened?'

'Oh yes,' said Doc Watson. 'I know that. Though I doubt it'll do us much good in the short run. I know what happened. How it happened. And who did it, come to that . . .'

Twelve

Jonah

P aolo Ursini woke from one nightmare into another that
was infinitely worse. To be fair, he didn't really wake at
all. There was only the most fleeting instant of horror-filled
consciousness between one state and the other.

Paolo's nightmare dream was a mixture of the last
conscious observations he had made, floating on the restless
surface above the lost *La Carihuela*, as the submarine came
up at him. It had looked so strange that he had not understood what it was to begin with. He had seen it – and experienced the full horror of it – like some unimaginable shark
wrapped in its shroud of ghastly netting. The simple terror
of the sight had engendered a kind of soul-deep panic in
him. That in turn had caused the strange half-waking sensations that had taken him like a sleepwalker through the water,
up the nets and aboard the monster itself to attack the fair-
faced man who stood above the gaping hatch. And to collapse
into a coma when the sensations – and the terror – proved
too much for his reeling sanity.

But with the coma had come the dream.

It was a dream in which he had been eaten by the monstrous
shark. He had felt his bones shatter in the grip of its terrible
jaws. He had known that his organs were crushed to soup and
jelly within him. He had felt himself sliding helplessly down
its gullet, head banging on the cartilage that formed its whale-
like throat. He had felt himself huddling in a foetal ball deep
in its abyssal belly as first cold saliva and then other food –
fish this time – and finally the scalding blood and broken bits
of some other victim had all showered down on him.

And in the dream Paolo had passed from the belly of the beast into the thudding, pulsing passageways of its gut. Had felt the clothes dissolving off his body. Had felt the acid scrubbing at his skin. Had heard the monster screaming for more victims with an overpowering bellow that was everything he understood of naked terror.

Or rather, everything he understood of terror until the fatal instant that he had opened his eyes, woken by that terrible, feral screaming.

He had opened his eyes to utter blindness. That had seemed as insanely logical as all the rest, as he passed from one state to another – for if his clothes and skin were dissolving in the gut of the leviathan, how could the soft jelly of his eyes have withstood the digestive corrosion? His nose and mouth were burning now as well, though the digestive juices consuming him smelt and tasted strangely of electrical fires. He drew in his breath to howl with the howling of the monster but the burning in his throat filled up his lungs and he choked into silence after all. Then the brightness came. Frail and dim as the luminosity on the lure of an angler fish down in the abyssal deeps it swam through the stench and agony towards him. And it showed him things that were even more terrible than a dream where he was blind and naked being dissolved in the belly of some monstrous fish.

It showed him that he was wedged in a tiny bunk under a compressing curve of metallic hull. The place where he found himself was simply overwhelmingly constricted. Filled with shadows that instantly attained the weight of earth lying on top of someone buried alive. He was a potholer trapped in a deep subterranean tunnel. He was helpless, buried under an avalanche. He was choking in the cellar of a collapsed building. He was wide awake in the bottom of his grave.

The tiny worm of claustrophobia that had lurked in his subconscious since childhood was transformed in the instant into a raging ravening dragon of madness that consumed him as utterly as the terrible whale-shark of his dream.

He started up, brown eyes wide, spittle flying from the corners of his delicately sculpted lips. Annie Blackfeather, holding the little torch whose light was far too paltry to

91

reveal the depth of madness in those staring eyes, put a gentle hand upon his shoulder and opened her mouth to soothe him like a mother. She expected him to lie back down obediently, for after all, had she not just finished stripping off his filthy clothes and giving him the gentlest of bed-baths to wash away poor Faure's blood which had covered him like red tar?

He hit her in the throat with his elbow so hard that he smashed her larynx and separated the third and fourth cervical vertebrae – and the spinal cord within them – as neatly as a guillotine. Annie was dead before she hit the floor. But such was the feral power of the beast the claustrophobia had unleashed that he caught up the first thing to hand – a metal bedpan – and smashed her in the face with that as well.

Then he grabbed the torch from her flaccid fingers and ran out into the choking darkness silently. As naked as the day he was born. As wild as his first primal ape-ancestor who had dropped out of the trees all fangs and claws to hunt the African prairies. As mad as Hannibal Lecter and twice as dangerous.

The next person to encounter Paolo was Chief Petty Officer Albert Monks. Monks was leading a team of men from the engineering sections who were tracing all the power lines between engineering and accommodation to make sure none of them had actually begun to burn. They were certainly smoking and smouldering in places. The air was heavy and hard to breathe. The lights of their two torches – Monks held one and a leading seaman another – shone in golden blades that told of fumes in the atmosphere. But there was nothing obviously burning. Monks, unaware just how far ahead of his team he had moved, switched off his torch and squinted with his streaming eyes, using the stygian blackness as a useful backdrop certain to betray even the weakest glimmer of spark, even the faintest flicker of flame. There was no sign. No sound, apart from the water noises and the faintest gasping. When Monks reached out, there was no heat in the clammy wall section he was following. He flicked on his torch and turned to call his little team together. And there, immediately behind him, stood a naked man. Slight, crouching, absolutely hairless.

'Hey!' said the outraged petty officer. 'What the hell . . .' And the terror-twisted beast that was Paolo Ursini perceived another threat.

The last thing Monks saw was the bedpan in the naked man's right hand. He hardly even had time to register that it was badly battered and liberally smeared with fresh blood.

The edge of the bedpan came down like an axe precisely on the widow's peak of Monks' swept-back hair. It hit high on his forehead immediately above the nasal spine and the superciliary ridges that bore his shaggy eyebrows, landing right between two slight frontal eminences, upon the suture where two plates of his skull met in childhood and fused together as he grew. There was a soft, almost squishy sound as the edge of the bedpan smashed the suture wide, splitting the skull nearly in half and causing such a powerful trauma to the frontal lobes beneath that Monks, like Annie Blackfeather, was dead before he hit the floor. And Paolo was gone before Monks' team pulled themselves out of the shadows; as silent and as swift as a curl of smoke.

News of Monks' murder reached Mark Robertson as he stood beside Doc Watson looking down at the battered mess that had once been Annie Blackfeather. 'You say you know who did this, Doc?'

'Yes, Captain. The first survivor, the man, is gone. It has to be him. The other one, the woman, is still here.'

'What did he use?'

'There's a bedpan missing. It was here five minutes ago and now it's not.'

'A bedpan? Christ! That's . . .'

'Insane. Yes. I know.'

'Insane?' Mark repeated the word. Watson never said anything unconsidered. 'You mean that literally? We have a madman running around the vessel? When she's in this condition already?' He gestured at the blackness, the silence, the gathering stench of smoke.

'You've got to consider it, Captain. If he wasn't mad when he came aboard then something's set him off since.'

'But *what*, in God's name? *Why*?'

'There was a guy I knew once went ape if you tried to restrain him at all. Even in fun, you know? We were in school together and I used to know him pretty well. But I pulled away in the end because he wasn't in control. It got so that if you laid a hand on him he lost it altogether. The red mist came down so to speak, and that was that. Had to give up sport wrestling pretty early on. Put too many opponents in hospital. Had to pack in playing rugby 'cause he would lash out in the scrum. Had to give up camping in the woods in the end. Started tearing sleeping bags apart. To rags and shreds. Like a werewolf, you know? Simply couldn't control it.'

'And that's what we've got here is it? Some kind of a lunatic werewolf?'

'Well, I'm no kind of shrink, Captain, but I have to tell you this. Battering strangers to death with a bedpan just simply isn't the kind of thing that a sane guy usually does.'

Mark Robertson nodded wearily.

His walkie-talkie hissed into life. 'Captain? Captain! Shit is there anybody there? This is Leading Seaman Smith. I'm on CPO Monks' team, working with Chief La Barbe, checking the lines for fire. Are you there, Captain? We got a *man down* here. I say again, *man down*! Over . . .'

The next man to encounter Paolo was Chief La Barbe himself. Unaware as yet of the deaths of Monks and Blackfeather, the chief was out in the dark alone, trying to work out some way of cannibalizing enough of the electrical circuitry to reawaken the power *Quebec* needed so urgently if she was going to survive. Fortunately, the chief had a visual – almost photographic – memory. He did not need his computer programs or even his books and paper schematics to tell him where the circuits were. And, just like the unfortunate Monks, he was well able to use a combination of slit-eyed observation, delicate sniffing and gentle probing to tell with almost perfect accuracy whether the cables, relays and junctions he was checking were on fire, had been on fire or were obviously damaged by fire.

La Barbe had just found a complete section that seemed blessedly undamaged. He switched on his torch for an instant to mark the place, then he swung round to head back to stores. There would be everything he needed there to get the cable out and to attach it to form a bridge that would bring back some of the power. To the pumps first. Then to the lighting, he thought, following the beam along a passageway, almost running in his excitement.

Stores was empty and, of course, dark. La Barbe ran in, torch beam swinging precisely and accurately to the areas he needed. Just as he knew every circuit so well that he could see it if he closed his eyes, he knew the disposition of everything in here. His picky insistence on always cleaning and returning everything to exactly the same place was certainly paying off now! He reached up for the tools he needed, and slipped them into the loops on the electrician's belt that he was wearing for the job. Then he turned, swinging his torch beam ahead of him, ready to rush back to the undamaged cable. And there, in the doorway immediately in front of him, was standing a stranger. What struck La Barbe first was the strange fact that he did not recognize the man at all. Only then did it register that he seemed to be naked.

The stranger was standing sideways-on looking fixedly back along the corridor La Barbe himself was planning to follow – back to the command areas and the crew's quarters. La Barbe switched off his torch. Why he did so, he would never know. Perhaps some understanding hidden far below any conscious thought warned him of the unimaginable danger he was facing here. Stores plunged into darkness. Darkness but not blackness, for the stranger was carrying a torch as well as something La Barbe could not quite make out. The backwash of the torch's beam illuminated the naked chest and clean-cut profile of the hairless head. And as La Barbe watched, too tense even to breathe, the strange, gaunt face turned slowly towards him. Nothing else moved. Not the torso, not the hand holding the dim little torch, not the bare feet that had brought the stranger silently here. Just the head. Swinging the face like a radar bowl towards La Barbe, mouth agape and gasping silently, teethe gleaming; nostrils flared like those of a hunting wolf, eyes like a cat's eyes gently glowing in the torchlight.

'Chief! It's the Captain! Can you hear me? Over?'

La Barbe looked down at his bellowing walkie-talkie, simply riven with horror. Then, terrified that he had taken his eyes off the apparition in the doorway, he looked up again at once. Instantly struck blind by the darkness.

For the doorway was black.

La Barbe broke his thumbnail on the switch of his big bright torch but he didn't even notice the pain. He shone the beam into the doorway and strained his streaming eyes to see. But the doorway was utterly empty. The naked stranger had vanished as silently as he had come.

The questing beast that had been the urbane Armani-clad, Armani-fragrant Ship's Engineer Paolo Ursini was driven by the simplest of desires – to escape. But he had no idea of where he was or how to get out. Anyone who stood against him – or seemed to do so – was crushed. Everyone else was, at the moment, irrelevant. But Paolo was not quite mindless. Even in his current state he understood that the thing he had used as a weapon so far was not an efficient tool. So, when chance offered him a better one, he took it without a second thought. Without any thought at all, in fact.

The closest that *Quebec* had to a chef was Leading Seaman Jacqueline Smith. It was to Leading Seaman Smith that the big cod had been brought after it had fallen out of the net on to Bob Hudson's head. And she had been in the process of preparing it when the light and power went down. It was a big fish, more than a metre long, fit, full and taken in the prime of life. And it could hardly have been fresher. After a long run leading a galley-team cooking frozen, canned and pre-prepared food at all the hours God sent on a submarine, it had brought out the cordon bleu in her.

She had gone to work with a will, taking off the head with great care and her largest Sabatier knife. She took out the fillets above the eyes and set the rest aside for stock. She

96

pulled out the guts as the head came off and put those in the bin for the ship's cat. She took up the Sabatier again and removed the fins and tail. Then she scaled it. The whole process was dazzlingly swift, for Leading Seaman Smith could have held her own in many a leading restaurant. And proposed to do so, the instant she had served out her time aboard.

Then she stood back for an instant, deep in thought – an artist considering her composition. 'Steaks,' she said at last aloud. 'It has to be steaks.' The Sabatier was a good tool – but for cutting up a fish this size she had a better one. So she set the big carving knife aside and reached for something bigger. Sharper. In the instant before the lights went out, she stood poised and as focused as a Samurai warrior, with a fifty-centimetre Solingen meat cleaver held up above the fish. The cleaver was her pride and joy: nearly a kilo in weight with forty centimetres of its fifty-centimetre length taken up with white-steel blade. The whole cleaver was German-forged specially hardened carbon steel, and the blade boasted a razor edge that would last for ever, all of thirty-five centimetres long.

She brought it down with force and accuracy on to the first section of the fish. But in the instant it took for the stroke to land, the light, the power, everything, died. She was lucky not to take her hand off. Shocked and confused, she left everything where it was and began to feel her way out into the corridor, trying to find out what on earth was going on.

When she came back fifteen minutes later, with a torch, an assistant and very little more knowledge, she was utterly astonished to find the partly prepared cod lying almost decorously in a battered bedpan on the chopping board. The fish's head, beside it, had been impaled by the Sabatier carving knife with a force that had taken the French steel right through the metal worktop.

And the Solingen cleaver had vanished.

Thirteen

Stirring

Robin Mariner began to stir just at the moment when, unknown to her, Paolo Ursini stabbed the blade of the Sabatier through the cod's head and the thin metal of the work surface underneath it with a noise like a gun shot that nobody else heard. She opened her eyes as Paolo – equally as unaware of her existence, for the moment – slipped silently back out of the claustrophobic little galley into the increasingly terrifying warren of corridors. Lightless, constricting, apparently airless – seemingly endless . . . She blinked several times to clear her vision, as the light from his listlessly carried torch gleamed along the edge of the meat cleaver's blade, bringing to vividness for an instant a ruby or two of blood. That was merely cod's blood; for the moment, at least.

Robin did not wake into darkness, but in many ways she would have preferred to have done. Instead she woke to the disturbingly theatrical sight of two men putting the broken body of a battered woman on to the bed next to hers. The grotesque little scene was made worse by the stark beam of torchlight which brought too much brightness to parts of it and sharp-edged, dramatic shadows to the rest. One glance at the way the woman's head was hanging off her shoulders told the all too widely experienced Robin that she was definitely dead.

Robin looked on without stirring or, for the moment, speaking. One man was tall, powerful-looking and black. He wore a naval-looking uniform beneath a white coat. Robin could not see badges or rings of rank. The other man was shorter, rounder and bearded in black with silver highlights on either side of his determined chin. He wore a naval uniform with four gold rings that told her what he was. Something about the place, silent and shadowy, lit only by the horizontal blade of the torch beam, told her where she found herself, unexpected though this was too.

The uniforms told Robin at once that she was on a naval vessel. Their accents in a moment would confirm it as Canadian. And everything else except the silence and the darkness – both anathema to submariners – told her she was on a submarine. A sub without light, power or propulsion. A sub that, from the feel of it, was sitting at the surface – for the time being at least. But then, wherever the sub had come from, it must have surfaced – and quite recently at that – to have taken her aboard out of the life raft, which was the last thing she remembered with any clarity. A surfaced Canadian navy submarine, then, where someone was slaughtering women. Or had broken the neck and battered in the face of one woman, at least. It seemed only sensible to her – if less than courteous and bordering on bad form, for they had clearly saved her life – to stay silent for the moment. And to observe events from under lowered lids as the strange men, deep in conversation, tucked the girl's corpse into bed and covered her with a blanket.

Especially as Robin was all too well aware that she herself was absolutely stark naked under her own flimsy sheet.

'They're bringing Monks in now, Doc,' said the shorter man in the captain's uniform. 'And I don't like it that I can't raise the chief.'

'I don't like any of this, Captain.'

'It's put us between a rock and a hard place. I'm going to have to reduce the work parties and set watches on everybody trying to get the power back. That'll slow any repairs we could actually practically get done. I'll have to set up search teams into the bargain and start trying to hunt this guy down before he does any more damage. And that'll slow the repairs still further. I'll have to stop rationing light and use all the torches aboard, even though we're blind and helpless when the batteries go. I'd better impound any spares we have in stores pretty quickly, now I think of it. All in all, if we don't act fast and get lucky, we'll still be chasing all over the ship in the pitch bloody darkness looking for this madman when we hit the bottom of the Atlantic Ocean.'

'Always assuming he intends to leave any of us alive,' answered Doc. His voice was rich, deep, reassuring. His drawl made his words seem almost cheerful.

'I don't know what he intends,' snapped the captain bitterly. 'I know what *I* intend – for him and all the rest of us. And that's enough for me.'

'Do you think there are any ships in the area?' Doc asked after a moment's silence.

'Well, I'm pretty certain there's at least one. The one that we ran over and hit as it sank. The one that's underneath us and still on its way to the seabed for all I know. The one these people came off in the first place, I guess.'

'I meant ships that might be in a position to help us, Captain. If we could find some way to get a mayday out.'

'I don't know, Doc. I don't even know if we're above water or below, though the motion of the hull makes it feel like we're still on the surface. I don't know if we'll ever be able to get a mayday out, even if we restore power, with all that damage up aloft. And I sure as hell don't know if there's anyone close enough to help us.'

'I know,' said Robin, unable to keep silent any longer.

And then, as the two men turned to look at her with their faces full of surprise and suspicion, she realized that she might not know for certain after all. For it occurred to her with terrifying force that the sunken vessel they were discussing might well be *Sissy*. But then, her calm good sense reasserted itself. How could a submarine have run over *Sissy*? 'What's your current position, Captain?' she demanded.

Mark Robertson looked across the brightness of the torch beam at the woman in the bunk lit by its backwash. The combination of sheet and shadow made every curve of her as plain as if she had been a centrefold. The ringlets of her hair gleamed like twenty-four-carat gold. But the power and command of her eyes and her tone focused him so completely that not even her body could distract. And, as obediently as any sea cadet, he told her *Quebec*'s last known position.

100

'How long have I been aboard?'

He answered that as well.

She did some sort of calculation in her head that required a fleeting frown of concentration, and a quick shake of the golden ringlets. 'Then I think I have some good news for you, Captain. Very close astern of you, if my calculations are correct, there is an immensely powerful ocean-going tug . . .'

When the team brought Monks in, Mark ordered them to pass the word that everyone aboard should assemble in the mess hall, then go and find the chief. He helped Doc deal with the second body while Robin dressed. Then the three of them went down to the mess hall together. It wasn't much of a hall, of course, but it was the largest single space aboard. Here, Mark completed a roll call that established everyone was present except for Blackfeather, Monks, Faure and Bob Hudson. That Robin Mariner was there – dressed now in overalls from the slop chest – and that the maniac with the meat cleaver was not.

Mark did not make a song and dance about it, but neither were Chief La Barbe, Lieutenant Chen and Sub-Lieutenant Gupta. With Monks' small but very select team, they were in stores retrieving every spare flashlight and battery they could find. They had gone there via the arms locker and La Barbe at least was extremely pleased to be carrying one of the very few sidearms aboard, for his encounter with Paolo had left him very shaken indeed.

In the mess hall, the captain briefly explained the situation to the assembled crew – and how he proposed that they should deal with it. He saved the news about *Sissy* for last, so that he would be able to send them out into the all too dangerous darkness with the hope of a light at the end of the tunnel. But when he accepted questions in a vain attempt to lance some of the boils of worry that were festering all too obviously and widely among his crew, he found that their iron discipline was beginning to crumble. Panic, indeed, was stirring. And there were barrack-room lawyers, safely anonymous in the darkness there, who would stir it further still.

101

'Why don't we just open the hatches and cut our way out, Captain?'

'I told you. We can't open the hatches in the hull without power. The conning-tower hatch system is out of service for the moment – though as soon as we get to work, I'll be sending a team up there . . .'

'But we can't work out there in the dark with this mad guy running around. How many people has he killed already?'

'Each work team will have a guard to keep a look-out . . .'

'Are these guards going to be armed?'

'You know we keep a very limited arms store aboard. There's nothing more dangerous than firing guns off inside a submerged vessel mostly made of steel . . .'

'So who gets the guns?'

'Some officers and some guards will be issued with firearms. I don't want to discuss the matter further.'

'Can we open the hatches when the power comes back? Cut the nets and get out then?'

'That is part of the plan, of course. But only as long as *Quebec* is sitting high enough out of the water. We know from *Chicoutimi*'s experience how much damage and danger can come if we let water in through a hatchway. And besides, we're in the middle of the North Atlantic. Where would we go?'

'On to this lady's tugboat, for a start . . .'

'If the tug *Sissy* makes contact, we'll decide matters at that time.'

'Just so long as the navy's main priority is making sure the crew is safe rather than the vessel.'

'Of course that will be the main . . . —'

'I wouldn't be too sure. These things cost millions and millions. We come for free.'

'I give you my word that the safety of the crew is the main concern of the officers not only of this vessel but of the command in Halifax and beyond. I think that's enough discussion for the present. Officers, you may dismiss your men to work now, please . . .'

Robin stayed with Mark when he had dismissed the crew

102

to their various duties. It was hardly a conscious decision and she certainly had no intention of telling him his job or trying to second-guess his orders or actions. But the command positions were where she would have been on any vessel of her own and these were where she felt the most at ease. Particularly as there was obviously nothing she could do aboard that was of any use at all.

Mark at first found her a distraction. Then he dismissed her from his mind. But then, after a while, when she had dropped a comment or two into the conversations he was having with his men, he began to use her as a sounding board for some of the plans and decisions he was a little less certain about.

For her part, Robin was used to this kind of approach. It was one she often shared with Richard himself, for, decisive and commanding – and occasionally overpowering – though her husband was, he enjoyed the camaraderie that a team approach could bring. Especially when he and she were the team in question. And Mark's priorities were simple enough. Power. Pumps. Lights. Communications. Ensure the sub was watertight and sitting at the surface. Some attempt to get men out of the vessel – but only if it was possible to get them back in again. Check the damage to the bow. Cut away the nets. Freeing the propeller would be a waste of time because they did not carry a spare shaft and this one was well beyond repair.

'So whatever else you restore, you can't restore propulsion.'

'That's right.'

'Then as soon as you have communications you need to clear a distress call and a salvage contract with your superiors.'

Mark gave a bark of laughter at that. 'Spoken like a woman with a tug boat close at hand!' he said. But his laughter robbed the wry riposte of any real offence.

'But that's getting pretty far ahead of ourselves,' she countered. 'Nothing much is going to get done in the immediate future with your unwanted guest running around spooking your work teams and distracting far too much manpower from more important work.'

'Back to the rock and the hard place . . .'

'Just as you discussed with Doc,' she agreed. 'And I concur. You do not want to be running around in the darkness still looking for this man when *Quebec* hits the floor of the Atlantic.' As if to emphasize her words, the submarine gave a sorry little heave and both sea-wise bodies felt her settle further by the head as the leak in the bows pulled her further down. Robin felt her short hairs rise and saw the frown on Mark's face. The way the sub was pitching now had almost settled to stillness. She sat with hardly any stirring at all. That could only mean that the hull was sitting so low that the waves were washing over all but her conning tower.

They were having this conversation at the base of the conning tower in fact, while above their heads a team was exploring the possibility of getting through to the emergency hatch. If they had looked up, Mark and Robin would have seen the flashing of the torches in the gaping shadows there. First, because they were merely talking, Mark had switched off his own torch. But hardly had they finished speaking than a beam fell down on them like a spotlight. Mark looked up. 'It's no good, Captain,' the leader of the team called down. 'The whole of the inside seems to have torn loose and shifted forward. We're not going to get up there in a hurry.'

'Thank you, Leif,' answered Mark formally. 'Come down now. I have another job for you to do.'

Robin and Mark stood back as a tall young officer and three crew men climbed carefully down on to the deck. As they stepped down, so they extinguished their torches until only the young officer's was alight. The beam of it rested on Robin suddenly, and a big square hand thrust into it, reaching out to shake hers. 'Leif Hunter, ma'am. Lieutenant. Navigating Officer.' In the backwash of the light she saw that rarity among the submarine service, a man almost as tall as her Richard. Square-jawed, freckled, with a lustrous mop of auburn hair that would have graced a fashion model.

'Robin Mariner. Captain. Thoroughly out of her depth,' she answered and returned his firm handshake formally. The corners of his deep dark eyes crinkled appreciatively.

A few moments later, Lieutenant Hunter and his three-man team were following Mark to the arms locker. Robin went with them, paying only scant attention to the orders the captain was giving his navigating officer. She was wondering how Richard was, now that Lieutenant Hunter's simple height had brought him back to mind. Was he worried about her? He must be! Had he worked out that she had gone over with the life raft? Yes – knowing him. Then what would he be doing about it? Searching for her, if she knew him. Searching for her unless he had been sidetracked somehow into a larger search for either of the vessels that had just collided here. And if he was, that would be all to the good as well. For it would bring *Sissy* here all the more quickly. And the decided downward slope of the forward sections through which they were walking towards the secure area where the arms were kept made her all too well aware of how limited time was becoming. And, indeed, the frown of concern that the slope of the deck brought to her face was compounded by the gathering silence. There were no longer any wave sounds slopping over the decks above. That meant the section they were in now must be entirely submerged.

But then, surprisingly suddenly, there came a throbbing pulsing through the stillness of the submerged hull. It was a stirring, almost thrilling sound that battered through the darkness like the thudding of life-blood in an exhausted athlete's ears.

'Hey,' said a disembodied sailor's voice, sounding not a little nervous. 'What's that, Lieutenant Hunter?'

They all stood listening. The throbbing thud grew louder and louder until it seemed to be stirring in the air all around them.

Then it stopped. And, in the sudden, echoing silence, Mark Robertson answered the crewman's question. 'Company,' he said, almost laughing with relief. 'We have company.'

105

Fourteen

Hunter-Killer

Like many another man and woman, Lieutenant Leif Hunter had allowed himself to be defined by his name.

Leif learned at his mother's knee about Leif Ericson, son of Eric the Red, who had sailed his longships round Cape Farewell from his father's Viking settlements in Greenland and had colonized Vinland in North America several hundred years before Christopher Columbus's birth. Leif's name had not been chosen on a whim: his mother, a statuesque, flame-haired woman with porcelain-white skin and a vivid rash of freckles, brought him up to believe that in her veins and his flowed Viking blood. By the time he went to kindergarten he was a powerful little warrior and a berserker of dangerous potential.

And it seemed that Hunter Junior had always known about hunters and hunting. So that when his demanding ex-WWII corvette-captain grandfather and exacting weekend-huntsman senior-executive father began to take him out tracking and shooting in the forests near their home, it seemed the preco-cious youngster was already as wood-wise as Hiawatha and a marksman to rival Hawkeye.

From the moment Leif joined the service he had tried for Canadian Special Forces, seeking secondment to the United States Marine Corps or the British Special Boat Service. The only thing that held him back was the difficulty of honing his physical perfection in the confines of a submarine. He was still fit enough to be on the short list for inter-forces exchange, however. And his father wouldn't have hesitated to take him out into the wilderness after grizzly or Kodiak

106

bears – if that had been allowed. All in all, his captain could not have chosen more wisely when he decided to send out an officer and a team of men into the darkness of the corridors and work areas to seek their psychopathic stowaway.

Leif Hunter led his team of three men from the point. This was not an act of foolish bravery. It resulted simply from the fact that he was the best equipped in every possible way to lead them – in physical terms, in tactical terms and in experience. He was every bit as good a hunter as he thought he was. He was also an excellent officer, and, although his responsibilities were largely in ship-handling and command, nevertheless he had made it his job to learn every nook and cranny of the *Quebec*. From truck to keel, from stem to stern, from soup to nuts, as they say. Or – in this case – from cockpit to bilge, from torpedo doors to screw. He had walked these silent passageways in full light and security light and even with his eyes shut – preparing for the kinds of tests the Marines or the SBS would put him through. Which was, coincidentally, perfect preparation for this very moment.

And Leif's captain had not sent him out unprotected or unarmed. He, like each man in his small command, wore a bulletproof vest and a toughened plastic helmet as though they were a SWAT team attending an armed siege. The men held a precious torch each but were using them sparingly. Their officer, however, held one of the vessel's precious SIG-Sauer handguns. It was the P226 – with the longer barrel, the fifteen-round clip of 9mm bullets and the tactical light mounted in front of the trigger guard. He held it in standard firing position with the light switched on and he followed the beam as though it were a torch. The guns were standard issue and were designed exclusively for use in the unlikely event that *Quebec*'s officers or men should find occasion to board another vessel. But, again, like Leif and his ambitious preparation, the SIG-Sauer was perfect for the task in hand.

From the control room, Leif led his little team forward. They crossed the upper heads and showers from one bulkhead door to the next, then scanned through the weapons stowage swiftly, for the second bulkhead door into the weapons area was particularly heavy and Leif felt it unlikely that one man could have opened it alone. They pushed as far forward as they could reach as swiftly as they were able and then they turned. They could not go further forward or further down below because of the leak in the bow that had flooded the areas around them in the absence of the pumps that might have kept it under some sort of control.

Leif led them up, however, into the spaces between the three forward hatches – the torpedo embarkation hatch, the ATP hatch and the forward escape hatch. Their quarry might well have managed to get himself up here, and the four-man team proceeded with care and concentration, in spite of the increasingly intrusive sounds of footfalls and tapping on the casing immediately above their heads. If anything, the promise of contact with the outside world made them more determined to have sorted out as many problems aboard as possible. There was no contact at this level back as far as the control room, so they went down two levels and began again below weapons storage in the non-commissioned crewmen's bunk area. Again their search was fruitless. All Leif learned – by pressing his ear to the icily sweating forward bulkhead – was that the areas from here to the bulbous bow were completely flooded now.

At this level, Leif knew, they could get a straight run down the boat, however. They worked their way back past the huge refrigerators, stocked with everything the crew might wish for in the way of 'fresh' food. Opposite these were the canned and dry goods storage areas – and these consumed a disproportionate amount of the hunt patrol's time for there were all too many places that might easily conceal a man. Then, grudgingly satisfied, they worked their way back past the heads and showers to the crew's mess, so lately the scene of the captain's less than rousing address – then on past the galley so recently relieved of its largest, sharpest and most dangerous meat cleaver.

Aft of the galley were the weapons-control areas. Aft of these, the engineering areas that took up fully one-third of the vessel's length from deck to keel. First came the engine room and then the motor room, each surrounded with a maze of stygian corridors full of smoke, shadows and short-tempered engineers guarded by bellicose crewmen and trigger-happy navigation officers. And aft of these, the areas of maximum physical damage where the propeller shaft had torn itself to pieces like a giant redwood caught in the heart of a twister.

Paolo was nowhere near the hunters. He was as unaware of them as he was of everything else – except his overwhelming need to escape. Though such was the depth of his psychosis he was not even aware of that. It dictated his actions and he obeyed it – but there was as little awareness involved as there was coherent thought. He was pressed against *Quebec*'s titanium-steel skin between the aft escape hatch and the Dutch breech. He was pressed quite literally, from the spread of his tongue past his breast and his belly to his thighs, knees, calves and toes. In the gloom thrown by the failing battery of his torch on the walkway beside him, he was tapping on the metal with the blade of the Solingen meat cleaver. Tapping, and waiting with a concentration either super- or subhuman for the tapping that would come in reply. Had he been the Paolo who would have better been associated with Ferrari than Jack the Ripper, he might have thought of sending a rudimentary message. An SOS or some such: dit dit dit, dah dah dah, dit dit dit. But he had the mentality of an animal now, and Morse code – like compassion, empathy, humanity – was far away from anything of which he was capable.

To Leif and the other hunters, the tapping on the submarine's casing was a distraction to be ignored. To Paolo it was like a summons from a higher plane. Each tap, each squeak of boot sole on the deck outside, had something of an angel's voice. Like Gabriel warning Lot to get himself out of Sodom. Like the Holy Spirit speaking so stirringly in Moses' burning bush. Like God Himself talking to Noah about animals, arks and floods.

Had anyone at that stage paused to consider Paolo as anything other than a mindless psychopath, then they might have predicted more of his actions than they did. But to them he was merely a hairless, naked ape armed with a massive

109

cleaver who had already killed two of their popular ship-mates and was likely to kill the rest of then given half a chance. He was frighteningly subhuman. Who aboard was going to empathize with him?

The other stranger, out of place and getting bored with following the captain around, was the one most likely to empathize with Paolo. And Robin certainly had the intelligence and insight. And perhaps, on an almost spiritual level, she was beginning to do so, for she too was seeking tight spaces that might lead to a quick way out. One of the things that had struck her most about Lieutenant Hunter was his size. And the team he had taken hunting with him – soul-mates all – were not small men. Looking around the crew as Captain Robertson had been addressing them, she had been struck by the fact that, for the crew of a submarine, there was a surprising lack of short and slight people here. She was certainly the slimmest and one of the shortest here – though she stood a solid five foot eight inches. Narrow-eyed, she looked for someone of her own build. And, as the captain dismissed his less than cheery command, she found what she was looking for. He was clearly of an Asiatic background – Filipino at a guess. He had a mature face but the body of a boy. He would have made an excellent jockey, she thought. He would certainly make a good companion for someone planning to worm her way as far up the fin above the conning tower as she could get, opening whatever hatches she could reach. For whoever was outside the vessel now, prowling around on the decks and tapping randomly, would be bound to check the main hatch there – especially if, as Robin acutely suspected, all the hatches in the main hull were awash.

'Excuse me, sailor, my name is Captain Robin Mariner, British merchant marine and Heritage Mariner shipping. May I ask your name and rank, please?'

The long eyes looked at her askance. But she had come in at the captain's shoulder and she had explained there was a tug probably coming. Perhaps even here now. She was much more attractive than any of the other women aboard. He was willing to be civil at the least. Particularly as the brusque manner in which she shook his hand made her chest move in an appealingly liquid and unsupported manner. Especially as she had managed to acquire that badge of truly elevated status – a torch. 'Leading Seaman Li, Captain. What can I do for you?'

'Who is your commanding officer?'

'Lieutenant Pellier, sonar.'

'I see. You don't have immediate sonar duties?'

'No, Captain. My section is assigned to guard duty, I believe.'

'Excellent. With your permission, Leading Seaman Li, I will ask Lieutenant Pellier if he can assign you to guard me. Then we'll explain to the captain exactly what I propose to do with you. And we'll see if we can scare up an extra torch to help you.' Once she promised a torch, he was hers body and soul – and would have been, even had she been built like the back end of a pot-bellied pig.

And so Leading Seaman Li found himself following Robin up through the vertical shaft above the conning tower so lately vacated by Lieutenant Hunter as she eased herself through the constriction that had excluded the large lieutenant. But she only achieved this at the cost of receiving some discomfort to her bosom and, unconsciously, of giving some pleasure – and the first of many intimately lewd thoughts – to Leading Seaman Li.

Like Hunter, Robin went first. She pushed the torch up through the narrow section, followed by her arms, extended upwards as though she were performing some kind of a dive. Her shoulders slipped through as her legs pushed her body up the ladder. Li placed her feet safely on the rungs she could no longer see, and this was particularly welcome when her breasts, unsupported by any underwear but elevated by the reaching of her arms, became crushed against the rungs that she was facing. The metal at her back seemed to be pushing tighter, as though she was caught in a massive pair of pliers. But sheer bloody-minded badness, as her mother used to say, forced her onward and upward. While Li, below, shone his torch up at the straining seat of her overalls, suddenly made all too clearly – and pleasurably – aware that

111

she was not wearing any more underwear below than she was wearing above.

Immediately above the constriction was a hatchway. As Robin reached up to spin the handle that opened it, Seaman Li came up close behind her, sliding through the narrowness like a snake exploring a rat hole. The deck above was strangely tilted, almost folded. Had it been made of anything other than metal, it would have cracked or split. But it was metal – so it had folded. The hatch sat in it at a crazy angle – and Robin suspected that all that was holding it closed were the bolts operated by the circular handle in the centre of its slightly domed shape. And she was right. As soon as she span it, the bolts grated back out of their sockets and the round portal began to creak open.

The hatch was heavy but at least it was counterweighted and designed to open slowly even when the power was off, so Robin was able to push it until it swung wide. Then she pulled herself up through it with a strange kind of a twisting motion, well suited to the strange environment they were moving through. For, instead of pulling herself directly upwards, Robin had to bend – as the deck head above her had bent – through the better part of fifty degrees.

Seaman Li followed suit, his mind full of appreciative memories of the effect her sinuous movement had had on the tightness of her clothing. He found Robin sitting hunched in a strangely twisted area, better suited to an old-fashioned fairground than a modern submarine. The hatch itself hung wide and one glance warned the experienced submariner that it would never close again without the employment of levers or pulleys. For the full weight of the metal hatch was hanging directly from its hinge, and what should have been a flat deck for it to sit upon was a kind of metal wave frozen in the act of breaking. But what had gone up had also gone down. The metal floor had folded away from the forward wall of the room, and had torn the ladder away with it. The upper hatch into the cockpit seemed square and undamaged – but neither of them stood any hope of reaching it, even had either been able to stand upon the hatch-handle of the solid little escape pod whose movement forward – levered by the snorkel or the periscope within the fin – had done much of this damage. Even had she stood upon his shoulders – which she was most welcome indeed to do – or had he stood on hers, the hatch would still have been well out of their reach. So that, regretfully, was that.

'We should go back now,' Li observed quietly. 'We can go no further. There is no point in just waiting on the chance someone will open the hatch above.'

'You're right, Mr Li,' she answered, her voice a little deadened. They had seemingly achieved so little. They may even had made things worse; certainly that hatch was never going to close again. Robin took a deep breath and thankfully failed to notice the added sparkle that this brought to her companion's eyes.

'I'll go first, then,' said Seaman Li with an unexpected cheeriness that she was utterly at a loss to explain.

But, even as Li was standing beneath the constricted section looking upward almost ecstatically at Robin's attempts to wriggle down without doing further damage to her chest, a strange unearthly screaming rang through the entire vessel. And all of a sudden it became obvious that her whole attitude and motion were undergoing some kind of a change.

The creature that had once been Paolo Ursini had followed the footsteps along the deck, almost oozing from place to place immediately below the casing. As Robin twisted her hips above the appreciative Li, preoccupied with the twin discomforts of a snagged button at chest level and a cuttingly invasive – not to say divisive – seam somewhat further down, so Paolo reached the point at which the deck just forward of the main access hatch joined the aft of the fin. With his face touching the underside of the casing deck and his head touching the foundation of the tower wall, the effect of the metallic screaming was doubly intensified in his already spinning skull. And, at the moment the screaming started, Paolo's torch beam flickered and rapidly began to die.

It was only the sound of *Sissy*'s metal guttering sliding home as the messenger pulled the towline into place, but to Paolo it was the Heavenly Choir and the voice of God all rolled into one. With feverish speed, he followed the fast-fading beam of his torch across to the sharp-etched tell-tale pattern of a grille. The grille was solid and by no means designed for people to come or go through. But then again, neither was it designed to stand against Solingen-steel meat cleavers. Moments later Paolo was down in the passage-ways immediately behind the conning tower itself. As he landed in the blackness of the passageway his torch beam died at last. He threw the dead thing aside with no thought and swung round, searching, his eyes as wide as his drooling, gasping mouth in the suffocating darkness. He was actually at a kind of crossroads. The passage he was in led forward past the control room and back towards the engine room. Lateral passageways also led into the AMS section and into the control area itself. It was, in fact, one of the busiest sections of the vessel, even under these circumstances. Had Paolo waited long enough, almost everyone aboard would have come past him. It must have been blind chance, there-fore, which dictated that it was Leif Hunter first. And, in the utter blackness of that lightless place, Leif's tactical light was a telltale giveaway that warned Paolo someone was approaching long before the little hunting patrol was anywhere near him. With the cunning of a wounded tiger, Paolo stepped noiselessly back into the pitch black of the cross-passage, and watched as the brightness silently approached. If he was actually thinking anything, it was that there was a torch coming. And he wanted a torch. Of course he could not know that the bright beam originated just in front of a trigger-guard and immediately below the barrel of a SIG-Sauer P226 automatic pistol.

If Leif Hunter made any mistakes, then they were the oppo-site of the errors his father and grandfather had spent so much time and effort warning him against. He did not allow his concentration to falter, even though he and his team had been from one end of the vessel to the other three times now without seeing hide nor hair of their quarry. He did not vary his pace, but proceeded slowly and with the maximum care.

He did not allow himself or his men to become sloppy in spite of the tedium of the hunt. On the contrary, he kept the concept of his quarry very vividly in his mind. And if there was an error, then this was it. For, during the seeming eternity of the hunt, that mental picture had indeed began to assume the power, the presence, the physical size, the almost human cunning and unlooked-for reasoning ability of the most dangerous grizzly bear. As Leif approached the crossroads in the tunnel, therefore, he unconsciously set his sights high and planned for some deviously cunning trap.

So that when this scrawny little bald guy, more like a chimp than a bear, just stepped out of the utter blackness round a corner, grabbed hold of the gun and chopped off his hand to get it, it was absolutely and utterly the last thing Leif was expecting.

Paolo, on the other hand, had no idea what he had really done. He whirled and ran away forward into the darkness past the control room under the conning tower towards the heads and showers there and the weapons-storage area beyond. His head was filled with the need to answer that heavenly, screaming summons. As he scurried forward, he fumbled with the strangely clumsy torch that he had found, consumed simply with following the brightness of its beam. Utterly oblivious of the facts that behind the torch lay an extremely deadly and powerful gun, fully loaded with fifteen 9mm bullets. Or that, still maintaining the tightest possible grip upon the gun, was the severed hand of Lieutenant Leif Hunter.

Fifteen

Power

News of what had happened to Lieutenant Hunter went through *Quebec* as fast as the Atlantic water would have if the forward bulkheads had failed, as fast as the realization that the submarine was under some kind of control and beginning to move more purposely forward. But the relief brought by one piece of news was utterly undermined by the other. Especially as *Quebec* was not yet moving under her own power, could not yet start the pumps needed to ensure the Atlantic did not in fact break in and remained in total darkness except for the torches. And this was especially worrying as there was now no way to distinguish a torch beam from a flashlight in the hands of a friend from a tactical light on a 9mm automatic in the hands of a madman.

Not until it was too late, at any rate.

Robin received the news as she and the strangely attentive Seaman Li were making her report to Captain Robertson. He of course received the news directly on his walkie-talkie from two separate sources. From Hunter's understandably shocked right-hand man, who reported the instant the incident had happened, to say, among other things, that his position was now redundant. And five minutes later from Doc Watson to report that he believed he could save the lieutenant's life in spite of the shock and blood-loss. But saving his hand, even if they could find it, was beyond his capability or indeed any likelihood that he could see.

Cometh the hour, cometh the man, thought Robin as she saw the steely glint appear in Mark Robertson's eye, and the commanding squaring of his chin. Suddenly he looked a lot

116

less like Santa Claus. 'Right,' said *Quebec*'s captain. 'The priorities have to stay the same. We'll have to hope the guards will at least give warning if this madman shows up, but we cannot allow ourselves to be distracted by anything – no matter how disturbing. The only way out of this that I can see is to restore light and power. Even if we're somehow coming under way so that the likelihood of losing the vessel is lessened, we still have to secure the safety of our people.'

'If you're under tow, you'd better start planning what you're going to say to the first man that speaks to you,' said Robin. 'With any luck at all it'll be my husband Richard Mariner and his tug *Sissy* will have got her line aboard you first. But I warn you, if it is Richard, he'll be looking to drive a hard bargain with you or your masters in Halifax. He's a man who's used to power and he likes to get what he thinks he deserves. You'd better be clear in your mind just exactly what you're going to say to him.'

'I'm going to say thanks a bunch but stay the hell out of my submarine until it's all secure,' said Mark decisively. 'No one comes aboard to muddy up the water until Psycho Bob is under guard or ready to go underground. Not even your husband, Captain: even if we do owe him our lives.'

'Wise enough. But then?'

'I'm going to say he's talking to the wrong end of the pecking order. He likes power? Then he needs to talk to someone with some power to make decisions – or at least to someone who has some clear and relevant orders from someone who has made some decisions. So there's no use talking salvage to me till I've had a good long chat to Navy Ops in Halifax – who will then refer me on to MARLANT HQ and they'll tell me to chew the good old fat with Admiral John Julius Pike. And they don't call him "Long John" Pike behind his back because he's missing a leg. Pike would as soon part with the navy's money as a pirate would part with Flint's treasure. So for once I won't be the only sorry bastard caught between a rock and a hard place.'

'Looks like the fun and games are only just beginning, then,' said Robin drily.

'You'd better believe it, lady,' answered Mark.

And as he spoke, the power came back on.

The first thing they were aware of was the light. One moment it was remarkable by its utter absence. The next it was there, all through the entire submarine, as though somewhere God Himself had spoken. Well, perhaps *whispered* rather than spoken – for the light was only at about twenty per cent power and was spectrally pale and thin. But it was light. It was there. It was, in fact, almost everywhere.

Then the air-con started breathing, blowing the stench and the smell of burning all around the vessel in draughts and breezes that brought neither freshness nor – as yet – warmth. Then, as the last metallic scream from the foredeck announced the 80mm tow rope bedding home, the pumps grumbled into life and the big old frame began to throb. The tilt on the deck grew noticeably shallower at once. The rolling of the hull became more noticeable as she sat higher in the water – but the pitching remained non-existent as her bow was no longer at liberty to rise and fall. And indeed, thought Robin cheerfully, it would not have any play to do so until the submarine's hull began to move more easily through the water as the tow got properly under way.

Mark Robertson gave a grin that flashed with almost piratical grimness. 'Right,' he said. 'That's more like it. Now we can really get to work!' He crossed to the communications area and depressed the All Hail. The NOW HEAR THIS rang through the vessel and he spoke. 'This is the Captain. Thanks to Commander La Barbe and his people for a job well done. Chief, I know you won't want to rest on your laurels and you'll have a list of priorities as long as your arm, but can you release Lieutenant Chen to me, please? I need the communications fixed because I have to talk to Halifax. If Captain Mariner's right – and she's been bang on the money so far – then someone's going to be knocking on the door at any moment now demanding to know how much this old tub is worth! And it'll likely as not be her husband, who by all accounts is a power to be reckoned with.'

*   *   *

118

Robin felt oddly excluded from the sudden upsurge in everyone's spirits. Now there really was nothing obvious for her to do. Now, suddenly, she had leisure to wonder whether or not it really was Richard who had taken *Quebec* under tow – or whether there was some other tug out there off Cape Farewell and Richard, with everyone else on *Sissy*, was actually at the bottom of the sea. Preoccupied, and for once lacking that almost mystical link that allowed her to read Richard's mind and surmise his intentions and whereabouts, she drifted away from the conning tower at precisely the same time as he was climbing the fin outside. By the time he had reached the cockpit she was halfway back to the infirmary, unable to think of anywhere she would be of more immediate use than there. By the time he was opening the uppermost hatch, she was lingering in the infirmary doorway. And when Richard started his conversation with the forewarned Captain Robertson, she was deep in conversation with Doc Watson, offering to help him with Lieutenant Hunter's arm.

Paolo sat in the dim twenty per cent brightness of the weapons-storage space looking down at Lieutenant Hunter's hand. Or rather, what the hand was holding. Just as the returning of the light had brought hope to everyone else on the vessel, it had brought a change to Paolo as well. He now realized why the torch he had taken had felt so strange. And, gripped by psychopathic hysteria though he still might be, he wasn't so mad that he couldn't recognize a gun. The booming of the captain's voice came and went throughout the boat. It didn't impact on Paolo at all because it came from inside, from below. He was only interested – fixated, still – by what was above. By what was outside. He slowly released the lieutenant's marble-white fingers and replaced their cold grasp on the grip with his own. He hefted the cleaver in his left hand and he began to retrace his steps to the bulkhead door into the place. So heavy and stiff that Leif, unknown to Paolo, had thought he could never open it on his own. So heavy and stiff that the last of Leif's patrol – unknown to either hunter or hunted – had failed to secure it again. A chargeable – almost a court-martial – offence.

119

Paolo lingered at the doorway with the cunning of a beast, sniffing the air and panting silently. All he could hear were water noises and pumps. But then, carried by the strange acoustics of the twisted mess within the fin above the conning tower, came a voice. A voice from on high. A voice from outside.

'Hello, *Quebec*! Can anybody down there hear me? Hello, *Quebec*!'

Paolo could certainly hear him. He looked up with wild, almost worshipping eyes. And there, immediately above his head, was a shaft leading directly upwards to the forward escape hatch. Paolo dropped the gun and the cleaver. He leaped on to the rungs and swarmed up them in an instant. The hatch cover, like the one that Robin had opened, was a domed circle with a round release handle at its centre. Paolo twisted it open, gasping and grunting like the animal he had become. He heard the bolts sliding back. He heaved with all his might. The hatch began to open.

And the cascade of water that resulted knocked the stunned man off his perch. Head over heels he tumbled downwards, and only by the grace of God did he manage to catch at one of the lower rungs to slow his descent. So that, in the centre of a wild cascade of water, he landed safely on the deck of weapons stowage. In a panic, he grabbed the cleaver and the gun and hurled himself through the heavy bulkhead door. Slipping and sliding wildly on the wet deck, he nevertheless managed to close the door behind him and secure it. Then he picked up his weapons once again and ran for the nearest refuge.

Paolo burst into the head and shower area. It was empty and silent. There were stalls along one wall. Beyond these there were several showers – uncharacteristically roomy – uniquely aboard the submarine. There were towels on rails opposite their doors. Paolo hesitated. He simply did not know where to run next. Strangely, the brightness – such as it was – seemed to have robbed him of the certainty, the initiative he had been able to access in the darkness. He was in any case lost and a little confused. He had come so near to freeing himself – only to be so cruelly hurled back down into his nightmare once again. The voices had betrayed him – though in his current state he hardly understood the concept of betrayal. All he felt under the bewilderment was a seething volcano of rage and hatred, companion to the uncontrollable animal panic. He took a step or two nearer to the shower stall. He hesitated once again, for some reason looking upwards.

The door behind Paolo opened. He walked forward once again, grabbing a towel as he stepped into the nearest hiding place. He needed the towel to hide what he was carrying. The nearest hideout was a shower stall.

So that Engineering Sub-Lieutenant Gupta, coming into the head for a much-needed leak on his way to check the forward pumps, saw only what one might expect to see in such a place: a naked man holding a bath towel going into a shower stall. The illusion was made yet more credible for the moment by the thunder of cascading water that was echoing through the place. Gupta kicked the three-quarter-length stall door wide and spread his legs against the slope of the deck. He unbuttoned the lower buttons of his overall and called to the man in the shower next door. 'Hey, you in the shower . . .' He hoisted himself out and added to the sounds of falling water as he continued his one-sided conversation. 'You'll be lucky if that water's hot,' he bellowed cheerfully. 'We've only just got twenty per cent of power to the lights, pumps, air-con and life support – hatches and so forth. And lucky to get that. There won't be anything other than lukewarm water anywhere outside the galley until we get into dock and do some serious repairs.'

As last words went, they were neither insightful nor memorable, but that was all Gupta got. He was looking down to tuck himself away and so he failed to see Paolo's shadow. Under the sounds of the pumps and the cascading water, he never heard the naked footfall.

The blunt side of Paolo's meat cleaver broke his neck in almost exactly the same place as Paolo's elbow had broken Annie Blackfeather's neck at the start. But from the opposite side, of course. The effect was just the same, though. Gupta went down like a felled tree. But there the similarity in the incidents ended. For Paolo had grown more cunning if no less desperate in the interim. This time he did not need to batter anyone's face in. This time he had a plan. And the plan had come with the realization that, like Adam in Eden, he was naked.

Paolo put down the gun and the cleaver. He pulled the flaccid body out on to the floor. Here he stripped off Gupta's overalls and footwear, dressing himself with feverish haste. Then, grunting with the effort, he sat the dead engineer on the toilet and locked them both in the cubicle. Then he dropped to his knees and wriggled out from under the three-quarter-length door. He picked up the gun and the cleaver and took a towel that would cover them. He hesitated for just an instant, then he took another towel and slung it casually, unremarkably, round his neck – so that, almost by coincidence, it covered his face from the eyes down, exactly like a mask.

Sixteen

Wait

Had Richard not waited in the cockpit, trying to inveigle Mark Robertson into something like a decision on the matter of towage terms, then the tow would have ended a great deal sooner than either of them calculated. But he did wait, insisting that he should be at least made fully conversant with every possible detail of the situation aboard. Making absolutely certain that Captain Robertson was ensuring one hundred per cent the safety of Robin – even if no one else could be protected to the same degree.

Then Richard waited a little longer, allowing Bob Hudson a word or two with his commanding officer in the certainty that Captain Robertson would want his first officer to contact Halifax from *Sissy* and begin some kind of negotiation in the face of his own temporary inability to do so.

As Bob and Mark requested some perfectly reasonable privacy, Richard looked back over the gaping ruin of the fin-top as the night fell properly, and he thought. At first, he thought how he would be surprised if even *Sissy*'s radio officer could do much to fix that lot. Immediately, he decided that he must make arrangements to bring a big transmitter over, if *Sissy* had a portable one aboard. Then they could drop the microphone on a long lead down the hole that Bob and his commander were talking through. But that would do for the morning, he thought. If he didn't get some sleep soon he would doze off where he stood. *What a day!* One way or another it seemed to have exhausted him so thoroughly that even Robin's doubly dangerous situation would hardly have him awake and worrying.

123

Mind you, he thought, almost dreamily, that was a situation that shouldn't be beyond Robin to keep under some kind of control. She had faced down many a deadly danger in the past – from the Russian Mafia smuggling women across the Great Lakes to assassins who blew her up in London. He realized with something of a start that, surprised – overwhelmed – as he had been by her sudden disappearance from *Sissy*, he had never actually believed that she was gone for ever. That she could ever actually be dead and gone. He guessed that must always be the way of it – until bitter experience came and taught you the terrible truth. Eventually there would come a situation that one or other of them couldn't handle. There would come a day when one or other didn't come back at all. There would come a night – first of many, perhaps, when the bed would be half empty and far too big. When the huge old house at Amberley would have too many rooms and too many memories – unless the twins were home. When the days and the nights would be forever far, far too long. For one of them or the other.

But then, suddenly Bob broke into his exhausted and uncharacteristically depressing train of thought. 'The captain says your wife can have a place in any command of his at any time, Richard. She's the perfect lieutenant – a damn sight better than me!' He gave a wry laugh. 'I guess the old boy's getting tired and stressed out over this. Hardly surprising, really! He says he's had enough for one day, anyway.'

'Haven't we all!' laughed Richard.

But then, as he and Bob finally gave up and let the harassed captain return to his crisis management, Richard paused one last time and waited a moment longer to elicit the gruff and hurried promise that he would be able to speak to his wife first thing in the morning – or even sooner in the unlikely event that *Quebec* got her communications back up. That was the best that even he could manage under the circumstances. It was by no means satisfactory, but, as with the tow, Mark Robertson's hands were tied by powers far beyond his control. In this case, *circumstances*, thought Richard wryly – which effectively bound them all. Then he straightened, turned and prepared to climb down the netting on to the benighted foredeck.

The foredeck was literally benighted now, and should have been almost as dark as the inner areas of the sub had been for most of today. But *Sissy* was shining her big aft-mounted arc lights on her tow. It was usual procedure – certainly on Tom Hollander's commands; especially if he had people over there.

The forward watch had gone now that the tow was bedded home in the guttering and pulling effectively. The officers on the bridge would keep an eye out of that conveniently aft-facing window as part of their formal watches; all they needed was light enough to see by.

And the effect of the lights was of crucial importance. For they were low enough to seem almost parallel to the surface of the sea. This made the dazzling blades of their beams delineate every whorl and ripple, every web of foam and spindrift, on the surfaces of the waves that were sluggishly washing over the submarine's still half-submerged hull. They also showed something that had been coming and going on and off all afternoon. Under the icy breath of the fitful breeze swinging northward now the sun was down, the water was gently steaming. There was not enough to make a fog bank yet, but it might well thicken up before morning, especially under light airs. It might have been thick enough even now to conceal what was going on. But, because of his position, Richard could see what the lights revealed almost as though he were looking down upon the lines on a living chart.

He half caught the first sign out of the corner of his eye. Where another man – especially one as physically, mentally and emotionally exhausted as he – would have shrugged it away, Richard paused. Bob Hudson collided with him, not a lot more compos mentis than Richard himself. 'What?' he demanded, as grumpy as a teenager roused early.

'That's what I was wondering,' said Richard. 'What is that down there?'

A wave washed up like oil, slow, black and gleaming in the arc lights. It rolled across the deck immediately in front of the fin, and as it did so – just as it reached the very apex of its sluggish passage over the boat, so it gave a strange kind of twist. The sleek black back was suddenly marked with a rash of white. The rash assumed a circular shape as though the water had developed ringworm or meningitis. A circle of lines appeared abruptly, seeming to contain the whiteness, controlling it into more compact roundness as they slid inwards with some strange and sinister purpose of their own.

'What's that?' asked Bob, befuddled.

'What's *there*?' asked Richard more forcefully, a cold finger seeming to trace itself down his spine.

'What? What d'you mean?'

'What's there? On the hull? What is underneath that disturbance, Bob?'

'The forward escape hatch. Oh dear God! The forward escape hatch! It must be open! Christ!'

'It can't be wide open or the water would be going down there like Niagara Falls. We may have time to put things right. You tell the captain. I'll go down and see if I can shut it. Then you get down and help me if need be.'

'Aye aye!' answered Bob sincerely, snapped into full wakefulness by something in Richard's tone as effectively as if he had just been given a cold shower.

A cold shower was the last thing in the world that Richard wanted, but of course that was what he was effectively going to get. He swung down the front of the fin as swiftly as he was able and slopped across the deck. A couple of big steps were sufficient. Then he was on his knees, with the blackness of the ocean washing almost to his waist. He pushed his hands elbow-deep into the back of the next wave, groping through the weave of the net for the hatch cover and the mechanism that would allow him to close it.

Bubbles ticked distractingly up the arms of his suit, on the inside above the flaring cuffs, warning that his pullover was soaking almost to the shoulder already. The strange lines of the micro-currents, swirling like tap water down a plughole, sought to pull his fingers into the jaws of the partly open hatch. His hands became almost as difficult to control as a beach-ball in seaside surf. And even when they found what they were looking for, they could not force the cover closed.

'Is there some kind of a trick to this?' demanded Richard hoarsely as Bob slopped up beside him, sending a wall of foam into his face.

'From what the captain says, the trick needs to be restoring a hundred per cent power.' Bob splashed down beside Richard. More water in his face, much of it down his neck – to meet the bubbling surface under the waterproof sleeves somewhere near his biceps. Everything underneath the suit was absolutely wringing wet now. He had an instantaneous thought that he could hardly have got wetter if he had just gone in for a swim. Then Bob's hands were beside his own, and the young first officer added a little explanation to this cryptic opening. 'The hatches are controlled by servo motors meant to balance the weight. Smaller and lighter than actual counter-weights, of course. But with power at only twenty per cent, we have to do eighty per cent of the work ourselves. And that may just be more than we can handle.'

'We need someone down there helping from the other side,' said Richard tersely. 'We'll never get it closed on our own from up here.'

'We do indeed. And if the areas below aren't almost fully flooded already, then we need them there before they are.'

'Someone strong and quick thinking,' said Richard.

'Someone up for a cold shower,' added Bob.

And the words came like a revelation to Richard. For cold as the water was, it was nowhere near as icy as it should have been. That was what the little wisps of mist had been trying to tell him all afternoon – but he had simply been too preoccupied to see their message. And it might be a crucially important message too. Warmer water meant they were out of the Arctic flow for the moment – where the water was icy, below freezing in some areas, only kept liquid by the salt and a great deal *thicker* than the average for the Atlantic as a whole. Instead they were in the out-wash of the Gulf Stream, where the water was warmer and a good deal *thinner*. *Quebec* should have been sitting high, like a swimmer in the Dead Sea, supported by the element sufficiently strongly to be able to read a paper while he floated. Instead she was like a child in a municipal swimming pool looking for some water-wings. How much difference could the two types of water make to *Quebec*'s chances of survival? Until they had a definite destination for this tow, perhaps they had better set a course up towards Cape Farewell and search out some thicker Arctic water that would make the sinking submarine just a little more buoyant for a while. He had better check with Tom Hollander as soon as he got back to *Sissy* . . .

But then he realized ruefully that worrying about salinity, water temperature and specific gravity was all almost obscurely theoretical. Not to mention considering setting a course for anywhere, let alone for Cape Farewell. Because, unless they got the hatch cover closed at once, *Quebec* would be lost long before he even got back to *Sissy*. And, he realized for the first time and with a considerable shock, there was an outside chance that the sinking sub would pull the tug down with it unless they were very quick-thinking indeed with their cable-handling.

But then he put all such abstruse speculation firmly out of his mind and concentrated on the task that was all too literally in hand.

Seventeen

Love

With Bob Hudson off the boat and Leif Hunter in the sickbay, Lieutenant Luc Pellier was effectively first officer. Furthermore, as the vessel was under tow, his duties as sonar officer were effectively surplus to requirement. It was Luc Pellier, therefore, who was ordered by his increasingly harassed captain to take the biggest, strongest team that he could find and go and close the forward escape hatch. To do it bloody quickly before it was too late – if it wasn't too late already. And then to try and find out which lunatic son of a bitch had opened the thing in the first place.

Though as far as Luc was concerned, the way the captain phrased the final order almost certainly contained the identity of the guilty party – or the captain's strong suspicion as to what it was. All the way up to the bulkhead door, the nervous officer kept his hands in his pockets, just in case. Though he was himself half convinced that the lunatic stowaway might still be in weapons stowage too far gone in his madness to remember how to open doors.

Although Luc's orders were specific – take the biggest and the strongest – they were not absolutely clear in one important regard. They didn't say take *only* the biggest and the strongest. So that when the other stranger, the one who called herself Captain Robin Mariner, decided to attach herself to the group that he was leading, bringing the useful, resourceful and reliable Leading Seaman Li with her, Luc was content to let her have her way.

Robin's decision to join the team was by no means as casual or motiveless as it seemed to Pellier. It was, in fact,

129

dictated by one of the strongest motives generally recognized: it was dictated by love. Hunter was asleep now, exhausted, shocked and sedated. There was nothing more she could do to help Doc Watson. And the little infirmary was depressing – filled with two and a half corpses as well as the wounded man, who, even drugged and comatose, was facing in his dreams the destruction of his most treasured ambitions. And in any case, she had become aware – for the news had gone through the vessel like wildfire – that Bob Hudson was up on the foredeck trying to close the escape hatch in question. And he had this big guy with an English accent with him whose name the captain somehow knew. Robin was sure she knew it too, though the accuracy of the scuttlebutt, like the availability of the power, was less than a hundred per cent.

Robin had nothing in mind more fully formed than a certainty that if she wanted to talk to her husband before tomorrow, then she should at least put herself somewhere she might have the opportunity. For whether he closed the hatch or not, he was not likely to stay aboard *Quebec* for very much longer. It was now, in fact, or never. And she suddenly discovered that, after the far too numerous near-death experiences of the day, she did want to hear the reassuring grumble of his voice and she didn't want to wait.

There were six of them, therefore, who approached the bulk-head door beside the heads. They were crowded into a short corridor with another big bulkhead door behind them. Pellier's team were more punctilious than Hunter's had been so all the doors were closed and secured after them as they proceeded. The door on their right leading away into the heads was an ordinary one made of wood veneer on a hollow frame such as might be found in any modern house. If things got out of control here when the metal door into the weapons section opened, it was likely to fail, burst open and allow the room to be flooded. Pellier ordered one of his men to check if there was anyone in there, therefore. The crewman just popped his head round the door and called, 'Anyone in here?'

There was no answer, so he shrugged and closed the door

130

again. So Gupta's body remained undiscovered for the time being. And indeed, it would have remained so for some considerable time longer had not Robin had an idea. 'Look, Lieutenant,' she said suddenly, 'I don't want to tell you your job, but you're just about to open a doorway into an area that may be flooded to some depth and here you have the one area conveniently to hand where water is not only expected, but is designed to drain safely away. Even the deck is extra strengthened and waterproofed in case the showers overflow. Instead of closing the door into the heads, wouldn't it be a good idea to try and get any water coming out of weapons storage *into* here, so some of it at least can go safely down the shower drains?'

Pellier shrugged in a way that betrayed his French ancestry even more clearly than his name. 'Sounds like a plan,' he said, rudely and almost dismissively. 'Let's go for it. We don't have time for a long debate in any case.' And so they proceeded, as Robin thought wryly, *Poor love, he's only so rude because I challenged his leadership. And his manhood.*

The British design team who had conceived these boats in the late 1980s had faced a bit of a quandary with this bulkhead door. On the one hand, there was a temptation to go for safety and put a strengthened glass window high in it, the same as in the other doors overlooking hatch areas – where safety after all should be the highest priority. But this hatch was in weapons storage and the bulkhead door would overlook that space. And here, of course, security was the highest priority. Even more important than safety.

The result of this was that Pellier, hesitating with his hands out of his pockets and on the bulkhead door-opening mechanism, had before him only a metre and a half or so of blank white-painted metal, heavily bolted and massively hinged. It would open outwards when released, and, for all that it was notorious for the unforgiving stiffness of the hinges, that was at least partly due to the simple weight of the door. Weight which, if released into motion by the power of a roomful of water behind it, was likely to squash the man who opened it like a fly.

'What I propose is this,' decided the young lieutenant after

131

a moment of thought narrowly observed by the men who formed his team. 'Captain Mariner and Leading Seaman Li will take charge of the door into the heads and showers. You will open it outward and angle it as best you can to channel it into the room and along to the shower stalls.' He nodded decisively, as though he and he alone had thought of this. 'The rest of you men will position yourselves with me, and push with all your strength against the door as I release the mechanism. Once it is unlocked, we will be able to ease back and release any weight of water in a controlled manner. Then, as soon as possible, two of us will release control of the door to the others and go into the weapons-stowage area where we will aid the men on deck in securing the hatch. In the meantime the door will be closed behind us until everything is secure and we are able to proceed to drain the area with more safety and control. Is that clear?'

The little command looked at each other and shrugged. 'Clear,' said one of them speaking for all, but he didn't sound entirely convinced.

'Sounds like a plan,' said Leading Seaman Li, rudely, almost dismissively. He was very much on Robin's side. Possessively so after his entrancement looking up at her all-too-tight white overall, and the way in which she contrived to fill it. But deep within the powerful little seaman the simple lust resulting from a long, lonely voyage was germinating into a genuine regard.

Robin too was less than convinced. It might well take all four of them to control the door. And, if that was so, then every inch wider they had to open it would make things worse. Better by far for her and Li to position the door into the showers as Pellier had ordered – then squeeze their slighter frames through the smallest possible gap beside the bulkhead door then go and close the hatch themselves.

'Mr Li, do you know how the hatch mechanism works?' she asked, sotto voce as they went to the wooden door and swung it wide.

'Naturally, Captain. I am as reluctant to drown as any man aboard,' he answered equally quietly. 'Therefore I know how all the safety features work.'

132

'Right, men,' ordered Pellier, oblivious to the muttered conversation at his back. 'Prepare to take the strain.' Four brawny shoulders pressed against the metal like a trainee rugby scrum.

'Would you follow me into weapons storage and close the hatch there if need be?' Robin persisted.

And Leading Seaman Li was blessed with a sudden vision of how she would look with her overalls not only breathtakingly tight, but transparently wet into the bargain. 'Of course, Captain,' he answered at once. Motivated by simple lust, if not quite love as yet, as Li's burgeoning regard and respect for the woman as a companion and leader was swept under in a flood of testosterone.

'Releasing the mechanism . . . NOW!' said Pellier, still oblivious to Robin's careful plans. And, thankfully, like the rest of them, unaware of Li's erotic fantasies.

The bulkhead door slammed back five centimetres before the struggling quartet managed to bring it under any sort of control. Water cascaded out from shoulder height, and thundered across the little corridor. It swirled against the wooden doorway held open by Robin and Li standing shoulder by shoulder, and swept obediently past the cubicles of the heads and away into the shower stalls, hissing and foaming as it went. Tugging at Gupta's ankles, and beginning the process that would upset the precarious balance of his corpse upon the toilet seat.

'Jesus!' hissed Pellier shocked by the weight and power of the monster he had just unleashed, hunching down to push back against the relentless pressure of the door with all his might. 'What the f . . . —'

But Pellier never finished the word. For four white fingers suddenly came reaching out around the edge of the door exactly level with his face. Four white fingers closed into claws with square-cut nails gleaming like shards of glass. Reaching out at Pellier's face as though trying to claw at his staring eyes. It was so sudden, so utterly unlooked-for, that the lieutenant sprang back with a shout of surprise and fear. The only explanation available to his shocked imagination was that the madman must be in there after all and wildly trying to claw his way out of the room. The door slammed open fifteen centimetres more at once; the cascade of water grew in volume exponentially and, like some strange white spider floating in the topmost wave of it, came Leif Hunter's missing hand.

With all the rest, it swept past the shaking door and into the shower stalls. Here it actually grabbed at the knees of Gupta's sagging body before it swept on into the nearest shower stall where it slid sedately down the inside slope of the whirlpool forming there, caught on the grate at the bottom and remained there through the rest of the incident.

But the water from weapons storage was out of control now – for the moment at least. Even with Pellier, shamefacedly back in position, the depth of the flood round the feet of himself and his men made it almost impossible for them to keep firm footholds. And without that, their pressure on the door failed even further. The door swung relentlessly wider and it became all too obvious even to Pellier that he could only get his men into the room and over to the leaking escape hatch if he let the door go altogether – and risked whatever consequences this might bring. Something he was clearly – and wisely – hesitant to do.

Robin tapped Li on the shoulder and waded forward. The water was at waist height now, so much of it had been released. The force was still considerable, but she could move against it. It was certainly strong enough to hold the flimsy thing of veneer and cardboard open as it swirled towards the showers and away down the drains. At the bulkhead door itself, she simply leaped up and in without hesitation, diving over the power of the out-rush. Completely unconscious of how revealing the soaking and transparent cotton of her overall had become. Particularly as the over*all* was actually over nothing – except her otherwise unclothed body. And Li followed her, eyes aglow and face fixed in an ecstatic grin.

With a guttural grunt of sheer physical effort, Pellier and his men began to force the door closed behind them.

Weapons storage was a large space fortunately empty at present, for it should have contained the sub's full cargo of torpedoes. Under the pallid light, however, it revealed nothing but empty racks sitting like reefs half in and half out of the flood. And falling from the deck-head up above them a torrent that would have done credit to the fiercest tropical downpour. Side by side, Robin and Li splash-waded across the room, still up to their waists in water. The effort required to move through the current was considerable – but it eased almost magically when the door closed behind them with a disturbingly final clang. The rungs leading up the wall and into the throat of the escape hatch itself were not too distant, and Robin filled her mind as she heaved herself across towards them with a simple set of calculations. If she wanted a word with Richard, she would have to go up the ladder first for she would have to be closest to the hatch. But she didn't really know how best to close it. So in actual fact Seaman Li should go up there first. He should be working on closing the hatch while she came up close behind him and tried to talk to Richard over the sound of the water – which she now realized would be very noisy indeed.

It was the noise that decided her in the end, making her mind up just as she reached the bottom rung. If she did allow Li to go up first then she could never really hope to talk to Richard. They would never be able to hear each other – she under that relentless roaring downpour and he above a layer of thick green water. She had an instantaneous cartoon-vision of her words coming up to him in bubbles, bursting into communication as they popped in the cold night air. The vision served to take her up the white rungs until her face was as close to the hatch as she dared put it. She felt through some kind of empathy rather than through any of her actual senses that Li was swarming up the ladder immediately after her. And then, with shocking vividness, after a moment of hesitation, she felt him actually clambering over her to reach the hatch mechanism.

'Richard!' she screamed in a kind of panic, suddenly all too well aware that Li was planning to close the hatch as quickly as he could. Which was exactly what she should be doing herself, of course. 'Richard! It's Robin!'

As Robin's quarterdeck voice boomed around the throat of the escape shaft, the downpour seemed to ease. Outside, the sub, another wave was passing and the trough behind it promised to uncover the hatch altogether for an instant. So that Richard, still kneeling with his numb hands fastened on the exterior section of the mechanism, beginning to slip back into the almost self-pitying train of thought as to how life would be without her, heard her voice quite clearly. Disembodied, seeming to come from nowhere and everywhere. As though she were already dead and haunting him.

'Robin!' He glanced around, utterly disorientated. 'Where are you?'

'Under the hatch, you great fool. Where else?'

'My God! How could they let you . . .'

'They couldn't stop me, Richard. I'm like a force of nature!'

'Too bloody right!' He had called her something like that often enough before. Her buoyant confidence filled him like a drug. 'How are you, darling?'

'Alive. And that's saying quite a lot after a day like the one we've just had! How are you?'

'Fine now. I was a bit worried earlier . . .'

'So I should bloody hope!'

'But I'm fine now. Big wave coming. We ought to get this hatch cover closed. I love you!' He called the last words down to her as the next wave swept in. It must have been the last in a series of seven. It was certainly big enough. It crested at chest level and completed the destruction of the last dry clothing under his supposedly waterproof outfit.

'Bloody hell!' shouted Bob at his shoulder.

Richard nodded grimly, thinking the lieutenant was talking about the wave, which had come very close to sweeping them both overboard.

'That is some kind of woman!' continued the submariner unexpectedly. 'After all she's been through today she still comes back for a goodnight chat. Jesus! If we could get this hatchway up you'd likely get a goodnight kiss!' He grunted as he felt the hatch begin to move. And Richard suddenly felt a really painful stab of regret that it was swinging closed at last. He heard her calling once again, like a forsaken

136

mermaid out of the depths. Then the hatch was closed tight and the wave was gone and the job was done.

'Jesus!' concluded Bob Hudson, babbling because of the strain and the excitement as much as anything else, his eyes bright in the arc light seeming to peer into Richard's very soul. 'I think you'd have done it, wouldn't you? You'd have opened the hatch if she had asked you and drowned the whole damn lot of them for one last kiss.'

'The things we do for love, eh?' said Richard, pulling himself upright without either a yea or a nay. 'The things we do for love.'

Which was almost – if not quite exactly – what Seaman Li was thinking some three metres below Richard, as he looked lingeringly up at Robin while she climbed wearily down the escape hatch ladder towards his lustfully worshipping gaze.

Eighteen

Damage

R ichard greeted the new dawn by coming up on *Sissy*'s deck like something out of Jules Verne's *Twenty Thousand Leagues Under The Sea*. He was kitted out in a drysuit and compressed-air breather, one of a team of three including the chief that Tom was leading down to assess the damage to the submarine's hull. To be fair, Richard had not been first choice to take the third suit but after his all too brief talk with Robin last night he was burning to get involved in some practical part of her rescue – and in no mood to take no for an answer. And even Tom had to admit that Richard was so widely experienced in maritime disasters that he was more likely than not to come up with some useful ideas. Useful in terms of focusing wiser minds as they argued against his naivety at the least. If they were lucky he might even come up with something out of left field – something so outrageous or so childishly obvious that no one else had thought of it.

The tow had seemed to have settled well during a short night made shorter still by a series of negotiations and discussions, face to face and over the radio. Nothing definitive had been agreed – it seemed that nothing much could be agreed until Mark gave a full report to Halifax and got some direct orders from Admiral Pike. And even Pike, suspected Richard shrewdly, would have masters to answer to in the Canadian Treasury Department or the Naval Paymaster General's Office if nowhere else. And in these days of twenty-four-hour media and knee-jerk politics where reputations could be made or marred in a sound-bite, there was always somewhere else. *Sissy*'s last job, for instance, an apparently simple mission that attempted to stop a burning tanker drifting on to an isolated rocky shore, had ended up splashed across the news worldwide with half the politicians in the European Union clawing to get involved, especially in front of the cameras, in awesomely uninformed comment and all too eager opinion-touting if in nothing actually practical or helpful.

But all the negotiations – even a lengthy and utterly esoteric discussion between Richard and Tom about the salinity and specific gravity of Arctic water as opposed to tropical – came to nothing in the face of one overwhelming fact. The sub was simply refusing to sit on the surface of the sea. Even with her pumps working – if only at twenty per cent – and even with the tow fully under way and proceeding towards Cape Farewell with all the speed reasonable in the circumstances, the long hull sat stubbornly fifty centimetres or so beneath even the troughs of the waves.

So, even if they could cut the nets away from above the escape hatches, it remained unthinkable that they should open them and try to get anyone out. Last night's adventure with the forward escape hatch had established that if nothing else. The first thing they were going to do, therefore, was to assess whether there was any chance of repairing the damage to the bows from outside the hull.

If they could even slow the inrush of the leak a little, it might give the labouring pumps a chance to disperse the weight of the water in her and raise the bows a degree or two. And who knew? Once the bows were in an upward slope, they might just pull the rest of the hull up with them. Fifty centimetres would just about do the job. Eighteen old-fashioned inches. It wasn't a lot to ask for, was it? Give me fifty centimetres – and I'll give back fifty lives. One centimetre for each life. That sounded like a bargain if ever there was one.

These thoughts were enough to take Richard to the square stern of the tug, and into the middle of two overlapping, almost conflicting conversations. Up until now, Tom – also heavily suited and ready to make the assessment for himself

139

with Richard and the chief – had been alone at the centre of the tirade. When Richard arrived, the conversation became three-way as the two main protagonists continued while Tom tried to bring Richard up to date with some of their concerns.

Bob Hudson was advising caution. Could they wait, he asked, while he got back in contact with Halifax? 'There's a hell of a lot of classified stuff in *Quebec*'s bow area,' he insisted, lapsing in his concern into almost impenetrable technicalities. 'The Type 2040 sonar is only the beginning of it. There's the CANTASS upgrade linkage and a bunch of hardware they put in there with the under-ice special upgrade that even I don't know about. It wasn't all just air-independent propulsion stuff by any manner of means! And that's just the inside. The hull is covered in more secret acoustic anti-sonar tiles than there are heat-resistant tiles on the space shuttle. Every single one of them is worth a fortune in its own right – as well as being worth God alone knows how much to Russia or whoever . . . Jesus. If you get a long look at the wrong stuff, or a handful of anything that secret, Admiral Pike'll be sending the Canadian equivalent of James Bond after your asses. Licence to Kill and all!

'I mean I shouldn't even be telling you most of this. If anyone at MARLANT finds out I've even said half of this then it'll be my career, my hide and my ass on the line as well.'

Sissy gloried in the possession of an officer called the winchmaster. The winchmaster's name was Gustav Van Allen but everyone called him Gus. He was a weather-beaten man from Port Elizabeth who appeared to have been carved from teak, who seemed to be about as old and wise as the rest of the crew combined, and who knew his job almost as well as he knew his own mind. And he suffered neither fools, youngsters nor hesitation gladly. And he'd already had a bellyful of the young Canadian officer. 'Look on the bright side, chum,' he snapped. 'Maybe it won't be James Bond they send after your poor little lily-white ass. Maybe it'll be Pussy Galore.'

Having dismissed his opponent for the moment, Gus

swung round on Tom and included Richard in his all too evident concern. 'Like I said before, the tow looks good enough and is apparently sitting well – though I've never worked with a loop-rig like this one. But I've had my men keep a close eye on the hawser and we're paying out, little by little, from the big port winch here. Paying out,' he insisted, glaring at Richard as though his frown would make everyone understand. 'Paying out from the port without pulling in on the starboard. A foot an hour, maybe more – and it seems to be speeding up. It's the only way we can keep *Sissy*'s stern from settling. And you must know what that means.'

Richard could see at once that it meant that the towline was getting relentlessly longer. And that fact in turn meant *Quebec* was moving further and further back. But he could not at first see the relevance of Gus's concern about the tug's square stern *settling* under the strain of the tow. But then he remembered one of his unreasoning fears of the previous night. That if they weren't careful, then the sinking *Quebec* might even be heavy enough to pull *Sissy* under. And abruptly, and with an icy shiver, he understood Gus's worry all too well.

'*Quebec* is sinking,' he said quietly. 'Little by little she's going down in spite of all we've done so far. And because she's already so low in the water, she's pulling us down too – or she would be except that Gus's men are giving her more line.'

'More rope,' agreed Gus grimly. 'The better to hang herself as they say. So, sonny,' the winchmaster swung round and confronted Bob like a drunk in a bar-room brawl, 'unless James Bond actually has your sorry ass in the cross-hairs of his sights then you'd better forget him. And MARLANT, Halifax and Admiral Pike into the bargain. It doesn't matter what the captain gets to see down there – whether it's sonar or radar or Babar the bloody elephant. It doesn't matter if it's CANTASS or your candy ass or your admiral's favourite piece of ass. We go down and try to plug up that collision damage in her hull, or *Quebec* goes down for ever – and we'll be lucky if she doesn't take *Sissy* along for the ride.'

141

But Bob Hudson was not some no-account boy to be dismissed by Gus Van Allen's sarcasm. He was an officer, used to making decisions and taking control. 'Very well,' he temporised, forcefully if a little pompously. 'I understand the urgency of the situation and the imminent danger of considerable loss of life. Halifax will take that into account, believe you me – these are their people! But I will need to inform MARLANT of your actions nevertheless.'

'All right,' said Tom equably. 'You run on up to the radio shack while we go over the stern.'

At this point in the proceedings Chief Engineer Christian Jaeger turned up, also in his suit, in a hurry and out of patience. 'Let's go, Captain,' he said shortly. 'Time's a-wasting and there's a hell of a lot to do.'

Richard slipped down into the water, trying to remember that he must regulate his breathing carefully. Immediately he was clear of the little dive platform hanging off *Sissy*'s stern, just above the restless waves, the harness he was wearing tightened and he became a miniature *Quebec*, as *Sissy* towed him across the surface of the Atlantic. Gus the winchmaster and his acolytes paid out the line that was attached to the harness, fortunately faster than thirty centimetres an hour, line that was designed to let him fall back slowly and settle deeper into the water just behind Tom and the chief. It was more than mere line, however. Richard was also dragging a fine communications cable that kept him in voice contact with *Sissy* – and with the other two divers falling back and down with him. At first it was quite difficult to angle his body so that he faced back towards *Quebec* while at the same time moving, effectively feet-first, backwards through the water. But he soon got the hang of it, helped by the fact that he wasn't wearing flippers on his feet. Then he was able to dismiss the feeling that he was being pulled one way, while he concentrated on moving carefully in the other, controlling his movement forward with easy motions of his hands.

The concentration needed to get it right, however, took his mind away from several unpleasant things that had forced themselves upon him right at the start. The disgusting taste of the mouthpiece on his already parched tongue, for instance – and the even fouler taste of the air that pumped out of it. The realization – now that he was too deep in it to do anything but keep a lookout – that the persistent warmth of the water meant that this was still the Gulf Stream. That the Gulf Stream was home of an almost numberless range of sharks and other dangerous predators. Predators that came and went though a disturbing mistiness even more marked under the water than its cousin the wispy fog had been above. It seemed that his face-plate was turning opaque with unsettling speed. And finally, most poignantly, there was the worry that Robin might after all end up trapped on a slowly sinking coffin that he could do nothing to rescue.

The snout of the sub loomed out of the murk with shocking suddenness. And it put him in mind of his initial concerns at once. For the shape of the hull was as elegantly aquadynamic as the body of a shark. And it was equally packed with latent menace. The similarities did not stop there, for the damage they had come to inspect more closely was under the nose of the thing, a little way back. And it cut across the lower curve exactly like a shark's mouth, gaping a little, viciously fanged with triangular shards of gleaming metal. Only the net and the tiles spoiled the illusion.

The net gathered into the gape of the damaged mouth like the bridle on a horse, the relentless grey squares seemingly welded to the hull all the way up to the gleaming surface of the water above. It was caught beneath the hydroplanes – and indeed seemed to have got itself wrapped around them almost as tightly as it was wrapped around the propeller. The combination seemed to have clothed the whole bow section of the sub with a harness of net above and below, but behind the hydroplanes the belly of the sub was free of nets. The main line of tension that Richard could see stretched back from the hydroplanes like the lateral line on a shark's body where the motion sensors and attack triggers lie. Above it, the net might as well have been an extra layer above the slate grey of the acoustic tiles. Below it, the web billowed out in ghastly skirts as though some part of the monster had been ripped asunder and left to gape and waver in the currents. Beyond the skirts of loose-flowing net, he could see nothing, but he knew well enough what the propeller must look like: he brought to mind a big ball of his mother's grey knitting wool with a couple of knitting needles sticking at hazard out of it. For the wool read nets and lines, he thought. For the needles read propellers all askew and useless.

Tom and the chief were in place already, and they were watching him with much more attention than he was paying to them.

'Richard?' Tom's voice crackled in his helmet. 'You all right? Over.'

'Fine, Tom. Just coming into position now. Over.' Only now did Richard register that there had been a buzz of crackling conversation passing unheeded through his helmet all during his preoccupied swim down here. 'In position. Over,' he emphasized, to show that he was back fully on line and focused on the job in hand now.

'OK, Richard. Chief, first impressions? Over.'

'It's worse than I had feared, Captain. There's no way we have anything aboard big enough to block this off. Nothing that we could deploy, at any rate. It's a miracle the internal bulkheads have held. The pressure must be immense. A miracle. And a very great credit to the men who built her.'

Tom took the chief's awed silence to mean 'Over' and he added his own observation. 'We'd better warn Captain Robertson to shore up everything that has water behind it just in case. Richard, any thoughts? Over.'

'Are you certain there's no way we could plug this? Even partially? Nothing we could fother in? Over.'

'Hornblower stuff, you mean? Eighteenth-century seamanship? Get Lucky Jack Aubrey on the case?' came the chief's voice, scarcely more enthused than Gus Van Allen talking to Bob Hudson. 'Like maybe we have a spare *sail* or something like that? Over.'

'Not quite, Chief,' answered Richard coolly, unused to being mocked or belittled. 'I was thinking maybe of one of your biggest fenders, something like that. Haven't you anything like a fender made of coir or some collision matting or . . .'

'It's a surprisingly good idea,' allowed Tom before the chief could pour more scorn. 'But we haven't anything that big. Not of coir fibre. Our biggest fenders – and they are pretty big too – are all air-filled.'

'Well,' said Richard, 'you certainly couldn't put a Yokohama fender in there. They may be big and damn near indestructible, but they are basically just rubber filled with air. The points of broken metal in the damage there would rip one to pieces in a second.'

'It'd be like something out of *Jaws*,' agreed the chief. 'Only bigger.' His tone was more placatory. Richard knew about Yokohama fenders – maybe he could pull his weight in other ways. His tone and the movements of his head also made it clear that Richard wasn't the only one who had seen *Quebec*'s resemblance to a shark. Like Richard, the chief was on the lookout against unexpected attacks.

'Like *Jaws* but ten times bigger,' agreed Tom nervously, unconsciously letting slip that even he was on the alert.

Gus Van Allen's voice came on the line then. 'That's another foot gone, Captain. Up to two feet an hour now. What d'you reckon we should do? Over.'

'Bridge. This is the captain. Over.'

'Bridge here, Captain. First officer. What can I do for you? Over.'

'Alan. You heard what Gus said? All I can think of to do is take the speed up. See if that will help matters any. Take her up another two knots. Then if nothing happens, two knots more in ten minutes' time. Got that? Over?'

The first officer repeated the orders. And the divers had to adjust their position in the water again as the speed picked up by two knots. The three of them swam around the net-masked face of the sub, testing – as far as they could with their hands – the tension of the lines. And their sensitive, experienced hands confirmed what their eyes had told them – that from bow to hydroplane, top and bottom, from the surface – or fifty centimetres below it – down the better part of eight metres to the keel, the net was tight and absolutely solid. Even the gathers in the torn mouth section of the damage were as immovable as if they had been formed of steel and set in stone.

At last, Richard thrust his arms gingerly into the gape then followed them with head and shoulders as he tested the tension deeper inside for himself, with Gus calling ironically, 'Keep your eyes closed in there, Richard. You don't want to see anything too *secret*, man.'

The three of them laughed wryly, but Richard's curiosity was piqued. He reached for the waterproof torch he carried at his belt and pushed himself in a little further, flashing the beam around. He was waist deep in the damaged area with only his legs sticking out when disaster struck.

Distantly, and with no sense of impending doom, Richard heard the first officer contact his captain from *Sissy*'s bridge. 'That's ten minutes at two knots higher, Captain. Go to four knots higher now? Over.'

'Go to four knots. Over,' said Tom unthinkingly.

Richard felt the water surge around him – but the change in pressure was slight and he didn't even associate it with the half-heard conversation. He flashed the beam around the cavernous space behind the tightly drawn strands of netting. All he could see was an incomprehensible mess of ruined equipment. As though there had been an explosion in a computer store. Nothing secret enough here to get James Bond out of bed, he thought, let alone down to Q section and out after the three of them.

On the thought, Richard drew his legs in and curled into an almost foetal position, preparing to pull himself out again. He paused for an instant, almost lying on his side, with his back pressing against the cradle of the gathered net. He switched off his torch and made sure that his line to *Sissy* was clear of the gaping metal fangs surrounding him.

But then, suddenly and utterly unexpectedly, the lazy stirring of the current into the gape of the damage became something else entirely. The balance of the pressure shifted drastically as, away inside the sub itself, a sorely over-tested bulkhead gave way at last. The doorway burst open releasing a flood of water into the vessel. And the weight of that water was translated immediately into pressure. And all of it came down on Richard, pressing him up against the netting in the strange gaping mouth as helplessly and immovably as the netting itself was pressed against the casing of the sub.

Nineteen

Bulkhead

With Seaman Li close behind her but her head full of Richard, Robin slopped across the weapons-storage area until she reached the bulkhead door. It was tightly closed, of course. She banged upon it and yelled, 'All clear and secure, Lieutenant Pellier. You can let us out now.'

The door opened immediately and Robin was almost swept off her feet as she tried to step out. Pellier himself caught her arm, however, and held her gallantly erect as she staggered through, looking like some kind of pre-Raphaelite painting with the wash of foaming water breaking around her hips – or, the way Pellier and Li were looking at her, perhaps that should have been Pirelli Calendar girl. Seaman Li followed immediately behind her, but there was no hand available to steady him, so he lost his footing and was simply washed away. Robin swung her wiry strength in behind Pellier and the rest so that the door swung closed quickly, but Li was still swept helplessly towards the showers.

As soon as the door was shut, Robin stepped away through the last of the dwindling flood and let Pellier and his men get on with it as she went into the heads to assure herself that Li was still all right. But as soon as she came through the doorway she knew that something was badly wrong. Li was sprawled in the final wash of water wrapped in the arms of a naked man. And the naked man looked dead to Robin. 'Li!' she called at once. 'Li, are you all right?'

The seaman heaved himself sideways, disentangling himself from the flaccid arms. 'I'm all right, Captain,' he said. 'But it looks like Lieutenant Gupta's not.'

Robin crossed to her wiry companion's side and helped him to his feet at once, then they both stood looking down. Engineering Sub-Lieutenant Gupta lay on his back and his head lay at an angle that was all too reminiscent of Annie Blackfeather's. Robin crouched down and reached out to feel the neck for a pulse, just in case. The temperature alone assured her that this was a corpse, but her touch rolled the head a little further over so that she and Li could see the mark across the back of his neck.

'We'd better get Doc up here,' she said grimly. 'Looks like he has another client.'

Lieutenant Pellier stuck his head round the door just at that moment. 'Is that dead hand in here?' he asked. 'We'd better get it to the Doc.'

'There are at least three dead hands in here,' answered Li. 'And we need to get them all down to the Doc.'

Pellier blenched when he saw what the seaman was talking about. 'Jesus,' he said. 'I'll send for him at once. You'd better wait, here both of you.'

'Yes,' said Doc five minutes later. 'This blow certainly killed him. Broke his neck as clean as a whistle. There isn't much in the way of swelling or bruising because death was instantaneous and you need the circulatory systems working to get much in the way of swelling or discoloration as a rule.'

'But, bruise or no bruise,' said Robin quietly, 'what would make a mark like that?'

'I don't know. Something straight and heavy. Narrow, but blunt.'

'Like a heavy meat cleaver? Only not the blade. The spine,' she suggested.

'Yes. That would do the job perfectly,' Doc agreed.

'If it might have been a cleaver, then it was likely our madman,' said Robin. 'And that's a bit worrying, isn't it?'

'Yes, it likely was,' agreed Doc. 'At least I hope the hell it was. We're all under far too much pressure as it is without someone else running around killing people in the showers. But why is the fact that it's probably the madman *worrying* as you say?'

149

'Two reasons, I'd say,' mused Robin. 'Maybe more than two. And they may well be linked to each other. Firstly, why would even a madman use a meat cleaver if he's got a gun? And secondly, why would he want to use the back of the cleaver when he's got a razor-sharp blade?'

Li chimed in at that point. 'Perhaps a madman doesn't know he's got a gun,' he offered acutely. 'Maybe he's too mad to know what a gun is.'

'Fair enough,' allowed Robin. 'So why not just hit him with it as though it's a club? A rock? Whatever mad guys use these days?'

'Other than chainsaws, you mean?' asked Li slyly.

'Because he hit him with the cleaver,' proposed Doc more seriously. 'Maybe the cleaver was what he had in his dominant hand. The right hand.'

'OK. I'll accept that. Then why the *back* of the cleaver? I mean not even a madman carries a cleaver back to front. That looks like a conscious decision to me – and *that's* what's worrying. If he made a decision then he had a reason.'

'Right,' allowed the Doc. 'Then what's the reason?'

'Think. You have a gun and a cleaver and you want to kill someone but you don't shoot them and you don't want to cut them. Why is that?'

Li and Doc looked at each other then at Robin. The penny still had not dropped. So she continued. 'So that you don't get blood everywhere. Most especially, you don't get blood on anyone's clothes.'

They understood then. Or they understood some of it. They understood at least the significance of a naked man coming into a shower room with only a gun and a meat cleaver to cover his modesty – then going out again after a murder still with the gun and the cleaver, but leaving a naked corpse behind.

'Jesus Christ,' said Doc. 'He's got himself dressed!'

'More than that,' said Robin. 'He's got himself disguised.'

Of all the things that needed doing aboard *Quebec* that night, fixing the damage to the vent in the upper-deck passageway aft of the fin was the least important. So that when Paolo returned to the place that he had first heard the Heavenly Voices, he was able to leap upward and catch at the edges of the hole, pull himself upwards and twist his slight body through. The crawlspace between the deck head and the casing was narrow but it had a restful familiarity to the man – or rather to the creature Paolo still was. It was dark in here but no longer pitch black. And anyway, he had his strange-shaped torch now. It was warm, too, for the twenty per cent air-con had started circulating a little heat – which rose, as heat will. And the man was insane, not superhuman. He curled up in the elbow where the horizontal deck met the vertical fin, rested his head on the arm that held the cleaver, placed the arm that held the handgun along the upper ridge of his ribs, hip and thigh, and simply fell fast asleep.

No one else aboard *Quebec* got much sleep. Most of them were convinced that the instant they closed their eyes – or even lowered their guard – the madman would appear out of impossibly unlikely places and hack them screaming into pieces. Their fear was not all childish; nor could it all be blamed on the media where such monsters roamed unchecked performing miracles of mindless violence. And in so doing making a fortune for film directors, actors, authors and journalists. There were genuine grounds for worry, not least the fact that he must have passed through the ship at least once after Gupta's death, unremarked and unsuspected because he was dressed in Gupta's clothes. That in itself bespoke a disturbing failure of focus amongst many of those aboard. They were so busy looking for a naked, slavering animal that when the real thing passed them in a boiler suit they noticed nothing at all. Inevitably, it seemed, the stress of their situation and the exhaustion that sprang from it allowed things to get out of proportion all too easily.

Robin for one could see this clearly – and, with it, the real danger that the nameless stranger presented. Not only that they were so fixated on one thing that they let another wander freely in their midst but also that as time went on and he remained undiscovered everyone aboard was watching out for him more and more carefully. And watching out for

151

their actual duties less and less. Which was a very dangerous distraction indeed.

Robin answered it in the only way she could, and with Mark's grateful blessing and full authority. And with Leading Seaman Li very close at hand. A couple of times in every watch through evening and the night she patrolled the whole vessel herself, from stem to stern. Or as far as she could get each way, which effectively meant from weapons stowage to motor control. She passed, according to her plan at least, like Florence Nightingale or Mary Seacole bringing brightness, calm, quiet and peace. And a brisk return to duty and responsibility for anyone failing or falling short. In *Quebec*'s current situation, they would be fortunate indeed to survive even if everyone worked together and pulled their weight. As things stood, it was all that Mark Robertson could do to stop more and more people deserting their posts to prowl the corridors and passageways in dangerous groups armed with anything that looked as though it would do serious damage to anyone. Tempers flared. Confrontations needed calming. Officers, commissioned and non-commissioned alike, who should have been monuments of calm reliability, became at the drop of a hat screaming martinets who would have found themselves right at home on the *Bounty*.

For Robin, in spite of her fond dream of spreading the light of reason and calm, it all came to a head over the bulkhead door in the forward sleeping area. She was pretty exhausted and increasingly short-tempered herself by the time the situation began to build. She had lost all track of time, especially as she had grabbed a couple of power naps courtesy of Doc and Li, who watched over her as she lay in the last spare sickbay bunk. She fondly supposed these naps to have lasted an hour each at most but in actual fact both Doc and Li had nodded off during their watch themselves, unknowingly protected from discovery by the fact that Robin's watch had fallen victim to her adventures in the life raft. Like Richard's steel-cased Rolex Oyster Perpetual, it was an analogue, but, unlike his, the water-resistance had failed and the timepiece was taking nearly two hours to get the minute hand round the dial. But this whole situation had its fortunate side, for only a couple of hours' solid sleep kept Li under control. For the leading seaman was whipping himself up into something akin to a frenzy of lust that was, at the very least, going to get him sacked as Robin's right-hand man – a situation in which he was proving invaluable to her.

Outside the submarine it was approaching dawn, therefore, when Robin awoke for the second time, fondly believing her watch when it told her it was still the wee small hours of the middle watch. Li had jumped awake immediately before her but had not yet found any way of invading her immediate privacy with his gaze – or anything more solid. 'Ah, Mr Li,' she said, uncharacteristically springing into full wakefulness without the application of teak-dark early morning tea. 'It's just after 03:00. Time for a patrol.'

She rolled out of the bunk, scratched the tousled golden glory of her head and slid on her deck-shoes, failing to notice for a moment just how many buttons had come undone below her throat. Something that made up to Li for the fact that her overall was no longer so transparent now it was dry. They set off side by side for the control room. The conning tower was manned, of course, but the watch officers were comatose and sitting silently. They hardly raised an eyebrow as Robin and Li came past, let alone a smile or a conversation. Still believing the timepiece that was nearly four hours slow, Robin pressed on, hardly surprised at the lethargy – a traditional part of the 00:00–04:00 middle watch.

At the forward end of the control room the passageway split. One part led straight through the bulkhead door into the upper heads and showers area where they had discovered Gupta's body. The other led to a steep companionway. Here Robin decided to lead the way down into the areas immediately below weapons storage. Since Pellier had sealed the door, the room remained full of water to a depth of nearly a metre and Robin wanted to see whether or not it was leaking down into the other areas.

The forward companionway took them down into the corridor leading past the lower heads and showers. Beyond these were the refrigeration areas on the right as they faced forwards towards the flooded bow. On the left there were the dry-goods stores. Robin opened and closed all the massive fridges, content with a fairly quick check through to establish that nothing was obviously wrong. Then she and Li turned left and went into the storage rooms. Here their checking was slower. There were shadowy little nooks and crannies all over the place and although their primary concern was to search for leaks, they too soon fell into the trap of keeping too much of an eye out for hidden madmen armed with cleavers and SIG-Sauer P226s.

Robin came out alive and dry but stressed and less than happy. Li, sensitive to atmosphere, was also on a short fuse. All of which made matters worse when they reached the next door forward. This was a metal bulkhead door with a strengthened glass window in it. The glass had been modestly – not to say mockingly – covered by a tiny pair of pink gingham curtains. For this was the crew's sleeping quarters.

Without thinking, Robin banged the traditional 'shave and a haircut' warning and went through the bulkhead first, swinging the heavy portal inward and stepping over the sill. She was only halfway through the door when she was stopped by a heavy shoulder and by something cold at her throat. She looked down to see the handle of the big Sabatier knife held in a hairy fist. Li came crowding close behind her and the sharp edge of the blade bit at her skin. She stopped, stunned, feeling weirdly as though she had stepped into some kind of pirate movie. 'Who goes there?' demanded a gruff voice in her ear.

'For crying out loud . . .' she answered. 'What in God's name . . .'

'That's not the password . . . ,' replied the gruff voice, even more threateningly, in a cloud of halitosis that came close to knocking her out.

'It's that English broad,' said another voice. 'Says she's a captain or some such.'

'Came aboard with Psycho Bob, didn't she?' The shoulder crowded, the halitosis intensified, the Sabatier thrust up under her chin. The knife blade really did tickle in a strange and unsettling manner. It made her wonder, was that perspiration gathering in the hollow of her throat – or was it blood?

'Yes!' she snapped. 'I came aboard with Psycho Bob, as you call him. And I also brought my husband's tug, which is all that's keeping you alive! I'm here with Captain Robertson's authority. Now stand back and let me do my job!'

The seaman with the Sabatier fell back and Robin stepped into the crew's sleeping quarters with Li on her heels like a bantamweight boxer looking for a prize-fight. There was a surprising number of people in here, women as well as men, all crew – no officers that she could see. People she had talked to in the galley as well as around the boat – which explained the Sabatier at least. 'Shouldn't some of you be on duty?' she enquired, simply surprised by the number of them.

They exchanged looks and shrugs. Li at her shoulder muttered, 'Leave it, Captain.' Or maybe it was just, 'Leave, Captain.'

But in fact Robin had come in here with a purpose beyond routine inspection. She pushed forward. The man with the knife fell back, his bark obviously worse than his bite. His dog's breath worse than both. The rest of the area was lined with bunks, most of them occupied but with few of the occupants even pretending to be asleep. In the pallor of the twenty per cent security lighting and the coffin-square regularity of the shadows, they looked like a set of extras from *Buffy the Vampire Slayer*. They even cringed back a little from the glare of her torch as though she had brought sunlight into their strange, stuffy, not to say *smelly*, vault.

At the forward end of the bunk area there was another bulkhead door, and this was what Robin had come to inspect. Here, as up above, safety had given way to security and the door was solid metal. It opened into the forward areas where the secret radar and sonar equipment were. Where, Robin knew all too well – as did they all, in fact – there were currently several tons of Atlantic water, pulling the bow-section relentlessly down.

The door was sweating like a villain in a police interrogation cell with the pressure starting to build. Robin had

155

been expecting that. The water was cold; the bunk area was hot, the metal was a good conductor. But she had not expected such a large puddle of water on the deck below the door itself. She frowned, kneeling for a closer look.

Just as she did so, the vessel seemed to give a stir; a kind of surge forward. There was a buzz of concern through the room. Robin looked up at the frowning Li. 'It's all right,' she said loudly, speaking to more than just her companion. 'The tug's just pushing our speed up by a couple of knots or so. Nothing to worry about.'

She turned back to the sweating door, her eyes narrow. Like a surgeon seeking the full extent of a cancer, she explored slowly and minutely. 'Li, is there a towel or something there?'

He passed her a spare pillow. She mopped the door dry with that, then sat back on her heels, watching to see where the sweating reappeared first. And, oddly, it was not on the painted surface of the door at all, but at the edge. All around the edge, in fact, as though the seal was beginning to give way. 'Can you pass me another cloth or whatever, Mr Li?' she asked. 'I just want to wipe this dry again.'

The submarine's hull gave that stirring surge forward once again.

Someone groaned, quite loudly.

Robin looked up to see Mr Li turning away in search of another pillow.

Someone groaned again and a tiny jet of water sprayed into Robin's eyes.

'LOOK OUT!' she screamed at the top of her voice and threw herself aside.

Just as the door burst open and the first few tons of Atlantic water exploded into the room.

Twenty

Pressure

Richard couldn't breathe. It was almost as though the physical weight of the water flooding into *Quebec* and being supplemented by an equal weight of water flowing relentlessly over him was piled up on his chest. He had the vague sense beyond the gathering agony of his suffocation that the hull around him was being battered by a giant with a sledgehammer. Then everything went silent – except for the agonized pulsing of his blood in his ears.

Choking, suffocating and on the verge of the overwhelming panic that would have consumed a lesser man, Richard fought to clear his mind. The netting cut into him as though he had suddenly been transported to a planet where his weight had been multiplied by ten. Only the speed at which his line was snaking past, sucked into the relative vacuum behind him, undermined the disorientating impression.

Certainly Richard's ability to move his torso and legs had almost completely gone. Only his arms seemed to have any kind of freedom at all. But his head seemed to be welded in place and his vision was darkening rapidly. For it was the pressure on his chest that was important. Solid bone and muscle of arm and leg could take it. Only the chest, filled with thin air and therefore fatally compressible, could really let him down, even under these extreme circumstances. But there had to be something he could do. There had to be something. But what?

He felt the nose of the sub jerk down as the weight of water pressing in on him was added to the weight already in her. And that gave him an idea. Depth and pressure were the same thing to a diver. And they were met in the same way – by regulating the pressure of whatever gas he was breathing. That was the crucial thing. Just as the pressure of water on a swimmer's ribs is so great that it is impossible to breathe through a snorkel deeper than a metre below the surface at most, so the pressure at any depth greater than that must be met by equal pressure back. Only when the balance of pressure is restored can the diver begin to breathe.

With a smoky black edge swirling round his vision, Richard groped for the pressure regulator on his compressed-air pack. He turned it gingerly, as slowly and carefully as he dared. Too much pressure might prove as fatal as too little and burst his lungs like balloons. He had an instantaneous cartoon vision of himself, over-inflated, zooming up into the sky. But then his lungs began to fill with air and his vision began to clear. More than just his vision, indeed.

'Richard! Are you all right?' called Tom, and Richard had a vague impression that Tom had been calling that for a while. The captain's shadow moved across his vision, close enough to make him jump but far enough away to stay clear of the suction crushing down on Richard.

'Here, Tom. And not likely to be going anywhere soon by the looks of things. Over,' Richard answered.

'How do you feel? Over.'

'I'll live, as long as the sub stays afloat. Over.'

'Listen, Richard, the chief and I have been thinking about that. The line to your harness is pretty strong. We could maybe get Gus Van Allen to winch you out of there.'

'Off-hand I'd say that if Gus could sort out the tangle to my line caused by the fact that it's been sucked back over my shoulder through the net, then, if he could get every-thing out of here past the sharp edges of the damage and pull it on out of the current, he'd still only find my chest and maybe my arms in the harness when he got it aboard *Sissy*. I don't see my head or legs moving much no matter what my chest does. Over.'

'OK, Richard. But the instant there's any lessening of the pressure there, you get out of there. Over.'

'Like a hare at a greyhound track, I assure you. And in

the meantime, I'll try and pull my line back out of the secret bits of *Quebec* and hope I don't pull out anything that would get James Bond coming after me after all. Over.'

'Right,' said the chief. 'But we won't just be sitting twiddling our thumbs either. We're in contact with Gus and the guys on *Sissy*, trying to come up with something smart. And I mean, the people aboard *Quebec* have to be doing *something*. Over.'

'I hope so. Over,' said Richard. Then he mentally added, *Oh God I hope so!* But of course it wasn't his own predicament he was thinking about.

The bolts and the hinges on the bulkhead door in the crew's bunk area all failed at once. The door slammed down the length of the room like a missile and would have destroyed the bulkhead opposite had it not been knocked off line by the bunks it was gathering up before it. In the end it span away to port, cartwheeled across the deck and smashed into the side of the shaking vessel. The noise it made was indescribable. So massive, indeed, that it drowned out the screams of the crew themselves – those who were hurt by the massive projectile, or terrified by what they saw of its passage. The only ones who were quiet were Robin and Li who had been expecting the catastrophe and the two gruff guards with the Sabatier who were turned into a kind of pâté as it smeared over the pair of them.

The noise the door made echoed through the hull for an instant – already overwhelmed by the thunderous inrush of the sea. 'Out,' screamed Robin. 'Everybody out!' She hurt her throat and saw stars with the power she put into the order but she might just as well have held her peace. No one stood any chance of hearing her in that roaring madness. Fortunately, it was absolutely obvious what everyone had to do and they all set about doing it with almost superhuman speed.

The flying door had cleared the bunks in front of Robin so she was able to take off like a cheetah chasing a gazelle. After her third step, when the water was already up to her knees and trying to trip her with the unrelenting force of its

159

currents, she discovered that Li was well in front of her. Close on his heels for once, she pounded down the room, tail-end Charley bringing up the rear. Incongruously, she saw through the drenched white of his overall that he was wearing garishly coloured boxer shorts. She turned her gaze away at once. It never even occurred to her what the transparency of her own soaking overalls had been showing lately.

As she ran, Robin began to scan around the place as though this was her own command. On either hand, the wreckage of bunks was beginning to heave and toss on the increasingly stormy waves within the place. But there were no faces in the billows; no bodies amid the wreckage. No hands held high in mute appeal for help. They were alone in the room. That was something after all.

But then she saw that the others who had so rapidly escaped the place were grouped around the door, swinging it closed against the knee-high flood as it gathered rapidly towards their thighs. And the door closed outwards, away from her. Once it passed a critical angle, the weight of the water on this side would slam it and it would never open again. 'Wait!' she called, her words as silent and pointless as everything she had said in the last ten seconds. They couldn't hear anything but the joyous roaring of the sea as it gulped down one more vessel. They wouldn't obey anything now but their terror.

But, blessedly, Li reached the door just in time. His presence and his own shouting would have made no difference at all – but his quick-thinking certainly did. He swung one of the floating bunks into the closing gap, jamming the metal of its foot between the heavy jaws. Then he leaped up on to the bunk itself and turned, his hand held down for her. Up she went with a leap and a heave, as though they were circus acrobats in performance. He took her waist and all but threw her through the gap then followed hard on her heels as the bunk began to come apart. Its foot folded inwards and it slammed away into the flooded room. The instant that it did so, the door, too, slammed.

They were floundering out in the flooding corridor between the fridges and the dry-goods store that was rapidly becoming a wet-goods store. Robin swung round, shouting, 'Secure it!' But again, her order was redundant. The instant that it was closed, a horde of busy hands pulled handles down and slid bolts safely home. Then they stood gasping and aghast as the pretty pink gingham curtains played out a little drama for them against the strengthened glass – as though it were a television screen.

First the thin cloth began to jerk and shiver as spray, then foam slammed hard against it. Relentlessly and with awesome rapidity, it was soaked and smeared against the glass, as tight as a layer of paint. But then the hems began to stir and little by little in a kind of bizarre strip-tease, the gingham squares were pulled away by the power of the solid water. A centimetre at a time it seemed, the curtains rose with the level of the flood, floating away into the vastness of it. Until at last they were waving like banners pulled away from the door itself by the tug of the ocean ill-contained behind it. And as the sad little flags fluttered helplessly, the deep green glass behind them revealed the relentless rise of the water until someone in the chief's team had the sense to isolate the circuits and kill the lights before the whole boat fused again. A few moments after that, anyone still there would have heard the distant sound of popping as though a net-full of party-balloons had burst. The water had hit the still-hot bulbs, shattering them one by one, and pressed its surface hard against the deck-head that was all that separated it from the flood in the weapons-storage area above.

Robin didn't wait around for any of this. The instant she was out and checked that everyone else in the corridor was safe, she was off up to the conning tower. She was fairly certain Mark would know what had just happened – he would feel it in the very fabric of his command – but she was equally certain that no one would have made any kind of detailed report or damage assessment yet. So eager was she to get up into the command area that when she slipped, she assumed simply that her shoes were wet. She didn't realize for quite a while that she had slipped because of the steepening downward angle of the hull.

*   *   *

161

Richard teased the line back out of the yawning chasm behind him a metre at a time. And as it came he called to Gus to pull it in little by little. It was more for the human contact than for any other reason, because being able to breathe had cleared his head. And his clear head could understand all too clearly how dangerous his situation was. If they didn't close the flood off inside the sub pretty quickly, then *Quebec* was off down to Davy Jones' locker with Richard wedged immovably in its jaws. And indeed, with Robin trapped helplessly somewhere in its slowly imploding belly. His body became almost preternaturally sensitive to any change in the sub's attitude in the water.

He catalogued almost every millimetre by which her bow was settling under the added weight flooding into her. He noted the way her forward motion moderated as Tom called *Sissy* to throttle back again. But he also felt at once how this made almost no difference to the pressure he was under or to the gathering rate of downward tilt. Even when both vessels came to an almost dead stop in the water, Richard's situation did not ease. The only way he would get any hope of relief, he knew, was if they closed off the flooded area and let the pressure equalize. And if they could do that before the sub began its final downward swoop.

But then, as Richard was a man who always looked for the positive angle, he began to wonder, if the sub was this finely balanced, perhaps it would be as easy to pull her head back up again. Say Captain Robertson and his crew did manage to close off the newly flooded area. Say *Sissy* could hold *Quebec* on the surface for a while longer yet – perhaps not take her back under tow, but hold her – what did they have aboard that would do the exact opposite of what the inrush of water had just done?

Richard had the answer in his head and was beginning to formulate a plan of action even before the current slackened, telling him that Captain Robertson's command had once again managed to save the day, and allowing him to pull himself gingerly out of the gaping steel-lined jaws at the front of the submarine.

*   *   *

'How many Yokohama fenders do you have aboard, Tom?' Richard demanded even as Gus was winching him gently back towards *Sissy*. Gently but speedily. They were all aware that Richard was low on air, having used it at a higher pressure and a greater speed than planned. And Richard himself was also wondering distantly whether what he had done in order to survive would place him at risk of the bends.

'They won't be any good to plug the gap, Richard. We've discussed that. The damage will tear them apart. They're only glorified balloons . . .'

'That's what I mean, Tom. That's what I want to discuss with you. If we've got enough aboard, couldn't we secure them to the netting at the bow of the sub and then shorten the lines holding them in place until they lift her straight up out of the water? That way, if we secure them correctly, *Sissy* might even be able to take her in tow again, if we have any kind of a destination to tow her to . . .'

'We have a destination,' Bob Hudson told them as soon as they came aboard. 'While you've been working on the damage, I've been working on Halifax. It seems that MARLANT has a big exercise running in the Labrador Sea. Another reason why it was so difficult to get through to the top brass. They're diverting several of their ships towards us as we speak. Admiral Pike himself is aboard. They want to rendezvous as soon as possible.'

'Where?' asked Tom.

Bob gaped at him, apparently nonplussed by his question, in spite of the fact that it was so obvious. But then Richard glanced over his shoulder and followed the young officer's gaze. Even he was shocked to see how far further down *Quebec* had settled since he had gone back to her an hour ago at dawn.

'We can't say how soon *as soon as possible* is until we know where they want us to meet them,' said Richard gently, recapturing Bob's attention as he finished pulling off his helmet and reached for a bottle of sparkling water conveniently in a cooler by the divers' boarding point.

163

'Oh. Of course. They want to rendezvous at Cape Farewell. But God, it looks as though we'll be lucky to get her there at all.'

'Oh, I don't know,' said Tom easily, almost confidently. 'I think we have a cunning plan.'

Twenty-One

Tension

Richard was back in his diving suit – still without flip-pers. Still in it, really, for he had hardly had time to towel himself off and visit the heads in *Sissy* before he was redeployed straight back aboard *Quebec*. But it was his own fault, he thought with a wry grin. *If you can't stand the heat in the kitchen then don't come up with any clever recipes*, as President Harry Truman might have said.

Richard's helmet was folded back allowing his face the heady combination of fresh air and sunshine, while still letting him talk to Tom, Gus and the chief a couple of hundred metres away on board the tug. The line joining him to *Sissy* was long enough to be occasionally distracting though there was less tension than might have been expected because, although it was so strong, it was also very fine and light.

There was a great deal less tension than recently in every-thing else about Richard also. He was full of the euphoria that comes with surviving a near-death experience. He had experienced none of the telltale stiffness in his joints that might have warned of anything like the bends. And, had Robin been anywhere other than where she actually was, anywhere else at all, it would have been a perfect day.

He was slopping carefully across *Quebec*'s foredeck and the water was up past his knees now, with wave crests occa-sionally slapping him in the lower belly hard enough to make him stagger. On the one hand he could feel the pulse of power and pumps in the net-bound casing over which he was walking – and that was good; on the other hand he was growing increasingly worried about being washed off her altogether – and that was very bad indeed. He was walking uphill from the bow towards the fin, thinking how utterly impossible it would be to get anyone out through the escape hatches now – and that, under the circumstances, was the worst of all.

Richard was completing the initial recce on the deck with Second Engineer Herbert, the officer who would have filled the third suit had Richard not done so earlier. Even securely tethered as he was, Richard needed a diving buddy. Never one to waste a voyage, Tom had ordered Sparks into the Zodiac with Richard and Herbert. Sparks was up in the fin now, trying to lower a hand-held transceiver on a line – effectively an old-fashioned telephone – into the command area. Beside the battery in the cockpit's sole he had the actual radio equipment it was attached to. When the system was up and running, Mark Robertson would be back in contact with the world. For as long as they could keep *Quebec* afloat.

In the meantime Richard was at work down here. Herbert – Richard had never discovered whether it was the engineer's first name or his second – was the strong, silent type. Which suited Richard well enough. For once, he wanted to think matters through, not discuss them. This was no time to go trying to spread the responsibility around. It was on his word and his word alone that the big Zodiac would bring the chief across with the first set of Yokohama fenders.

Each fender would come ready prepared for the job in hand. And that in itself would be the result of a great deal of work and commitment from the tug's crew. For each one would come with a snap-on attachment ready to anchor it to the net on the sub as well as a series of attachments designed to allow a system of lines to be attached to it.

If everything went according to Richard's plan, each fender would float on the water – its indestructible air-filled buoyancy holding it aloft. It would be attached at the top to the netting as near to the surface as possible so that the drag would not pull it back out of place and dissipate its upward thrust when the tow began again. It would not be attached to the netting itself, but to a tight line mounted against the netting that would allow this anchor point to move up and down vertically. Or rather, if all went well, it would allow the fender to sit still while the net rose up beside it.

Below each fender, a strong line would run through a pulley attached as low as possible on the net wrapped round the sub's side. That line would run to a tow bar where it would be carefully attached according to some pretty complex calculations that the chief's acolytes were crunching now. To maximize the effect that Richard hoped for, all the lines had to be cut to a precise length and attached to the bar in the correct way so that maximum power would be exerted when the lines were tightened against the buoyancy of the floating fenders. For the plan was that the tow bar with all the lines from the fenders would then be attached to a heavier line that ran back to *Sissy*'s central winch, and all the individual lines would be tightened from the tug when the time came.

When the tow was under way again, the weight of the sub itself would still be carried by the loop of the main tow rope running through the guttering on the foredeck. The buoyancy of the Yokohama fenders at *Quebec*'s sides would be controlled by the lines running to that lateral tow bar which would sit in the water just ahead of her. And that bar, with the lines attached to it, could be pulled slowly towards *Sissy*, so shortening the distance between the floating fenders and the pulleys at the bottom of the submarine. That way, with careful and delicate winch work, and if those crucial calculations were correct, all the lines could be shortened together, little by little, as the tow proceeded.

And, logically, the shortening of those lines would begin to pull the bottom of the sub up towards the Yokohama fenders on the surface, until the upward power of their irresistible combined buoyancy began to lift the bow itself back towards the surface. And when this happened, the fenders would effectively slide down the vertical lines secured to the sub's side. And they would in theory do so until they met the lowest pulleys and the sub was sitting up above the surface of the sea like a bather sitting on an inflated rubber ring.

If the weight of the water already aboard the sub would allow it. If they had sufficient fenders. If they could all be attached safely. If they could all be secured to the tow bar correctly. If the net held, when and if they were all in place according to Richard's plan.

That was the theory, at least. It wasn't all that mind-numbingly brilliant when you looked at it in the cold light of day, thought Richard, a cloud of depression darkening his sunny disposition suddenly. Except that it really did seem like the only chance they had.

But it didn't actually begin to address in any kind of detail the extra challenges of starting the whole Heath Robinson contraption moving through the water towards Cape Farewell once again. These problems were probably the sorts of things that could be dealt with as they appeared – planned for or not – as they proceeded. On a 'suck it and see' basis. But if they spent much longer discussing and planning and contingency-predicting *Quebec* was going to slip away from them in any case.

Which was why Richard was here in his diving suit with the taciturn Herbert standing listlessly watching him as he tried to turn an apparently good idea into a solid, practical fact.

The good news was that they had plenty of fenders. One of the joys of the Yokohama inflatable fender system was its flexibility. *Sissy* normally ran with half a dozen inflated and in place, three on each side. Her work often occasioned the need for many more, however, and so she always carried spares. She carried many more than she usually needed because she carried them deflated, like party balloons in a packet. Richard could have three aside, or six, or nine if he really needed them – and if he and his team could control all that cordage and tension.

Which Richard thought they might, his confidence beginning to return a little. Amongst all his other experiences he had done some 'proper' sailing. He had crewed the experimental *Katapult* series of multihulls that his company manufactured. He had even crewed one in the Fastnet Ocean Yacht Race only a year or two since. And, as if that wasn't enough, he had been on the charity committee running a training ship for deprived youngsters, the four-masted square-rigged tall ship *Goodman Richard*. He had worked aboard her, running up the rigging side by side with the kids, for as long as his heart, lungs and legs could stand it. Ropes and rigging, therefore, held very few fears for him, no matter how many fenders were attached.

And these were not your average Yokohama fenders either, fine though those pieces of kit were. For the specialized work that *Sissy* undertook, Yokohama had produced a specialized fender. It was twice the usual size and therefore of greatly enhanced capacity. Enhanced capacity, of course, meant enhanced buoyancy. It was just a case of deploying it.

Richard pulled his headpiece into place and adjusted the setting on his compressed-air tank. *Here we go again*, he thought. 'Right!' he said to his buddy Herbert – and to anyone else who was listening. 'Let's go!'

Richard had not come empty handed, for he needed to do some measuring if his plans were going to have a realistic chance of fitting in with the calculator-generated accuracy of Herbert's mates in *Sissy*'s engineering section. He hung against the starboard side of the still vessel, therefore, and took the forward edge of the net-wrapped hydroplane as his first point of reference. Here he anchored a waterproof measure and took out the first of his waterproof pencils and his diver's pad. He had swapped his beloved Rolex for a digital diver's watch which promised to keep going long after he sank without trace and drowned in the depths. It also had a calculator function chunky enough to be workable with gloved or numbed fingers.

With Herbert's help Richard quickly established that it was just less than six metres from the leading edge of the hydroplane to the open jaw of the damaged bow. A few more minutes' activity established that it was fractionally less on the port side. Here, Richard extended his examination aft to include the width of the hydroplane itself in his calculations. And that gave him another metre to play with, say seven in all – and near enough the same from the bottom of the hydroplane to the foredeck.

The fenders would crowd together at the surface, but they

could be expected to sit two deep if need be, thought Richard, increasingly consumed by his plans and calculations. If he anchored the first one at the very edge of the damage, then it would sit one metre in front of the central anchor point and one metre behind. He could start with four two-metre fenders against the side itself, therefore, anchoring them two metres apart, each anchor-point halfway along the fender's length. There would be some extra room around the hydroplane perhaps, but that would be all to the good. And the two anchorage points initially would be seven metres apart vertically. He saw no reason why he should not plan for three more anchorage points at seven and a half metres down, placed precisely between the first ones, like seats in a cinema or theatre. Seven fenders a side – that should exert several tons of upward pressure. Enough to make all the difference, surely. But the vision he had so recently entertained of his visits to *Goodman Richard* made him think of something else as well . . .

'Right, Herbert,' he said decisively. 'Let's get the chief into the Zodiac, shall we?'

Chief Christian Jaeger insisted on checking all of Richard's proposals with a minuteness that could only be described as Teutonic. But at least it had the considerable benefit of carrying a great deal of weight when he announced himself satisfied. As though Richard had had a design accepted by BMW or Mercedes-Benz; to be a part of his beloved if less than perfectly British Bentley Continental or of the 400+kph Bugatti Veyron that Volkswagen made.

Once Chief Jaeger said, 'Yes,' then it really was full steam ahead. And the first thing Richard did was to relinquish his suit to a real working diver and go and have a shower. The retaining lines were rigged on the sub's sides precisely on Richard's marks between the aft edge of the hydroplane and the rear of the damaged section by lunchtime – four at seven metres vertical, three between at seven and a half on the port and the same on the starboard.

Threaded on each rope was a stainless-steel ring that would slide easily up and down it and to which the ring attached to the fender would clip. At the bottom of each vertical rope was the pulley through which the line would lead in from the towing bar and up to the ring on the fender when it was in place. And it was here that Richard became involved so directly once again. He threw himself back in the Zodiac and powered across for a further talk with the chief. Then the number-crunching began again. For Richard had remembered that on the *Goodman Richard* the rigging had employed a range of blocks and pulleys. He and the chief agreed that they could place a single block on each fender and a double block on the bottom of the guide rope. Then the line from the fender could run directly down to the first section of the double block, back up to the single block then down to the second section of the double block before running away to the tow bar. This would at least double the pull of each fender for the investment of an extra fourteen or fifteen metres of line. They might have used double blocks top and bottom – or triple or quadruple – but *Sissy* was not a cargo vessel and she did not have more than a dozen double blocks in her stores. Still, thought Richard, the little he had managed to add to his original idea meant that they were going to rig the equivalent of twenty-eight fenders.

By the time the first of the Yokohama fenders arrived, all rigged and ready to go, Sparks had completed his work on the fin and Mark Robertson had a two-way contact with the world. Richard stood back on *Sissy*'s stern, busily overseeing the ropework, and talked the disbelieving submariner through the plans that were being put in place on *Quebec*'s bow sections. Then he handed the handset over to Bob Hudson so that the sub's first officer could confirm what he had said and then add the news from Halifax and MARLANT. Then they cleared the air for Mark to get through to those vital contact points and talk the thing through himself with his superiors. Richard wandered off immediately after his own brief contact, all too well aware that if he stayed he would start demanding to talk to Robin and that, under the circumstances, would be inappropriate. Almost as inappropriate as it was natural.

He still had not had a chance to talk to her when the chief

and his men returned, having attached all the fenders to the sides and secured all their lines to the tow bar. 'OK,' said Tom. 'Let's get under way. Chief, I'll be calling for power at your earliest convenience. Just the tow at first, though you'll want to take up any slack in the Yokohama line, Gus.'

The winchmaster nodded as the chief and his engineers disappeared below.

Tom took a deep breath, inflating his lungs to their fullest. Then he exhaled luxuriously, turned and said, 'Let's go up on the bridge and get this show on the road, shall we, gentlemen?'

Richard was included in the invitation and went up with the others. He stood at the rear of the bridge-house looking away aft through the window there, thinking that the last time he had done that – a little more than twenty-four hours earlier – the huge rogue wave had been poised to fall on them. Then the water had been like a mountainside made of glass. It had been hurling towards them with unimaginable speed, ferocity and destructive power. Now the sea was calm. The three lines stretched back from *Sissy*'s stern to *Quebec*'s stem. Two of them were thick, bright and beginning to straighten out of their dejected droop. The third, the Yokohama line, was beginning to pull the tow bar towards them and the fourteen fat black balloons of the Yokohama fenders were beginning to come alive above the green-glazed shadow of the sinking submarine's foredeck.

The radio buzzed with an incoming message. Sparks stuck his head out of the radio room. 'That's Captain Robertson for you, Captain Hollander,' he said. 'Told you he'd get off the line to Halifax the moment he felt us moving.'

'Put it through on private, Sparks,' said Tom decisively. 'I want a quick chat with him person to person before we go for open broadcast.'

Richard dismissed the conversation from his mind and concentrated on the view again. The dripping towlines were out of the water now. The fin of the sub was beginning to generate a tiny white bow wave of its own. The tow bar suddenly broke through the waves and skidded unhandily along the surface, fourteen lines spreading out behind it like strings to some enormous puppet. Any moment now the fender lines would feel the strain and begin the delicate task of bringing the front of the sub to the surface.

A line from one of his favourite scary films came into his head out of the blue. He put on his best Robert Shaw voice paraphrasing Quint the shark-hunter from *Jaws*. 'She can't stay down with fourteen barrels in her. Not with fourteen she can't!' he whispered. And, as in the movie, the words were almost a prayer.

The scene now could hardly have been more different from yesterday's or from the terrifying one in the film he was thinking of, but the tension Richard felt was, if anything, more acute.

Twenty-Two

Air

Mark Robertson had assumed that things would be easier once he was back on the air, but he could see all too clearly that he had been terribly mistaken. He had supposed that a call to Halifax, MARLANT, Admiral Pike, or whoever accepted such distress calls, would get him sorted out. Or if not sorted out then well on the road to being sorted out.

But even with the warning Bob Hudson had been able to send them from *Sissy*, Halifax had been slow to offer anything like the guidance that Mark needed. Perhaps because the situation was so unusual, financially complex and fraught with political bear-traps. And, of course there was also the combination of fatally uncalculated factors – the existence of a major naval exercise that involved many of the main decision-makers likely to be of use to him and the simple – so far unremarked – fact that it was the weekend.

In many ways, *Quebec*'s situation itself was hardly unprecedented because of the *Chicoutimi* incident in October 2004. But it seemed that Halifax even had several problems with using that incident as an exemplar for their actions and advice on this occasion. The first problem was that the help so swiftly offered to *Chicoutimi* had all been almost 'in house'. It had been offered at almost a moment's notice by the Royal Navy, the US Navy, the British Coastguard. Ministry had talked to ministry, service to service. Now someone somewhere had to make decisions about commercial towage rates. Lloyds Open Form insurance agreements. With whom, indeed, Canadian naval vessels were insured in the first place. And who in the legal department might know that. Who in the legal department, indeed, might be available at all. Failing the legal department, they needed to look for guidance from someone in the Treasury if not in the navy. And either legal or Treasury meant someone in Ottawa, not someone in Halifax.

And whoever was responsible in Ottawa when they finally tracked him down, it seemed, put them all on hold again and went for further consultation, needing to spread a little responsibility for when the news hounds at home and abroad got the scent of this.

MARLANT, the Canadian Atlantic Fleet, was in any case focused on the Operation Storm exercise in the Labrador Sea and Admiral Pike was a part of that. Although he was currently aboard the flagship, *Athabascan*, the admiral was now out of contact because Operation Storm included a twenty-four-hour dead-air simulation to prepare the fleet for the effects of a nuclear strike on communications across the North American continent. They were four hours in with twenty to go, and even if a real nuclear attack occurred, the admiral had decreed that the simulation should not be breached.

Not that it could have been, thought Mark grimly. Because if there was a real nuclear strike then communications really would be down in any case – just as the simulation suggested – and Admiral Pike would still be unobtainable. No. To get to Pike now, Mark would need to go through the Secretary of State or the Prime Minister, and neither of them was available to him. In theory, he thought grimly, he could have asked the Queen for help – she was as likely to listen to him as anybody else. It was lucky indeed that the admiral had agreed to send a rescue squadron to meet *Quebec* off Cape Farewell in the last few moments before the dead-air simulation started.

But in actual fact, unknown to them all, things had just begun to get even more complicated still. While the craft involved in Operation Storm, seaborne and airborne, were tracing their courses over the waters of the Labrador Sea, so the air up high to the west of Baffin Bay was beginning to twist and turn. Global warming was attacking more than just

175

the ice cap on Greenland itself. The steady settled high-pressure chill that usually covered Victoria, Somerset and Baffin Islands was beginning to break down. An unseasonable tongue of warm air span eastwards out of the Aleutians, carrying Arctic albatrosses before it, to skim over hunting grounds that even now were warmer than in the highest high summer. Such an anomaly would normally have bounced south to plague the desert vastness of the sub-Arctic Canadian tundra. But instead it gathered force up here, speeded by the unseasonable warmth. And what should have been a snow tiger that lost its way in the limitless pine forests that are home to the moose, the wolf and the Wendigo, began to grow into a dragon that would come thundering out over the Davis Strait in little more than twenty-four hours' time.

In the meantime, Mark was at least able to begin his detailed incident report, but he soon found himself frustrated by the fact that the incident was still ongoing. He reported how they had experienced the surge beneath the rogue wave and the effect it had had on his command. He described the collision as best he could and how that – and its effects – had been handled. He summarized the surfacing and the attempt to complete the rescue of two people from the water. He recapitulated his realization that the sub was wrapped in nets and the results of that when the nets' lines got wrapped in the propeller. He was just about to start outlining the actions of Psycho Bob when he realized that he actually knew so little about the man that there was almost no point in going on.

Instead, Mark simply said, 'Is there a Fleet psychiatric consultant I can talk to? I have a situation here that could use the advice of a good psychiatrist.'

The man on the other end of the phone was the duty officer in the emergency room at Fleet Headquarters. He had been on duty all day and he had been the recipient of Bob Hudson's first contacts nearly six hours earlier. Since that time he had briefly raised Admiral Pike and tried to get hold of a wide range of people who were supposed to be on twenty-four-hour alert for matters such as this. Names in legal, names in Treasury, names in MARLANT itself, including the senior officer in charge of the submarine section, Chief of Staff, Submarine Operations, Commodore Hubert Hickey. And he had had no success at all. But he knew that when the commodore found out what had been going on, then somehow it would be his head on the platter.

'Look, Captain,' he answered wearily now, 'I don't know what *time* of what *day* it is with you out at Cape Farewell, but here in Halifax it's sixteen hundred on a sunny Saturday afternoon. And if you think you're going to find any kind of a doctor anywhere other than on a golf course, then you really *do* need a psychiatrist.'

The man the crew of *Quebec* had christened Psycho Bob woke up with a start. There was no light, but there was sound. All around him the angels were talking. No, not talking – calling. He could hear their fingers tapping on the outside of the hull. He could hear their voices echoing up and down the fin beside him. But he did not quite understand what they were telling him to do. He was very clear in what was left of his conscious mind, however, that he was still trapped down here and he had to find a way out or he would die – whether the angels helped him or not. Though such rational and reasoned thought was just a tiny glimmer of light like a match flame lost in the massive, yawning chasm of his feral, uncontrollable animal terror.

He rolled over, muttering to himself almost silently. The light on the SIG-Sauer flickered on again – very nearly at the end of its power. But it gave enough brightness to focus on the dull glow coming up through the hole in the corridor deck-head that he was using as a trapdoor into his hiding place. He shook the gun and the beam brightened, then he began to worm towards the hole. He carried his chopper and his flickering torch but he forgot the towels he had been using as his pillows. This meant that when he dropped into the corridor aft of the command area he was no longer able to disguise himself.

And, to make things worse for him, the crew through which he had moved almost like a ghost last night were

much more alert now. Alert and jumpy. Alert, jumpy and –
although the biggest Sabatier knife was floating in the flooded
crew's berth, tapping on the deck-head with the rest of the
rubbish there – most of them were armed. The galley staff,
trying to make some kind of meals as Mark insisted on standard watch routines, were almost in despair – even the butter
knives were gone. Down in engineering, Chief La Barbe was
reduced almost to inarticulate rage as he catalogued the lack
or absence of almost every large, long or heavy tool.
Lieutenant Pellier, now responsible as acting first officer,
was by no means alone in thanking God that the arms locker
was tightly secured, or all the guns would have been gone
as well.

Or, he was glad of it up until the shocking moment that
Psycho Bob dropped out of a hole in the corridor deck-head
in front of him and leaped towards him like a rabid tiger
waving a SIG-Sauer P226 sidearm and a meat cleaver.

Luc Pellier had just been at a brief meeting with the irate
and snappish captain, where he had been made vividly aware
of a series of shortcomings in *Quebec*'s handling of the situation so far. In the manner in which they had all seemed to
stagger from crisis to crisis – each one worse than the last.
In the less than perfect efforts being made at local level to
get her up on the surface and off to somewhere safe and
secure. But most of all and most especially, in the simply
jaw-dropping manner in which they were being helped and
advised by Fleet and Defence at home.

'Sort it out yourself, *Quebec*,' Mark summed it all up
stormily. 'And Long John Pike may send a pair of water-
wings when he comes back on the air. Air! That's all we've
had so far! Hot air.'

'Yes, Captain.' Luc didn't know what else to say.

'And in the meantime this man Richard Mariner is trying
to keep us afloat with a dozen or so balloons. While they
tow us God knows where across the North Atlantic! It's
laughable. A sick joke. And just a lot more hot bloody air,
if you ask me! And God alone knows what good it will do
if another bulkhead fails like the one in the crew's quarters.'

'Yes, Captain.'

As chance would have it, Robin appeared part way through this section of the tirade. She ran lightly and silently up the companionway and into the command area just in time to note the bitterly stressed captain indulging in one of the most human of failings. Transferring his anger and disappointment from those friends and family who had let him down to the stranger who was trying to help. She was for once alone, having been back down to check the bulkhead door into the crew's flooded quarters again while Li was looking in on Hunter – following her orders – to assess whether that all-too useful young officer might be in a position to lend a hand again. So to speak.

Robin said nothing when she heard Mark deriding Richard's attempts to keep them all afloat, but when Mark caught the steely glint in her normally lambent grey eye, he abruptly changed his tone and his focus. From frustrated complaint about their situation, he snapped into practical plans on how to improve it.

'Right, Lieutenant Pellier. That's our next focus. Go down to engineering and talk to the chief. It'll be faster and more efficient than calling him here then sending him back again. I want a plan drawn up to strengthen every bulkhead that has any water at all behind it. I want power back up to fifty per cent by the next watch to the pumps if nothing else, and if that can't be done I want a detailed report as to why it can't be done. And I want Psycho Bob found and put out of action. Permanently. Is that clear?'

'I'll get right on it at once, Captain.' Luc saluted – for the first time in a while – and included the startling blonde woman in his gesture. She was every inch a captain, after all. Then he turned smartly away and almost marched out of the control area, going through the list of orders in his head like a schoolboy preparing for a test. He got right on the last order a damn sight sooner than he planned to, however, and in a far more personal way.

The door out of the command area heading aft into the corridor towards engineering was like the door into the heads – ordinary dark mahogany veneer over a honeycomb of cardboard cells, like any door in any British council house built in the last thirty years or so. It looked solid enough but was about as substantial as brown paper. Luc pulled it decisively open, stepped through, turned to close it carefully, and turned back to proceed down the corridor. In the moment that it took to close the door Psycho Bob appeared, like some kind of madman's magic trick. Luc didn't even have time to blink, let alone gasp, gape or call out, before the slight figure in the filthy overall was flying towards him waving cook's cleaver in one hand and Leif Hunter's SIG-Sauer in the other. Luc never registered which weapon was in which hand but the truth of the matter made all the difference in the end.

Paolo had the SIG-Sauer in his right hand. But because he had been using it as a torch, this was as much of its function as he understood now; and all he really registered about it was the weight. He was not even holding it by the grip. He hit the strange officer in the head with it therefore and knocked him sideways across the corridor to bounce off the wall and spin back against the door which rattled in its frame. He did not go down, however, so Paolo hit him again with the solid weight in his right hand. Spraying blood, the man slammed back so heavily that the door cracked, but still he stayed erect. More in frustration than anything else, Paolo swung the cleaver in his left hand, ready to strike out with it, feeling nothing more than another club-like weight, unaware that the blood-crusted blade was uppermost.

And the door opened.

The reeling man in front of Paolo rolled away, collapsing backward and inward. And there, immediately behind the falling man, stepping forward indeed to stand protectively over him, was one of the creatures that had been calling to Paolo all along. He never doubted that it was an angel. The glittering curls, tumbling to frame the still, perfect oval of the face. The smoky eyes, now blue, now grey. The long straight nose, full mouth and determined, slightly dimpled chin.

His hands fell listlessly to his sides. He gasped and half smiled. 'Mi angelo,' he said in his first language, Italian.

180

The face floating before him almost smiled. It seemed to have come straight from the frescoes, galleries and stained-glass windows of his Tuscan Catholic childhood. It could have been by da Vinci, Correggio, Raphael or Michelangelo. And it was almost the last thing Paolo saw.

Robin stood astride Luc Pellier and tried to stare the madman down. The movement down the corridor that she could just see over his shoulder told her she wouldn't have to hold him long. But then if he started swinging that wicked-looking cleaver, she thought, she wouldn't be able to hold him back at all. But the moment of confrontation lingered. The stranger gaped at her. His hands dropped to his sides. He almost smiled, as though he recognized her – more than that, recognized her as an old and dear friend. 'My angel,' he whispered in Italian. Though it didn't begin to occur to Robin that he meant it literally.

Then there was a crisp sound, halfway between a smack and a crunch. The stranger's eyes rolled up and his knees buckled. He went down like a demolished chimney to reveal Leading Seaman Li behind him lifting a nasty-looking adjustable spanner for a second blow. 'No!' she said. 'He's out cold. That's enough.' She swung round to face the captain. 'Right, Captain. First order obeyed. We'll get the chief on task next and we'll deliver these two to the infirmary on the way. I'll organize a secure place to hold our Italian guest and sort out some way of restraining him safely when he wakes after his head's been checked and tended. Then we'll see what we can do to get this boat back up on to the surface and our people out into the fresh air.'

Twenty-Three

Storm

During the next twenty hours, things aboard both vessels seemed to improve little by little as *Sissy* resumed *Quebec*'s tow towards the rendezvous with MARLANT's ships at Cape Farewell. Their situation seemed almost idyllic in many respects as *Sissy*'s massive motors turned the four shafts that made her propellers thrash the gently heaving water and moved the whole floating circus forward at three, then five, then seven knots.

And while she did so, little by little, Gus the winchmaster and his team tightened the Yokohama line and eased the tow bar nearer to *Sissy*'s stern. Even in the early hours when Gus was forced to slacken off the main tow rope, he slackened the Yokohama line more slowly – and that in turn simply allowed the submarine's hull to fall back harder against the lines on the Yokohama fenders themselves. And this, perversely, had the effect of hastening the approach of that magic moment when all the forces balanced then reversed – and inch by inch *Quebec* began to surface once again.

And in *Quebec* herself things seemed to be getting better. The atmosphere lightened the instant the scuttlebutt got round that Psycho Bob was safely under lock and key. Once Robin had overseen that and – ever the humanitarian – had made sure that her strange Italian was as safe from the crew as they were from him, she took over the job of shoring up all the bulkheads. Whether they seemed to be at risk or not, every door or wall that contained water aboard was bolstered by buttresses made of wood or metal, solid or pipework, whatever the chief could supply.

And when the chief could supply no more, the ingenious and widely experienced Robin, living up to the reputation of a Mr Hood who shared her name, led her equally cheerfully ingenious team in search of things to cannibalize, reuse or simply steal. Wooden doorways vanished from their frames and appeared squashed flat against steel, spreading the load of broken bunk-legs, wedged in place with everything from substantial volumes purloined from the library to thicker chopping boards borrowed from the galley.

Now that the danger was over, kitchen equipment began to be returned – and the food improved as a consequence. The chief's tools also magically reappeared in engineering and, apparently also as a consequence, half power was restored to the pumps by the end of the first watch after Mark's gruff order – and to everything else within the next.

The two vessels proceeded busily through a ridge of high pressure that calmed the air and flattened the sea from Cape Race to Cape Wrath across the North Atlantic, and seemed to linger with its centre on Cape Farewell. A calm afternoon gave on to a balmy evening, which was followed by a cool, still night. In the early evening, the sea steamed lazily, but by the change of watches at 20:00 when the second dog watch became the first night watch, the steam was gone. No one really noticed this, except for Richard himself.

Richard stood out on *Sissy*'s afterdeck, watching the three lines of the tow ropes. Under the brightness of the tug's big arc lights, the Yokohama fenders crowded against the sub like a pod of pilot whales living up to their name and guiding the stricken vessel home. Their backs were black and gleaming and they heaved in easy interaction between the gentle tug of the towlines and the easy swell of the sea, each with a little bow wave at its jaws. Further back, the fin also had a bow wave, its simple white smile twisting out of shape occasionally as the wakes of the fenders played with it.

The central winch clattered abruptly. 'Another fifteen centimetres in,' called out the winch man to Gus who was over in the shadows by the port winch. 'That's good,' the winchmaster growled. 'And nothing paid out here for four hours now. We may be turning a corner here. But it'll be a while before we can be sure.'

'Another long night, then,' chimed in Richard quietly.

'Aren't they all, at sea?' said Gus gloomily.

Richard had never found it so. Or he hadn't until last night, which had seemed endless, short though it had been in the end. With Robin in such danger – and so far out of contact, while still so close – minutes had really dragged for once. But he didn't want to enter into a lengthy discussion about it, particularly as tonight didn't promise to be much better. So he gave one of his most noncommittal grunts and turned away.

The darkness of the forecastle head was as welcoming to Richard as its loneliness and silence. Though all three things were relative and illusory, of course, he thought. It wasn't really dark at all – there was a low, full moon that looked disturbingly close to the earth. Heaven help low coasts with the spring tides under the pull of that thing, he thought. And God help any werewolves too. He studied the face of the pale gold disc as though he could see into the dusty depths of the Sea of Tranquillity itself. But then, passing high across the uppermost curve, there like a stark black crucifix and gone in a whisper, the shape of an albatross passed.

The moon was so huge and bright that the stars behind it seemed to dim. And yet there were so many of them and they too hung so low that even had the moon been down their glittering constellations would have given light aplenty. Even the sea ahead seemed to be glowing – beyond the luminescence that *Sissy*'s bow wave was kicking up. Less romantically, perhaps, there was also the light from the bridge windows up behind him. Though Tom would soon be dimming them as the night watches proceeded.

And that was part of the reason why the loneliness was illusory too. For even though there was no one else on the foredeck, he was certain that the watch officer, the helmsman and probably the captain into the bargain were all watching his back as he stood hunched at the point of the rail down here.

But the silence seemed more real. *Sissy*'s motors were

184

turning powerfully but slowly. The winches had settled. Dinner was over and everyone other than watch-keepers was beginning to settle for the night. The muffled ship sounds were easy enough to factor out. The bow wave was a restless tumble, but it too was muffled by the tug's slow progress. The gulls had finished with the raucous fever of their evening feed and were mostly bobbing invisibly on the gently breathing ocean with their heads tucked underneath their wings. There was no wind. *Sissy* was at that point on the curvature of the earth that does not fall beneath the favoured paths of even intercontinental airlines, so there were no sound-footprints treading like distant thunder through the night. There was only, suddenly, and surprisingly close at hand, the haunting song of a whale.

And Richard realized then. The clarity of the air which had brought the moon and stars so close. The purity of the waves that no longer felt the need to steam. The coolness of the headwind – what there was of it at seven knots through a dead calm. The faintest smell of cucumbers and cheese. The high, lonely cross of the albatross passing briefly against the massive moon. The lonely song of the whale.

'We're in Arctic waters once again. Is she sitting higher?' he asked Gus moments later, when he was certain the icy currents were well wrapped all around both vessels.

'D'you know, I think she is. Though I can't say why for definite. And it'll be a while before we can be anything like certain, mind.' Gus's tone was faintly incredulous, but hopeful – almost cheerful suddenly, even in his characteristically cautious caveats.

'Good. *Great*, in fact. I'll see you later. If it's not one thing then it's another: I'm just popping up on to the bridge to make sure Tom has the watch officers briefed to keep a good lookout for icebergs.'

On the bridge, Richard updated Tom on their entry into the new water, though he made no comment on the way *Quebec* seemed to be reacting to the thicker, saltier element. For all he knew, the cold would do them a disservice by contracting the air in the fenders and stealing their buoyancy away. Calculation of the forces and counter-forces was probably beyond even Chief Jaeger's number-crunchers. It was so far beyond anything Richard could attempt that he dismissed it out of hand. He had more important things to worry about, starting with icebergs. It was on a night like this, after all – save for a little ice-born mist – that *Titanic* met her doom.

But even as Richard stood there, thinking about *Titanic*, Sparks thrust his head into the command bridge. 'Call for you, Captain Mariner,' he announced. Richard went through at once, his mind still full of thoughts of disaster, trying to work out just how bad news had to be to chase him with a message this far away from civilization. But in fact the call had come hardly any distance, and wasn't bad news after all.

'Mariner. Over,' he barked into the hand-held radio transceiver, feeling his stress levels and blood pressure beginning to rise.

'Hullo, Mariner,' came Robin's voice, as huskily familiar and intimate as though it had just crossed a pillow to his ear. 'I've stolen Mark Robertson's handset and he's not getting it back for the better part of this watch. Now. How're you doing, darling? Over . . .'

Admiral John Julius 'Long John' Pike stood on the command bridge of his MARLANT flagship the *Tribal*-class destroyer *Athabascan*, looking north into the Davis Strait. Behind him on the darkened bridge the flag captain and his officers moved with quiet efficiency about their various tasks as they simulated danger and tragedy. But the admiral's baleful attention was fixed on the watch officer, Third Lieutenant McCunn, who had called him here to discuss the weather with him.

It was night of course, but the darkness up there in the north was more than mere absence of daylight. It was absence of starlight and moonlight too. It was absence of any memory that light had ever existed – as though God had woken on the first day of Creation and said, 'Let there be Dark.' But the darkness there was by no means steady or consistent. Even as the admiral looked, a fork of lightning slashed down

186

through the sky, revealing the wild whirl of clouds around it so briefly that the vision only really registered on his subconscious.

'It's heading south now, you say,' he demanded of the anxious watch officer crouching over the weather monitor.

'Yes, Admiral. It's as tight as a hurricane and really small as depressions at these latitudes go. A thoroughly nasty piece of work. Its pressure gradients are so steep and it's moving at such a speed that it hardly gives any warning at all. But it'll hit with incredible force when it arrives. The winds will top Force Eleven within twelve hours I would say, unless it finds some way to dissipate all that force.'

'But it'll run *south*, you say?'

'South and east, Admiral. It'll be over us within the watch then it's off down the coast of Greenland, as near as I can predict.'

'Heading for the cape?'

'Cape Farewell? I'd say so. Definitely, Admiral. It won't go anywhere near the mainland. And as you're calculating no doubt, that's a blessing at least. All our people at home on dry land will be safe enough in their beds unless it shifts back on to the westward track all of a sudden. But do you want to break the dead-air protocol?'

'What, on the assumption that when some madman lets off a dirty bomb in New York, New York the weather'll *stay just fine* for the occasion?'

'I see what you mean, Admiral. Of course, Admiral. But you'll want to warn the others? Operation Storm?'

'On the assumption that you're the only competent weather predictor we've got in the whole Atlantic Fleet? Jesus, if that's the truth, boy, the sooner we know it the better, wouldn't you say?'

In spite of his long chat with Robin that put many of his fears to rest; in spite of his talk with Gus which convinced the pair of them that *Quebec* was indeed beginning to pull herself back towards the surface, in spite of the fact that *Sissy* was sailing gently through calm seas on what still promised to be a prosperous voyage, Richard slept badly

187

that night. And he greeted the dawn in a dark and uneasy mood.

On the face of it, there was no reason for Richard's pre-occupation, for everything that had promised so well last night had, if anything, improved overnight. Mark Robertson reported to Tom at 08:00 that all aboard *Quebec* had passed a peaceful night and he asked that his Captain Mariner's love be sent to Tom's Captain Mariner. Gus reported, little short of awestruck, that the Yokohama line had pulled in well all through the night – to such good effect, in fact, that the guttering which contained the main tow and the raised section it was snugged against occasionally broke the surface. By the noon watch, he calculated cheerily, they might risk a man or two on the foredeck to see what difference their weight might make. And Tom himself reported that *Sissy*'s progress in the night had averaged nearly seven knots. If they kept this progress up, they would be able to rendezvous with Admiral Pike's vessels at Cape Farewell before sunset. Allowing, as Mark informed them, an afternoon of detailed communication with the vessels as they approached the meeting point – for the dead-air simulation should finish at 13:00 hours on the dot.

What was it, then? Richard wondered. What element of the promising situation was out of place? Something so tiny as to be almost impossible to see. Something so subtle, indeed, that no one else had seen it yet. Something so obscure, in fact, that even he could not put a conscious finger on it, but must be content to let it sit there at the back of his mind like an itch he could not scratch. As the day wore on, he found himself returning time after time to the forecastle head where he had spent his quiet time last night, watching the black-etched outline of the albatross cross in front of the massive moon.

There was nothing of equal magnificence to see today, however. There was the green heave of the sea, blue-backed where it caught the light. The water was clear and Arctic still, and yet innocent as yet of the telltale signs he knew so well from his work at either pole that warned of big ice nearby. There were dolphins in the distance and seals in the bow wave, but mostly there were the raucous gulls calling and diving. Calling and diving. There was no longer any of the Arctic odour in the air – that compound of berg and bergy bit, although he noticed the wind was shifting. Then he was surprised to realize that he could feel a wind at all after the dead calm of the last few hours. There was the steady prairie-flower blue of the sky reaching away to the far horizon. Seemingly far beyond even the cape that was their destination. So far ahead and so high above that it seemed to darken a little at the top. And there, with its back against the dark stain of the troposphere above the still and crystal air, precisely in contrast to the albatross against the moon, there was the purest, whitest, wisp of cloud.

Twenty-Four

Cape

They all arrived at the rendezvous off the Cape within a couple of hours of each other. Richard in *Sissy* towing Robin aboard *Quebec* was slowest but had least far to go. Admiral 'Long John' Pike in *Athabascan* came much faster and brought both *Huron* and *Iroquois* with him. But the outriders of the storm came fastest of all.

Richard knew the storm was coming almost from the moment that he had seen that white cloud like the wing of an albatross against the utmost top of the sky. He did not need the warnings that Sparks began to bring with increasing regularity to a frowning Tom. He did not need the tidal wave of information that exploded from Admiral Pike's weather-beaten fleet the instant the dead-air protocol was past. He felt it coming on a deeper level. And he feared it. So he began to draw his plans accordingly.

'It'll hit at the worst possible moment,' he said loudly and formally to Tom, Chief Jaeger, Gus the winchmaster and Bob on *Sissy*'s bridge in the early afternoon. They were speaking a little stiltedly because they had open channels to Mark on *Quebec* who had Robin and Chief La Barbe listening, and to *Athabascan* where, no matter who was listening, only Pike seemed to be speaking. It was important to get as much as possible agreed now – for communications would not be quite so easy when the weather closed down. And once the weather did close down then they would have precious little time to save *Quebec* and her people.

'We'll lose communications with you first, *Quebec*, because we'll have to send someone over to close the hatches or your control room will start to flood with rain and spray . . .'

'And we know what that did to *Chicoutimi*,' inserted Pike.

'Precisely. In the meantime we'll all have to do risk assessments. Or redo them. Mark, we'll look to the Yokohama fenders and the flotation system out here. You'll need to assess which shored-up bulkheads are most likely to fail if the going gets really rough.'

'You're sure we're not riding high enough to start taking people off, Richard?' Robin asked.

'No. I'm afraid not. We might be able to risk it in an hour or two, depending on wind and weather at that time, but at the moment we've only managed to put you back at square one, I'm afraid.' Richard crossed to the rear of the bridge and looked out across the complexities of the afterdeck, the tow and the Yokohama line. 'You're exactly at the point you were when the forward escape hatch opened and flooded the weapons area. By the way, has that area been drained enough to allow access or must we work with the aft escape hatch?'

'No. It's still flooded. We can use it if we absolutely have to but it would be better if you could come aft.'

'OK. And no way out through the fin?'

'Only a couple of us are slim enough to get through the damage done when the periscopes broke and the escape capsule moved. And we can't get up to the cockpit from there any more at all.'

'OK. After escape hatch it is for preference, but forward one if push comes to shove. Admiral Pike. We've explained the situation to you. What practical hands-on help do you envisage giving us?'

'We're able to transfer fuel to *Sissy* in case she's running low – you must be going through bunkerage pretty fast out there and I guess it won't help matters if you have to slow down or stop. We're rigging *Huron* and *Iroquois* with lines and winches so that they can go alongside *Quebec* and take your Yokohama-fender system aboard the instant that we get to you. That should lift *Quebec* right out of the water. As long as the nets she's wrapped in hold. Then it's all a done deal.'

191

'And as long as we have calm weather and time enough to get that all in place,' warned Richard, sceptically, glancing up at the square white battlements of cloud beginning to gather overhead. 'What else?'

'My men are ready and prepared to go in our inflatables and take any survivors out of the water, of course. We have a team of divers getting prepared on each of the ships. Halifax and London have both wired us details of the internal layout of the sub, so they're being briefed in case they can somehow get aboard. Maybe through the damage to the bow you told us about. We've got the infirmaries ready. We can send in our shipborne choppers at a moment's notice . . .' The admiral's voice wavered a little.

Richard understood the no doubt highly uncharacteristic faltering as a sure sign that the admiral knew as well as he did that there was almost nothing any of them could do if the bad weather moved in too quickly and remained against them for any length of time. What they needed was a very special-ized type of craft – a small fleet of them for preference. Mini-subs, support and repair vessels, specialist tugs even more task-specific than *Sissy*. But among all the offers of help that Sparks had received during the last thirty-six hours, there had been nothing of any use – cruise ships exploring the Greenland coast and the scientific station at Cape Farewell itself, a couple of Cunarder *Queens* halfway between New York and Europe, tankers and container ships bound to and from the St Lawrence Seaway, trawlers without number. All welcome for their support. All, in the final analysis, even less use than Pike's warships. The simple fact was that they were too far away from the obvious sources of relevant help and the situation itself was so unusual that unless *Quebec* could be kept afloat – and *Sissy* kept under full power – for another week or so, then there was no chance of anyone helping them.

So they were going to have to help themselves. And fast, he thought, as a pattering of raindrops splashed across the busy towing deck he was looking down upon.

Richard stood on *Quebec*'s foredeck for what he suspected was just about the last time. The waves washed past his knees, and were beginning to gain sufficient force to make him stagger. 'Tighten the Yokohama line,' he ordered Gus – for they were desperate enough now to put the whole contraption at risk by pushing matters to their limit. There was an intensifying groan that seemed to come from all around him as the central winch gathered in the lines with ruthless force. *Quebec*'s head tried to shrug the weight of the ocean aside as the fenders attempted to force themselves under the surface – and the whole lot tried to tear the netting off the hull altogether.

But Richard's system was designed to work with the forces around it, easing the sleek hull upwards little by little as the fenders pulled against the anchor-points near the damaged keel. Forcing things to move so fast was simply to risk losing it all. The groaning came again, seeming to boom out of the vessel he was standing on, to throb in the hollows of the damaged fin behind him, to boom out of the slate grey of the gathering weather smeared across the lowering sky dead ahead. He found he was sweating, as though the massive forces unleashed by the relentless tightening of the Yokohama line were tearing his own solid frame apart. The waves washed over the shining black whale-backs of the drowning balloons at the submarine's head, breaking and foaming then re-forming as they slid across the drowned swell of the hull half a metre down. They groaned again, all fourteen of them in a chorus of protest taken up by every line below them and every strand of net around them. Richard could feel it in the soles of his feet like some kind of Inquisition torture. 'That's it, Gus,' he called at last. 'She'll come apart if we tighten any more now. We'll try again in a while when things have adjusted here.'

'OK,' came the reply.

The terrible noise stopped at once, but the soles of Richard's freezing feet continued to burn as though he were walking on burning coals. He turned. Bob, his buddy on this expedition, was already halfway up the fin. He was all set for a bellowed heart-to-heart with his captain. And it would be Bob – and maybe Richard if Sparks was too deeply involved with MARLANT radio traffic – who would be coming that last time to take the radio and to close the hatch when the weather got too bad to risk letting it into the sub. And that wouldn't be too long now, thought Richard.

He hesitated, for a moment, looking around. The sky behind them was milky, washed with striations of high white cloud. Above them it was dull, though the rain had stopped again. Ahead it was grey and darkening – and closing down towards the increasingly restless surface of the sea. Away left, the ocean gathered into a vague rain mist as another squall swept south of them, a skirmisher ahead of the main army of the storm. To the north, on the right hand, the air was clear enough to show on the furthest horizon a solid smudge of darkness. And that was it. That was their destination and rendezvous point. That was Cape Farewell.

But even as Richard established in his mind the certainty of what he was looking at, the sight of it was washed away by another, north-running squall, as though the whole view were a wet watercolour running into a misty grey mess. 'Better talk fast, Bob,' Richard bellowed up over a sudden bluster of wind. 'Or you'll be closing that hatch on this visit after all.'

Richard and Bob were back within the hour. The sea was much more restless now and the rain came driving icily on a north-easter that was in itself so cold that it was a wonder the rain could exist at all without turning to hail, sleet or snow. The two men swarmed up into the cockpit atop the heaving fin, its movement so much more violent, it seemed, than the pitching and rolling of the deck below. And they weren't a moment too soon, Richard thought, watching the way the rainwater was swirling down the hatchway like bath water down a plughole. As it went it completed the destruction of the radio they had been too slow to retrieve after all. And made little cascades off the cable spiral leading down to the hanging handset that no longer carried Mark's words to the world. 'Any last words?' He bellowed to Bob.

'Anything?' Bob bellowed down the gurgling gape of the hatch.

'Nothing here,' called Mark faintly in reply. 'But is Richard Mariner there?'

'Here!' shouted Richard.

And Robin's voice shouted up to him with unexpected clarity and force. 'See you soon,' she called.

'Help's on the way,' he called – though he had told her before – and everyone aboard knew what their plans were. 'So hang on in there. And remember, I'll never give up. I'll never stop looking . . .'

Bob's hand smote down on his shoulder then and he glanced up. An even more vicious squall was battering in over the tossing shape of *Sissy*. Another couple of thousand tons of water was cascading from the sky. Without a further thought, Richard slammed the hatchway shut and Bob secured it. Then the squall hit and Richard began to wonder whether he and Bob would get back aboard the tug themselves.

Athabascan came round the cape less than an hour later. She was running at flank speed with a big white bone in her teeth, the only bright thing in the grey-on-grey of the picture. Battleship-grey destroyer running through a steel-grey ocean under a slate-grey sky. Even her running lights seemed dimmed by the rain beating down on her. *Iroquois* and *Huron* were close behind her sailing in line, but almost invisible in the gathering murk. For they seemed to bring the full fury of the tight little storm with them.

Richard watched their approach from *Sissy*. His work on *Quebec* was done for the moment. She was sitting higher in the water now than ever, but still they dared not open the hatches for the Atlantic would simply pour into her even now. And that massive reservoir of water would be all too fully supplemented by a relentless downpour whose power and simple weight of precipitation would shame the fiercest tropical monsoon.

But, more worryingly still, the rain was accompanied by wind squalls of intensifying fierceness that whipped up the waves all too efficiently into a spiky chop the better part of two metres high that seemed to come from all directions at once. It was a credit to the design of the Yokohama

195

tow – and the sturdy workmanship that had gone into it – that the whole Heath Robinson construction seemed to be standing up to the battering. But *Quebec* was beginning to yaw and roll as she pitched. The fin kept catching the wind like a sail – the power of it all too easily visible as the water streamed this way and that off it, torn into fluid patterns like sand off the top of a Saharan dune, like ice crystals off the crest of a glacier. The strain on the real tow was beginning to tell all too clearly and Gus bellowed in from the thunderously streaming deck that he was back to giving the corkscrewing vessel more line. And easing back on the Yokohama tackle into the bargain.

'With you in fifteen,' rasped Pike over the airwaves.

'And not a moment too soon,' replied Tom courteously. 'We're finding it increasingly difficult to keep things under control here.'

'I hear you,' snapped Pike. 'Now, let's just run over our approach manoeuvres again. Looks as though we'd better get it right first time . . .'

Richard stood in his allotted place – one that he had chosen for himself. He stood shoulder to shoulder with Gus the winchmaster and Bob, watching intently as *Iroquois* and *Huron* eased themselves against the fenders clustered thickly on *Quebec*'s sides. *Athabascan* held back – but only a very little, scarcely more than *Sissy*, who was preparing to let her tow rope run to twice its current length. The falls were tumbling already from the hastily rigged cranes on the forecastles of the two destroyer escorts. On each fall hung a marine, like the winchman on a coastguard helicopter being lowered to a drowning man. They would secure the falls to the fenders and, as soon as it was all secure, the ships would, in very precise concert, lift the submarine out of the water. That was the plan at least. And it was a natural extension of Richard's own. Except that, like the last desperate tightening of the Yokohama line that they had tried themselves, it made no allowance for working with the elements. That crucial element of the original design had gone by the board with the arrival of the storm.

For with the sunshine and the calm, time for manoeuvre had vanished into the screaming murk.

'Those Yokohama fenders are doing another first-rate job!' bellowed Bob as the shrinking foredeck suddenly seemed very small and frail between the two towering warships as they pitched and yawed astride her. The fenders stopped groaning and started to scream. The sound of rubber trapped between acoustic tile and solid steel sounded like fourteen pigs being brutally slaughtered.

Richard just nodded in reply, and dashed his hand down his streaming face, knocking the water out of his slitted eyes with brutal abruptness. He nearly broke the battered beak of his own nose – but noticed neither the pain nor the spontaneous tears it brought. He dashed his hand across his face again and whipped the spray off his fingertips. 'All secure,' came the order over Gus's transceiver. 'Slacken your towlines.'

Sissy eased away as the lines from the two big warships tightened. The heaving sea between them seemed to boil. The black-backed fenders bobbed helplessly in the massive cauldron. Then, under the relentlessly irresistible pull of the massive ships' cranes, they began to rise out of the water as though they were real balloons. And, after a few breathless moments, the battered foredeck of the submarine hove into view as well. And even the fury of the vicious little storm was smothered by the cheering that tore so many hundred throats.

Cheering or no cheering, the moment the submarine's deck was clear of the surface, the teams went down again. This time they had cutters. The net was hacked apart over the forward hatch. And, Richard assumed, over the after hatch as well. The forward hatch was all he could see. And he began to cheer again with all the rest as he saw the first figure ease itself up into the dreadful day. *That must be Robin*, he thought. *And yet . . .*

For fifteen minutes more the sub hung in place as figures streamed out of the forward hatch and were guided up to the boarding nets hanging from the vessels' rails. It was hardly more of a scramble up aboard the sleek warships than

197

it had been up on to the top of the submarine's fin, thought Richard. And they must have sent Robin off first, with the halt and lame, the sick and the wounded. Then the crew and officers in the order familiar from countless routine rehearsals. The only man hanging back must be Mark Robinson. The captain always the last to abandon. In the finest traditions of the service. 'See anyone you recognize?' Richard bellowed to Bob.

'I don't know. It's hard to tell in all this. And *Sissy*'s pulling away quite fast now . . .'

He might have said more, but his words were lost in the strangest sound that Richard had ever heard. It was as though a massive mainsail on the four-master *Goodman Richard* had torn. Had ripped asunder quite slowly. So that individual threads and lines could be distinguished as they snapped apart. And infinitely more loudly than the destruction of such a sail might be. And the whole, terrifyingly, echoing from under water like the bells in a sunken cathedral.

'Oh shit,' said Bob. 'That's the net.'

'Too right,' agreed Richard. 'I hope to God they've got everyone off, because . . .'

Even as he spoke, the submarine dived. One minute it was there, then it was gone. 'Cut your cable,' said Richard to Gus. 'If you don't she'll pull you under.'

Gus hesitated, and Richard could see why he might, given the price of cable and the length of the stuff they had just fed out. But he knew what was happening now as though he could see it. And he knew what would happen in the immediate future with a kind of scientific prescience. Like a chemist observing a reaction. Like a physicist recording a well-tried experiment.

Quebec was on her way down, free of the nets at her fore-castle. The added pressure of her dive would be popping open even the best secured of the bulkheads as the Atlantic relentlessly squashed the last of the air out of her.

Pike could see this too. 'Cut your lines,' he ordered *Iroquois* and *Huron*. 'Or she'll tear your winches out.'

As the submarine sank, the fenders would float and *Sissy*'s towrope, with the Yokohama line, would stay tangled in the netting between them. But at five metres down, or at ten or fifteen, the lines around the propeller would tighten. The fenders would vanish in a twinkling and if *Sissy*'s towlines were still in place, the power of the sub's crash dive would pull her under the water as well.

'Gus!' he rasped again. 'Cut the tow or she'll pull us down!'

As though in slow motion, Gus turned at last to obey. And Richard watched him until a new distraction burst in upon him. The transceiver hissed into life. 'Captain Mariner?' came an unfamiliar voice, oddly deep and reassuring.

'Mariner here.'

'Captain. My name is Watson. Petty Officer First Class and *Quebec*'s medic. I have some bad news, I'm afraid.'

'Yes?'

'I'm here at the bedside of Captain Robertson, who escaped from *Quebec* by the skin of his teeth and got pretty badly injured in the process. And he has asked me to tell you that Captain Robin Mariner and some others under her command went back below at the last moment, sir. He wanted me to tell you that they didn't get off in time, sir. I'm afraid to say they're still aboard *Quebec*.'

Richard said nothing. There was nothing left to say. He stood there, stunned, waiting for his mind to race into rescue mode as the three towlines fell away, severed at his command. But all he could think was that he had, quite literally, just cut off his last hope of pulling Robin back out of this.

And no sooner had the three lines settled into the roiling water than the fourteen Yokohama fenders between the razor-sharp bows of the destroyers jerked under the surface and out of sight as though they and the vessel they were tied to had never existed at all.

Twenty-Five

Farewell

Robin stood for a moment in the freezing downpour looking upward as Richard's last words echoed down to her.

'I'll never give up. I'll never stop looking.'

Then the upper hatch closed with a *Bang!* that sounded unsettlingly final. The dangling handset on the great long line of spiral cable gave a terminal twitch, but hung in place like a length of dead ivy. And the downpour stopped. The effect of the words on her was the opposite of what Richard intended. The simple phrases brought home to her the hopeless enormity of her situation. It was as though until that moment she had been living in some kind of a fantasy where everything was guaranteed to come to a happy ending. All of a sudden she felt helpless and utterly alone. As though he had known she was bound to die and this was his last farewell.

But Robin did not stand there in the icy puddle of despond for long. Ever someone who reacted to depression with action, she swung round to Mark, sparking with febrile energy. 'Right!' she snapped, abruptly consumed with burning rage that she should have allowed herself to get into such a ridiculously life-threatening situation in the first place. 'What's next?'

Robin spent the next hour undoing some of her own handiwork and then finishing something that the heavily bandaged Pellier should have tackled in an ideal world. But this pitching, tossing, heaving and groaning little world was very far from ideal. She went through from the command area into the corridor outside the heads where Gupta's body had been found. The doorway into the heads was open now, for the door itself was part of the system shoring up the bulkhead door into the flooded weapons-storage area beneath the forward escape hatch.

With Li and a couple of others that she had built into a useful little general-purpose team, Robin set about undoing some of this very precisely fashioned work. Her objective was simple. Instead of wedging the bulkhead door tightly closed and containing the flood in weapons storage, she wanted to wedge it thirty centimetres open. Then she wanted to hold it there while the water that stood between the crew and the forward escape hatch flooded through the open doorway into the heads and drained away down the plug-holes in the shower stalls. The pumps were back to fifty per cent power now and *Quebec* was hardly running in secret mode, so everything from bilge to bog water was being pumped straight out into the Atlantic.

It was done within the hour. A very active hour, far too full of work to allow fear and depression to get a grip. Some fifty minutes later, Robin was able to remove the makeshift buttressing and step through the fully open door into a shallow lake contained only by the raised rim of the bulkhead behind her. What struck her most in the darkness of the cavern was the way the water was heaving. Perhaps it was the way the light was coming through the door behind her and reflecting off the restless wave-tops. Perhaps it was the fact that she had almost expected things to be calm and quiet in here – in spite of the increasingly extravagant motion of the hull. But it was as though she had stepped into a strangely contained maelstrom.

And the noise! The hull itself was groaning as it rolled, pitched and tossed. The tow-point up above was growling as the submarine heaved and yawed. The lines against the sides thrummed and quivered with tension, attaining deep bass notes like the strings in a wild orchestra. Each Yokohama fender had its own individual squeak, grumble and grunt. Every one seemed to reverberate like an ill-pitched drumskin under the solid booming batter of the wind, like the band of some devil's army beating the retreat.

At first, Robin could not place the irregular but insistent

tapping that seemed to echo up as though there were mermen beneath her feet trying to get up and at her. Then she remembered just how full of floating debris the flooded crews' quarters downstairs were, even before the lights exploded under the pressure of the icy surge. But the water sounds washed over all. Slithering, rippling, tinkling, pattering, hissing, sloshing, slapping, thumping, battering, bellowing and roaring – coming from outside and inside, far and near, above and below.

Robin spent less than ten seconds in soaking up all these fearful impressions as she strode purposefully across to the ladder and swarmed swiftly up to the forward escape hatch. She reached up for the handle and tested it lingeringly, on the verge of giving in to that insane yet overwhelming desire to open it. Her preoccupation was broken almost at once, however, by a broad beam of brightness that struck up from shockingly close below her. 'Everything OK up there, Captain?' came Li's voice from somewhere around her knees.

'Fine,' she answered briskly. 'Now, what's next?'

But as if in answer to her question, *Quebec* gave a kind of double heave, first one way and then the other, as though she had been slapped on both cheeks by a Frenchman challenging her to a duel. The groaning and grunting of the Yokohama fenders became at once an outraged squealing. And even as Robin and Li stood looking up at the tight-closed hatchway, the first footsteps splashed down on to the deck scant centimetres above their heads. 'Sounds like the cavalry's arrived,' sang out Li cheerfully.

Then the fenders really started screaming.

'That or the local pork butcher,' said Robin, quietly ironic, climbing down. The surge of hope that went through her was tinged with an all too lively awareness that things could still go wrong. Wasn't it in *Jaws*, she thought, that Quint had given that speech about going down with the *Indianapolis* and being attacked by sharks for days on end? About how the most terrifying time in the whole terrifying experience had been when rescue had arrived and he was just waiting to be lifted out of the water.

* * *

It was Mark's turn to spark now, with a combination of relief and restless energy. Like everyone else aboard, the captain knew what must be going on. The moment that they had planned for, trained for – and prepared for ever more religiously as their hope ran out – was only mere minutes distant.

They were so close to safety now.

And, like Robin, he was all too well aware that so many things could still go wrong.

Mark caught Robin's eye as she and her team stepped dripping into the command area. 'Forward hatch?' he asked.

'Free and clear, Captain,' she answered formally. He beamed at her, his face suddenly cherubic with relief and excitement.

They could all feel it now. The whole demeanour of *Quebec*'s long teardrop hull had changed. Her increasingly wild movements were contained. Her oddly truncated pitching – down-strokes brought up short against the buoyancy of the fenders – was gone. Instead there was a settled, steady, upward thrusting. The decks were tilting slowly, but upward, ever upward. The inner workings of their ears, attuned so carefully to motion of all sorts, told them that they were rising – as though in a very slow lift car. And the strange relentless roaring from all around was the sound of ton after ton of water pouring off her decks and into the stormy enormity of the Atlantic.

Then they all heard the footsteps on the decks above. Footsteps that rang and echoed, their reverberation no longer dimmed by a metre or so of water. The decks at least must be above the surface now.

'To your emergency positions,' ordered Captain Robertson, his voice rasping with ill-controlled emotion. 'Prepare to abandon ship!'

Robin's position was with the wounded. She had taken on many tasks since she had been pulled aboard, but she had kept coming back to Doc Watson's little kingdom. And she hurried back there now, fighting the urge simply to give up and get out. Like some medieval nun half in love with martyrdom. Like Joan of Arc. The occupants of the infirmary were mostly beyond rescue, she thought grimly. It was a brutal but practical requirement of the situation that Annie Blackfeather, CPO Monks, Lieutenant Gupta and what was left of poor Faure should all remain aboard until the vessel was absolutely safe. This was a fighting unit, after all. The wounded deserved selfless and heroic help. The dead were not worth dying for. There was no way that the lives of the living should be put at risk for their fallen comrades in situations as desperate as these.

Watson would be bringing Leif Hunter up, but Robin had no way of knowing who else might be hurt down there. And it was as well that she checked, for the restoration of light and power had by no means come free. Engineering Lieutenant Chen had received a range of burns to her hands and arms – then a badly twisted ankle. She could neither walk unaided nor support herself on crutches. Robin's arrival was providential, therefore. She took the suffering woman round the waist and helped her out into the corridor in the wake of Watson who had the groggy Lieutenant Hunter draped over his shoulder. She noted the little icebox (which did not have ice in it any more, but offered a chilled and sterile environment) that Watson had in his left fist. It contained Hunter's cleanly severed hand, of course.

'How did you do this?' she bellowed to Dorothy Chen as they laboured along the corridor side by side. She needed her quarterdeck voice even though Chen was so close to her because the outraged squealing of the fenders seemed to be rising to new and overwhelming heights. And the simple volume seemed to alleviate the raging frustration that seemed still to be consuming her.

'Twisted the ankle falling off a ladder,' bawled the laconic engineer, then she had to pant for a moment to recover the energy expended on the volume of the words.

'How did you come to fall off a ladder?' persisted Robin as though she was somewhere in Austria calling from one alp to another.

'Got a shock when the system I was isolating shorted out.'

'What system was that?'

'The one to the lights in the crews' quarters. I understand things got a little damp in there.'

Robin recognized that she was by no means the only mistress of ironic understatement aboard. 'You could say that. Yes,' she said more quietly; but it was unlikely that Chen actually heard her.

The conversation, punctuated by pauses and grunts, was sufficient to take the women to the command area. Here Mark was overseeing the orderly evacuation of his command through into the flooded weapons-storage area and up out of the forward escape hatch. Chief La Barbe would be doing the same at the aft escape hatch, Robin knew, sending his teams up out of the motor room. She knew this because there were only navigating officers and crew down here.

Lieutenant Pellier was standing officiously beside Mark, looking like some sort of Sikh with the thickness of the bandage round his battered head. In the midst of all the calm and orderliness, he was armed with one of the SIG-Sauer handguns, as though he was really expecting riot and mutiny.

'You four had better jump the queue,' Mark said gruffly, able to speak almost at normal volume as the screaming of the fenders settled into a ululating whimper.

'That's not a queue,' observed Robin drily, scanning the obedient line of well-disciplined and patient submariners. 'There's only a dozen or so. You should see the crowd at the Peacehaven Post Office every Saturday morning. Now *that's* what I call a queue . . .'

But she followed Watson through into the weapons area as she gave her utterly impenetrable little speech. For the sake of Dorothy Chen at least, she eased to the head of the patient line. Ironically, she found herself just in front of Seaman Li, who was waiting hopefully at the foot of the ladder, looking up at the busy figures of the oh so welcome strangers going to and fro up there. Happy to go up ahead of her for the first time since she had come aboard.

'There's usually blood on the carpets by noon,' she finished the bitter observation that no one else had any chance of understanding, placing her charge immediately behind Watson's.

But either the phrase Robin spoke just behind him or the

sight of the ladder immediately in front of him – or, perhaps, both – had an electrifying effect on Leif Hunter. Enough of an effect, certainly, to jerk him out of the near catatonia induced by Doc Watson's painkillers. He froze in the automatic act of reaching for the nearest rung with both his hands. He stared at the bandaged stump of his right arm for an instant. He gave an inarticulate cry. He tore himself out of Watson's grip and turned. '*Where is he?*' he demanded, fixing a disturbingly drug-widened and wild look on Robin.

It took Robin just an instant to realize who Hunter was talking about, though the stump he was waving in her face should have given her a clue. And it struck her with an almost physical shock that she didn't actually know where *he* was at all. She had had neither the time nor the inclination to spare a thought for Psycho Bob since Li had hit him with the spanner and carried him away. And she realized with a frisson of genuine horror that she had come within a hair's breadth of abandoning ship without him – and leaving him alone in there with only the corpses for company. Very likely all the company he would ever have, on the last long screaming ride down to the ocean floor that they all feared so much – and he feared more than all the rest of them put together. And, oddly, that fact seemed to make her more bitterly angry than everything else put together.

Robin turned to Li, her gaze almost as intense as Hunter's. 'Where did you put Psycho Bob, Li?' she demanded.

The seaman's long, dark eyes became almost shifty, sliding away from the frowning intensity of her wide grey gaze. 'We put him beyond the sick bay,' he admitted. 'There's some really secure rooms there.'

That was enough for Hunter. He was off.

'Far beyond?' demanded Robin. 'How far beyond?'

Li shrugged. His eyes wandered up and to his left. Dorothy Chen was halfway up the ladder now. Although her girlish hips were far slimmer than Robin's, the seat of her overall was tight enough to outline each seam and every stitch of the underwear beneath it in almost shocking detail. Then Watson was there behind her, taking her weight with an arm round her waist and preserving her dignity. Li looked back at Robin. Saw in her face the beginnings of realization; almost of accusation.

'Show me,' she said. And it was an order, direct and unmistakable. Spoken by someone who had commanded supertankers. Given by a woman to a man she had discovered in flagrante delicto – or obviously experiencing illicit pleasure – as the law will have it.

And he obeyed.

Robin and Li pounded into the command area almost side by side. 'What is going on?' demanded Mark. 'First Hunter . . .'

Robin paused, her rage subsumed for a second, by suspicion. Pellier had moved. He was right over by the door leading back towards engineering, as though he had followed Hunter there on his mad dash through. Her eye fell on the lieutenant's hand. It no longer held the big SIG-Sauer. 'We've left someone aboard, Captain,' she said, shortly.

Revelation seemed to come to Mark and his lieutenant both at once. 'Psycho Bob!' breathed Pellier. He looked down at his empty hand almost in mime, thinking too obviously and articulating too slowly, like a bad actor. 'That's why Leif took . . .'

'Thanks a bunch, Lieutenant,' snarled Robin. 'Well, we'll just have to hope we can beat your left-handed Wyatt Earp to his gunfight at the OK Corral. At least we know exactly where we're going.'

'You see these people off, Luc,' ordered Mark. 'Then you abandon. I'll go with Captain Mariner.'

'No, Captain,' Robin said decisively. 'Three's a crowd as it is. You wait here and keep things clear for us. Warn the navy boys up there that there might be a short wait. And if push comes to shove you get off yourself. We'll be back with our unwanted guest as quickly as we can. And I meant what I said to Pellier – Hunter will be looking all over the place while we go straight in and out. Shouldn't take more than five or so minutes. And Hunter will certainly come back as soon as he realizes his quarry has already gone. He's out for revenge, not suicide. I'll bet you can still see all of us up the ladder first. Captain's privilege and all . . .'

'Oh and Captain,' added Li. 'Is there another P226 handy? The tactical light could come in useful, if nothing else . . .'

'Do you have the key?' asked Robin as the pair of them pounded along the corridor past the infirmary. She glanced at her watch. 'We don't want to be standing around when we actually get to the door . . .'

'We're almost there anyway,' Li answered her. 'Just round the corner here. And the key's . . .'

Li was clearly about to tell her that the key was in the lock, thought Robin, suddenly ablaze with rage and frustration once again. Because the information was redundant. The door stood open now – with the key still there. And the tiny little store room behind it was empty – except for the blood splattered liberally all over the place.

The pair of them froze, side by side, staring into the red-smeared vacancy of the place. 'How did he do that?' screamed Robin. 'How did Hunter find him?'

Li's mouth opened and closed soundlessly. He was in more than enough trouble with this delicious woman already without admitting that they left Psycho Bob locked up in there, bound, in the dark, howling like a rabid wolf. But the situation saved him, for as he searched for an answer in the sudden echoing quiet after their wild rush and half-shouted conversation, the strangest noise filled the air all around them. It was a slow tearing sound, as though the whole of *Quebec*'s long hull were suddenly made out of canvas and something was inexorably ripping it apart.

The deck on which they were standing – no, staggering – was abruptly at a decided angle. The downward slope steepened until, within a heartbeat, they were both sliding backwards down towards the galleys under the control room itself. The ripping sound stopped – or, if it did not then it was lost beneath the roaring.

'Nets have torn. Sea's coming in. We need to get to the conning tower then up into the emergency pod or we'll go straight down with her,' bellowed Robin in her quarterdeck voice. The one she had used to Chen only a quarter of an hour ago in almost exactly the same place. But it relieved none of the twisting anger and frustration now. And she did not see whether Li understood what she was saying or not. Because then the lights went out.

Li switched on the tactical light under his SIG-Sauer P226 and the pair of them pulled themselves to their feet, beginning the near-impossible task of getting themselves up into the command area. The time for anything other than immediate action was long past. There was hardly even time for the incandescent rage with which Robin considered the near certainty of her own death. And the destruction of the lives of everyone who loved her, parents, husband, children . . .

Li led to begin with because he had the light and the local knowledge. But Robin crowded him relentlessly for she was more decisive, quicker thinking and had experienced disaster not unlike this before. So simple odds dictated that she wasn't likely to be so lucky twice.

They had ended up at the T-junction ending the passageway just forward of the galley. The wall they slid into and the deck down which they had slid were at a near-forty-degree angle. They walked with their shoulders sliding along the wall, therefore, until the opening of the companionway gaped before them. Water was pouring down this already, but with a little ingenuity they pulled themselves up out of the worst of it, and climbed upwards hanging from the banister. The movement of the air being pumped through the passageways by the relentless pressure of the water was almost at gale force now, and it made things nearly as difficult for them as the water itself. Certainly, the hissing roar that it made – combined with pockets of increasing pressure high enough to hurt their eardrums, made communication effectively impossible.

They fell out into the passage leading to the control area and would have slid helplessly down again – except for the fact that it was seemingly just about to flood full of water. Here Li froze, for all he could see below him was an apparently bottomless black well framed in the open doorway down into the command area. He flashed the torch under the SIG up the slope towards engineering. The passage was clear and seemingly full of air. He started to climb at once, but Robin caught him and pulled him back with all her wiry strength. 'The pod!' she screamed. 'It's our only hope!' Side by side they slid down into the black maw of the flooding well beneath.

The surface was covered with debris but none of it proved heavy enough to hurt them when they tumbled into it. The lake of black water was deep enough to break their fall – deep enough indeed, to make them half swim, half flounder over to the mess at the bottom of the fin. And it was getting deeper every second, courtesy of the foaming fountain that stood immediately above the forward door whose gape now led down into the weapons-storage area where the forward escape hatch still stood securely open, letting in the ocean at an unimaginable rate. Here they were able to use the fallen column of the broken periscope to guide their feet past the whirling currents unleashed by the open hatch. Robin was even able to reach the handset on the spiral wire which still hung there, although it had been useless since well before Richard had slammed the upper hatchway.

The coil of cable was strong enough and secure enough to let Robin pull herself forward. As she moved, her fickle, adrenaline-fuelled mood began to change a little. Here was something practical that Richard had left her – and it was helping her towards a safe haven. Even the water seemed to be trying to help her now, for it had broken her fall if nothing else. On the other hand, Li's tactical light flashed over her shoulder as he fought to follow her, sometimes showing her where she was going, more often disorientating her with unexpected shadows.

But then another, steady, light came on.

Robin looked up at it at once, simply stunned – and Li did the same, flashing the SIG's light upward where he looked. And there, in the doorway above them was Hunter. And his presence shocked Robin out of her near-catatonic preoccupation. How Hunter remained there was a mystery, for he was holding his SIG in his left hand and waving the stump of his right while blood cascaded out of him almost as swiftly as water was foaming into the sub. Robin was so surprised that she lost her footing and slid back into the icy water. Only Richard's trusty phone cord allowed her to keep her head above water. Whether Hunter really saw her she never knew. She only saw him because of Li's light and that must have dazzled the man.

But Robin was of the same build as the hunter's quarry, except for her chest. And even her riot of hair had been slicked back into a sleek skull-cap now. Hunter opened fire at her at once, believing she was Psycho Bob. The water little more than a metre in front of Robin exploded in a pattern of shots and she flinched, knowing that the trajectory would follow the light-beam shining through the heaving liquid on to her chest. On to her heart, in fact. But there was no impact. Hunter's face screamed with mad frustration – though she heard nothing but the mayhem around her. He fired again. Even the gun was seemingly silent, though her ears were really beginning to hurt her now. And breathing was hard because of the throbbing of the air. Again the water exploded as the pattern of bullets hit home little more than a metre away from her. But, magically, nothing happened. And it seemed to her at last that she understood. The water was her friend. The water might be consuming the submarine around her, but the water would not let her die. Certainly not while she held on to Richard's blessed cable. She was so full of internally generated drugs now, so far up the natural high of action at the edge of death, that she never really considered the simple science that was normally so dear to her. The hydraulic requirement that water, which cannot be compressed, should react to the impact of the speeding bullet as though it were steel.

Then Robin did hear a shot. It seemed to come from some distance, but its effect was close enough. Hunter's face slammed back as though someone had kicked him in the forehead. And indeed, when he looked down at her again, his eyes wide with simple amazement, he seemed to have developed quite a bruise on the white skin above the bridge of his nose. About two centimetres above where his eyebrows joined. He nodded at her wisely and folded forward, tumbling down into the room. The confusion of his landing swamped

Li and came near to washing Robin away. She threw herself over to the fallen man, however, and tried to tug him also to safety. Li squeezed past her as she did so, with a shake of his head that she only saw in the submerged light of the two lost guns as it shone up from under the surface. There was just enough brightness for her to see that it wasn't a bruise on Hunter's forehead and that she was wasting her time with him now as surely as if he had been Blackfeather, Monks, Gupta or Faure. She turned and followed Li to the last, faint hope of survival, pulling herself up along Richard's twisting telephone line, madly convinced that the cable and the water were actually on her side.

The ladder up into the fin was almost impossible for Robin to climb now, for all her weight was thrown forward by the angle of the sinking submarine. The whole weight of the vessel – with the Atlantic up above it – seemed to press on her back and crush her breast down on to the constricting rungs. Worse than that, she was climbing away from the last lingering glimmer of light into a simply sepulchral darkness. Under any other circumstances, she would never have made it. But as she lingered there for a moment, agonized and terrified, feeling the water beginning to flood past beneath her into the last safe sanctuary aboard, she seemed to hear Richard calling his last wild promise down to her. And that fact made her so flaming angry that she simply had to go on no matter what.

'*I'll never give up. I'll never stop looking.*'

She couldn't have him wasting the rest of his life looking for a stupid bloody woman who couldn't even climb a ladder in the dark, she thought grimly. She couldn't have her father mourning a daughter dead before himself. She couldn't let her children down. And so, screaming with rage and frustration, she heaved herself on upwards after all.

Until someone from the real world kicked her in the head.

They kicked her in the head so hard that her vision was dazzled with brightness. But then she realized that the brightness was real. And no sooner had that registered on her reeling mind than a face thrust down out of the light towards her. It was battered, cut and bleeding, blood-bedabbled. Eyes gaping. Screaming mouth literally foaming. Great white teeth outlined in red. It was there, scant inches from her own, just long enough for her to see that it was Psycho Bob.

To see and to scream in return, thrown nearly as deep into mad panic as he by simple shock. Then the face was gone, and in its place two bodies locked in mortal combat. This time she saw the foot coming and jerked back out of its way. Then she steeled herself and pulled herself up the last few centimetres into the strange-shaped little room that was hardly big enough to contain three bodies – and two of them fighting wildly. She reached back behind her, wrenching up Richard's phone on its spiral of flex. Then she reached down for the last time and swung closed one of the only three hatches left aboard that would work now that the power was down.

No sooner had she done this than she was looking for some kind of a weapon. The brightness was coming from the open entrance to the emergency escape pod and she knew that there were useful items in here – compressed-air canisters at the least. One of those would make a very effective cosh. Under the circumstances, probably a fatal one. But she was really beginning to run out of patience here, she thought grimly. She reached in to heft out one of these, noting distantly that her hands were shaking as though she had advanced palsy. A sudden close encounter with Psycho Bob could do that to a girl, she decided. She had probably wet herself into the bargain but who would ever know?

She pulled out a canister and a whole mess of kit came with it – face mask, mouth-piece, regulator, Mae West, locator beacon, the lot. She was still dreamily trying to separate her murder weapon from the life-saving tackle when the need for it abruptly ceased. The two heads of the wildly wrestling men smacked together with a meaty sound loud enough to register on her cringing ears. Forehead to forehead they gave each other the Glasgow kiss goodnight and then, like two ball-bearings out of a Newton's cradle, they bounced apart to hit the echoing metal behind them just as hard. The little room was, suddenly, full of peace and quiet. And utterly unconscious bodies.

Robin didn't hesitate. She reached over for the first one.

It was Psycho Bob. His wiry frame was easy to move because his wrists were still firmly tied together – in spite of the work his teeth had done on the knots, the cords and a good deal of the flesh and bone nearby. That explained a great deal of the blood, she thought, as she dumped him in the pod and settled him comfortably, like a mother tucking a child into its cot. Then, a little less easily, she did the same for Li. She slapped them both quite hard – Li, of course, the hardest and for all sorts of reasons – but neither showed the faintest sign of coming to.

Robin hesitated, then. Of course she did. For there was only room for two aboard the pod. But the leader who came back down for a missing man, even though she knew nothing about him except that he was murderously, madly terrified, could not desert him now. And Li, secret lecher or not, had proved a good man in the end. A good man and a good friend. After all, had saved her life not once but twice. He too deserved the best chance she could give him. And she was awake and could fight for life. To leave either of the others would be simple murder.

And she simply could never live with that.

'That's it, then,' she told them. 'Time's up, boys.'

And time really was up, too, for she could feel water deepening all around her and that meant that the hatches were beginning to fail again.

She swung the door into the escape pod shut on the two men whose insensible bodies filled it absolutely to capacity. She picked up the canister she had selected as her weapon of choice and strapped it on – she just had room to do so now that she was oh so alone in the tiny room. She settled the mask in place and adjusted the regulator. She had a final burst of inspiration and tugged the spiral phone-flex free. She lashed one end of it to the nearest handle on the capsule and the other to the webbing of her canister harness. She tied it to the back, still, miraculously, thinking ahead. Then she was ready. She hit the release button and she closed her eyes.

The top of the fin blew off in sections, controlling the influx of water. This was designed to safeguard the release-sequence of the pod but it did enough to protect the body of the woman clinging grimly to it into the bargain. The movement of the pod, which had done so much damage to the inside of the fin, also had one more hidden effect. It meant that the little missile, instead of being launched towards the surface like a rocket leaving Cape Canaveral, eased out almost delicately. So that it was not until it was well free of the sunken submarine and heading upwards past the tethered, falling Yokohama fenders with all the buoyant joy of a balloon escaping on a windy day, that she finally lost her grip.

And even then, the flex stayed true and all the knots held good, allowing her body to fold, face down, with her strong back heading for the surface and her tender bits all folded around the life-giving air bottle. Like a plant breaking through concrete.

So that when *Quebec*'s escape pod burst through the stormy surface and settled, riding the swells like an indestructible cork, the body of the fainting woman bobbed up less than ten metres away from it, supported by the auto-inflated life-jacket. And both of their emergency locator beacons began to broadcast in unison.

Tom Hollander had met some focused people since he had assumed command of *Sissy*, but he had never met anyone even faintly like Richard Mariner. Long after everyone else had given up hope, Richard remained on the command bridge, looking out over the grave of the sunken submarine. And it was his absolute and unremitting faith that held the others there with him, like some kind of magic spell. Tom, at his shoulder, glaring out with him into the stormy murk. The helmsman holding the heaving vessel steady so that they could continue to search ahead. Alan, *Sissy*'s first officer, and Bob Hudson, who was still aboard, both poring over the radar, side by side. Chief Jaeger down in engine control and Sparks in his eyrie up here.

It was Sparks who found her first. 'I have a standard emergency beacon,' he sang out all of a sudden. 'No! *Two* standard emergency beacons . . .'

'They're *Quebec*'s, according to the automatic radar

215

readout,' confirmed Bob with simple wonder. 'That's the escape pod by the look of things. And one of the survival kits. Dead ahead and less than four kilometres distant! Jesus. Who'd have thought it was possible?'

And Tom Hollander's first lieutenant jerked his tousled blond head sideways to shoot a glance across at the quiet man who stood towering beside *Sissy*'s wiry captain. 'He did,' he answered quietly. 'He *knew* it was possible.'

'We will proceed to recover the beacons and whoever is with them, please Tom,' said Richard Mariner quietly, his voice gravelly, rumbling with strain, fatigue – and hope. '*And we go to the top of the green.*'